About the Author

ELISABETH MARRION was born August 1948 in Hildesheim, Germany. Her father was a Corporal in the Royal Air Force and stationed after the War in the British occupied zone in Germany, where he met her mother Hilde, a war widow.

As a child Elisabeth enjoyed reading novels and plays by Oscar Wilde, Thornton Wilder and never lost her love of reading novels by Ernest Hemingway, or short stories by Guy de Maupassant.

In 1969 she moved to England, where she met her late husband David. Together they established a clothing importing company. Their business gave them the opportunity to travel and work in the Sub Continent and the Far East. A large part of their working life was spent in Bangladesh, where they helped to establish a school in the rural part of the country, training young people in trades such as sign writing, electrical work and repair of computers and televisions.

For inspiration she puts on her running shoes for a long coastal run near the New Forest, where she now lives.

Also by the author:

The Night I Danced with Rommel: Hilde's Story
Liverpool Connection: Annie's Story

CUCKOO CLOCK NEW YORK

ELISABETH MARRION

SilverWood

Published in 2015 by SilverWood Books

SilverWood Books Ltd
14 Small Street, Bristol, BS1 1DE, United Kingdom
www.silverwoodbooks.co.uk

ISBN 9781096753087 (KDP paperback)

British Library Cataloguing in Publication Data
A CIP catalogue record for this book is available from
the British Library

Set in Sabon by SilverWood Books
Printed on responsibly sourced paper

For David

Prologue

Florida, October 1998

Was it Elisabeth or David who had spotted it first? They could not agree on that, but both had been in agreement to stop at the Antique Mall near Redington Shores that afternoon. It would be cooler in there. The air-conditioning in the car had packed up again. David should have stood his ground and bought the other one, he said. The car he really wanted. Too late for that now.

Their entry was announced by a little 'ping' from the bell above the door. The woman behind the counter looked at them briefly, but dismissed them as tourists who had just come in to have a nose around. Touching most items, asking for lower prices on this and that, only to leave without a purchase. Business had been slow lately.

She stood up to follow the couple.

"Can I help you?" She had reached the end of the store, the place where you could leave via the back door without being noticed.

"Cuckoo, cuckoo, cuckoo." The little yellow bird bowed his head with each announcement. Then it looked at them before it shut the small door angrily behind it. That was the cue for a group of dancers to make their entry. Round and round they turned to the sound of the music.

"That is so cute," Elisabeth said with excitement.

David shot her one of his looks, the one which said, "Don't be too enthusiastic otherwise the price will go up."

"We are closing soon," the woman said.

"But it is only three o'clock. The little bird said so."

"It is much later than that. The clock does not keep time very well. It has been running slow from the day my husband brought it back from a house clearance in New York. He said the weights don't seem to be the originals." The woman noticed the look the two exchanged and cursed herself. Me and my big mouth, she thought. They would have never noticed until it was too late. There was a big sign out front: BOUGHT AS SEEN – NO RETURNS, it said in large letters. She had made the sign herself after a customer bitterly complained that the tea set he had bought had cracks in it. He had wanted to show it off to his elderly mother: a proper tea set like the one she used to own many years ago, and he had looked a right fool, he said, when the tea poured through the pot and stained his mother's best white tablecloth.

"Can we have a look at it?" It was David who asked the question.

She puffed: now she would have to get the ladder. Where was the young man she only employed recently? Most likely out the back smoking a cigarette, or worse.

The doorbell sounded again. Two women were trying to wiggle a young child in a pushchair through the door.

"We are closing," the shop owner shouted, hoping they would go away. Children would finger everything they could reach, leaving their sticky marks behind, and she had had some breakages because of them. Vigorously denied by their parents, of course. No discipline anymore. She had stopped going to her favourite restaurant, Ballyhoo at Redington Beach, as the kids had put her off returning. Parents these days just let them run wild.

At least these people did not bring their child into the shop.

"Can you take it down?" Her thoughts were interrupted. She took a deep breath and pulled the nearest chair from underneath an old table. The legs seemed a bit wobbly, but it would have to do. No way was she going to leave the store unattended.

She struggled to get the clock off the wall. It had to be the one highest up, of course. As she handed it down to David, the price ticket, which had been attached to the back, floated to the floor. Elisabeth picked it up.

"Forty-seven," she said, looking at him again. David held on to the clock, and Elisabeth saw the little round opening at the back.

"It has some writing inside. Let's have a look. Hold it just like that." She put her eyes closer to it. "There is a faded label attached. It says Mordechai Goldstein on top, and underneath it says 1937."

"Come on, Liz, we have to go. Don't forget the new people who moved in on the top floor have invited us to their party tonight."

The shop owner lost interest. No sale again, after all the trouble she went through to get the clock down. She reached out to retrieve it from David.

"Don't move. Tip it slightly backwards – there is something else. You will never believe this – it says Hildesheim, Germany."

"Does that mean anything to you?" The owner's attention turned back towards the couple.

"That is where I was born."

A sale! If the customer had not picked the price ticket off the floor, the owner believed she could have easily added fifty dollars. After all, it had been made in the woman's hometown.

Wouldn't it be strange if the watchmaker and Elisabeth's family had crossed paths at some time?

Chapter 1

Hildesheim, Germany, 10 November 1938

Esther tried to listen for her father in the room next to hers, but any sounds in the house were drowned out by the riots outside.

"Father, we have to hurry. Just take a few things, as we discussed. Hurry, Father." She was not surprised that she did not receive a reply. Her father was a proud man.

Even the love for his only child could not persuade him to accept defeat.

"I think you are panicking for nothing," he said, putting his head round the door. "Our family has been a respected member of this community for centuries. Why do you think anything would happen to us now?"

"Father, we don't have the time to discuss it again. Please, just do as I ask."

"No, I have made up my mind, I am not leaving. You can if you want to, but I still believe in human decency. I am staying here. This is our home."

Esther sighed and put her woollen coat down. She was glad that vanity had not overtaken her common sense when she got her coat. Yes, the fur coat had been very tempting, and her friend had not understood why she did not buy it instead, but what she had really liked about the one she chose was the heavy lining. She had bought it last year when things were still a little easier.

"I am nearly done here and then I am helping you, Father. Only one small case each, remember? We can both take a rucksack as well and pack some provisions. Your jacket is done, now give me your coat."

He came back and threw it on her bed. His coat was not as heavy as her own, but it would have to do. She was an excellent seamstress: a trade she had learned from her mother before she was so cruelly taken from them. She felt her mother's presence in this room, and knew this would be the last time.

Finished! She lifted the coat off the bed several times as if she was weighing it. After that she let her hands glide over it from the top to the bottom. Not bad. Unless they knew, nobody would notice. She was also confident about her father's jacket, but his coat would present a challenge.

Esther took her mother's gold necklace and matching bracelet, the stones already removed. Now just her rings to conceal and Esther was done. Her father came back into her room and saw his gold pocket watch still untouched on the blanket.

"What about my watch?"

"No, you take it and put it in your waistcoat pocket as usual."

"But why? Surely it would be the first thing to lose."

"Father, we can't travel without any jewellery. Nobody would believe us, and then they would carry out a proper search. Is that what you want?"

Mordechai had no intention of agreeing with his daughter. My Esther thinks I am a fool, he thought. Better that way. There was one thing he was not going to leave behind and he had packed it at the bottom of his rucksack. It was quite bulky and heavy, and he only had a little space for provisions on top, but unless she insisted he unpack and show her everything he planned to take, there would be no way she would find out until it was too late.

They opened their front door as the sun was rising. Esther looked up. No clouds, but dark, angry smoke blew across the sky. It could have been a wonderful day today, she thought. Esther did not want to look to her left, but temptation was stronger. The synagogue was still smouldering. There were broken windows in the houses opposite; open doors, and items of china smashed on to the street. Other doors had red swastikas crudely painted on them.

"Come on, Father, it is time for us to leave."

The Kessler Strasse seemed deserted. They kept their heads down and tried to go as fast as Mordechai would manage. Esther had been worried about him for some time, and looked at him now. His once straight frame seemed to have shrunk and stooped, as if all his fighting spirit had left him. Maybe we should have left sooner, she thought. She took her free hand and placed it into his, something she had not done since she was a small girl. He turned round and she saw his grateful look and felt his hand take a firm grip.

Walking down the main shopping street they carefully stepped over broken glass from destroyed store windows. Esther glanced into some of them. The stores had been looted. Frau Neuberger was outside her toyshop near the market square, sweeping glass from one corner into the other without much purpose. She looked at them with a blank expression, bent her head down and carried on. Mordecai pulled away and was going to speak with her, but Esther resolutely held on to her father, preventing him from going and shaking her head.

Further down the road they saw people queuing at the station long before they reached it. Wordlessly they joined the queue, and soon other people stood behind them. Men in SS uniforms marched up and down the unmoving queue, assisted by boys from the Hitler Youth.

"Papers!" one of them barked.

Esther saw three women with pushchairs coming towards them. She recognised two of them: Maria, Egon's wife, and her friend Hilde. Egon was one of the doctors

Esther had worked with at the hospital. Maria had spotted Esther and tried to come over, but was stopped by one of the pimply youths.

Then Maria's friend shouted at the boy. He looked at her, his face bright red, and let Maria pass.

"Esther, where are you going?"

"Maria, it is no longer safe for us here. They have arrested most of the men this morning, including my Ibrahim. I had to promise him that I'd try and leave with my father today. Egon gave me your brother's address. I will be in touch with him. God bless you, Maria."

Chapter 2

"Move it, Jew!"

Mordechai felt a stabbing pain in his back and stumbled forward, almost falling over a black suitcase in front of him, but a child, no older than ten, managed to stop him hitting the floor. He turned round while getting his balance back, and looked straight into the barrel of a gun being held by a male in a brown uniform.

"Father!"

"You'd better watch your father. He does not seem to be steady enough to travel by train. We could arrange for a lorry to pick him up if you prefer." The same pimply youth who had spoken to Maria's friend, standing right behind the man with the gun now, grinned. He was obviously trying to get approval from his accomplices within earshot. From where Esther stood, she could see he did not seem as sure of himself as he wanted them to believe. He kept glancing nervously over at the woman still standing there with Maria, watching the scene.

Whatever she had said to him had certainly made an impact.

"Go on, we have better things to do than stand here in the freezing cold with you all day. The sooner we get rid of you, the better."

To Esther's relief, the queue started moving. She turned round to wave once more to Maria, but she and her friends had gone on and were halfway down the Bernwardstrasse.

"Where does the train go to?" Esther then asked the elderly woman in front of her. Esther had helped to pick up her box, and wondered how she would be able to take it with her wherever she was planning to go.

"*Savta*, I will take it, I am strong," said the same child who had earlier managed to stop Mordechai going down all the way to the ground. He picked it up and lifted it on his shoulders. The weight of it almost made him fall backwards, but before his grandmother could persuade him to put it back on the ground, he straightened up and proudly smiled.

"Hanover. This train will only take us as far as Hanover, and from there on, I don't know."

"Esther, but we want to…"

"Yes, Father." Esther interrupted him quickly, fearing other people would be able to overhear.

She took her father by his arm and kept willing him to come along faster, worrying that there would be no room left for them on the train. The platform was full of luggage and people opening carriage doors, pushing their belongings inside before climbing in themselves. Mothers handed their small children to total strangers in the hope of securing a place.

"Father, you go first."

"But Esther!"

"Tickets!"

"We don't have any."

"How do you expect to board the train then?" The guard outside was placing his whistle to his mouth, ready to blow it to attract the attention of the SS man at the other end of the platform, but stopped before the sound could penetrate the air.

"Dr Rosenthal, what are you doing here?"

"Heinrich, thank God it is you."

"Where is your husband?" Heinrich did not wait for Esther to reply. He lifted her suitcase off the floor "Come. Let me through," climbed up the train steps and started walking through the train, pushing people aside. He spotted two

16

small boys sitting opposite their mother and grandmother. "You two, on the floor. These seats are taken."

He beckoned Mordechai and Esther to hurry and pointed to the seats. "Wait," he told them, and was gone.

Esther felt the other women staring at her and felt uncomfortable. She was just about to say something when Heinrich came back. "Dr Rosenthal?"

Esther got up and went towards him.

"Take these," he whispered, and handed her two sheets of papers.

"What are they?"

"These are travel permits for rail workers' family members. You will be safe with these so don't worry. But you will have to travel all the way to Holland. I don't know where you were planning to go, but if you want to use these you have to go to Holland."

"Thank you, Heinrich."

"No – thank you, Dr Rosenthal. God be with you."

"And with you, Heinrich." Esther went back and sat next to her father.

"Do I need to be afraid, Esther?"

"No, Father."

"Who is that man?" he whispered.

"His daughter was a patient and it was me who operated on her."

"But that is your work, Esther."

"They called me from the hospital and I went in."

Esther's father did not reply straight away; then he said, "It was that Sabbath, now I remember."

Chapter 3

Nobody in the carriage spoke during the hour it took to reach Hanover. A mad scramble by Esther's fellow passengers followed their arrival. Everybody wanted to leave the train, trying to find a connection as quickly as possible. She wondered briefly where most of them were heading. Maybe it would be best to follow some of them, but where to? She had made no real plans, and had no tickets other than Heinrich's papers. Their journey was set.

Esther picked up her father's rucksack to assist him to put it on. She hardly managed to lift it off the floor where it had stood between her father's feet since the train had set off.

"Father, why is it this heavy? You will never manage to carry that. We have to take something out."

"Esther, you told me to bring provisions, so that's what I did. Now, give it to me." With determination, he took it off her. He first slipped his right arm through, then his left, shook it several times until it sat where it was most comfortable, took his small suitcase and went through the carriage door. He turned round and said, "I am not as useless as you may think, Esther. Now, let's go to Holland. God only knows why."

"Tickets!" Again, they were greeted by a guard when leaving the platform their train had arrived at. Esther tried to look as calm and confident as she could, hoping he would not hear her heartbeat, which to her seemed to echo through the large station hall. He scrutinised the family rail pass from Heinrich. "The railway papers should carry your name."

Esther felt an ice-cold wave running from her neck all the way down her back, the same time as the heat was rising in her face.

The guard handed the sheets of paper back to her. "The train to Amsterdam leaves from platform three in twenty minutes. You'd better hurry."

They had to fight their way down a set of stairs, being pushed around by other passengers. There seemed to be a mix of people all around them. Some looked like businessmen, some farmers pushing their carts, mothers and children, older children with their schoolbags and many young soldiers in various uniforms. Esther had no time to linger and study any of them closely. She nearly slipped on broken glass in the main hall, and glanced to her left and saw a row of small store windows broken. One of those still intact had the word *Jew* painted on it.

The steam from the roaring trains ready to depart made it difficult for them to see. Esther turned to her left, scrutinising the platform numbers.

"Come on, Father, it's this way."

Esther had spotted the train they needed to take in the distance and pulled her father along with her free hand. The suitcases, although small, made it difficult for them to move more quickly. Esther worried that her father was getting tired at this early stage of their journey. There was no time to waste; he could rest when they found a seat. Esther pushed him on, and finally they stood on the platform. There were no signs on the train showing its destination. She hoped for the best and headed for the first carriage door.

Another guard outside the train shouted, "Tickets and ID." With shaking hands, she once again took out Heinrich's papers and the requested IDs. Questioning looks went between the papers, IDs and their faces.

After a while, the guard sighed and said, "Heinrich Bauer is a cousin of mine. I don't recognise you as a member of my family, but if Heinrich gave these to you, he will have had his reason." He helped Mordechai to climb the steps, lifted the two suitcases up and watched Esther entering after her father.

"Have a safe journey, Dr Rosenthal," he said, nodded, and closed the door behind them.

"Let me go in front of you. I will be quicker, and can have a look to see whether there are any empty seats." Esther started to walk along the long corridor. This train was different to the first. It had individual compartments which opened by a sliding door. Each of them had enough seats for about six people. In the middle of the carriage, she spotted a compartment which was almost empty.

She opened the door, took her rucksack off and placed it on the middle seat. She heard her father's laboured breathing behind her.

"Father, would you like to sit by the window?"

Mordechai nodded thankfully, pushed his suitcase inside with his left foot and took his rucksack off. He placed it in front of the seat.

"I'll put it up on the rack."

"No, my rucksack stays where it is. Stop telling me what to do. I knew this was a bad idea. We should have stayed at home."

Wordlessly, Esther took each case and placed them on the space above their seats.

"Excuse me, are those seats taken?" The family who had stood in front of them in the queue at the station in Hildesheim now pushed their way in without waiting for a reply. Esther let out a sigh of relief at seeing familiar faces. The same boy who had prevented her father from falling took the seat next to her after helping his grandmother and presumably his two sisters to store their belongings. The little girl started crying when the train moved.

"Don't cry, Johanna, we will be there soon."

"I want my father."

Esther tried not to stare at her and directed her attention towards the window, but the steam prevented her making out any of the surroundings.

"Esther, did you bring something to drink?"

She immediately rose to her feet, opened her rucksack and got out the flask of hot, sweet tea.

"Are you not feeling well? Would you like something to eat?"

"Just a drink."

The taste of the still warm liquid ran through Esther's body, and momentarily she relaxed.

Esther nodded off after she had settled down again, and was awoken when the train started to slow down. She could make out the name of the station: *Bielefeld Hbf*. With a sudden jerk, the train came to a complete stop. From where she sat, she noticed black smoke rising from the distance to the left. She felt a sudden shiver.

The doors opened.

"Papers."

The usual routine followed. Shaking hands fumbled through pockets and held their papers to the guard, who looked at them and handed them to the person behind him for further inspection. They looked at the papers, then at Esther and her father, and handed them back without saying anything.

"Where are you travelling to?" the guard then asked the grandmother.

"Hook of Holland."

Instead of handing their tickets and IDs back, he dropped them on the floor in front of her, gave her one more look and closed the compartment door. The boy had already jumped to his feet to pick them up before Mordechai could move. Esther pulled her father by his sleeve, beckoning to him to sit down.

The next station the train pulled into was Dortmund. This time Esther saw the billowing smoke in the distance a long time before the train stopped. After that, she no longer dared to look.

Her father seemed to be asleep most of the journey, or, as Esther thought more likely, perhaps pretending.

Before the train reached Venlo, there was a long wait while Border Control, accompanied by SS in their black uniforms, scrutinised everybody's ID. Esther heard a commotion outside her open compartment door, and other doors slamming. Looking out of the window to the platform, she saw a group of young men, arms raised above their heads, pushed forward by soldiers using the front of their rifles, making them walk quicker. After what seemed to Esther an eternity, she heard the guard's whistle. The train pulled with a jerk, started to move forward slowly, and stopped again.

Esther froze. What next? Had their luck run out? But then the train gathered speed.

"Look, Esther!" Her father pointed excitedly out of the window. "Esther, we are in Holland now. Nothing can happen to us here."

The train slowed down and stopped again. This time the guards looked different. They politely checked everybody's papers, tipped their caps with the ends of their fingers, and said, "*Welkom op De Nederland.*"

They reached Amsterdam in total darkness. They had left their apartment almost twelve hours ago. Besides the tea earlier in the day, they'd had nothing to eat or drink. Esther had got them as far as here, but now had no idea what to do next. Mordechai, a little unsteady on his feet, took his belongings and went ahead.

The station seemed empty compared to all the hassle they had left behind. Mordechai stopped in the middle of the hall and looked around. "There," he said, and strode on. Outside a wooden telephone booth on one side of the great hall, he stopped, took his rucksack off, placed it on the floor and opened it.

"Father, what are you looking for?" He did not reply, and pulled out a little black book and his wallet. "You brought your address book?"

"I could not leave it behind."

"I told you to burn it."

"Esther, lucky I did not listen to you." And he opened the booth door.

"Whom are you phoning, Father? We don't have any Dutch guilders."

Mordechai took out a coin and showed it to her. It was a little silver Dutch ten cent piece which her father had carried with him as far back as Esther could remember.

He went into the booth, picked up the receiver, looked for a number in his book and started dialling. Esther heard a little click when the coin dropped. She then listened to her father whispering to somebody in Yiddish.

After a few moments, he put the receiver back and picked up his belongings.

"Now what do we do, Father?"

"Now we wait."

Chapter 4

Shortly after midnight a vehicle stopped in the road opposite the station. Esther shook her father awake; he had fallen asleep on the only bench. The stationmaster had asked them to move on around 10pm. When Esther did not immediately react, he had said, "*Ik moet de deur op slot doen*," rattling a large set of keys, and she had nodded that she understood. "*Het spijt me.*" He had looked apologetic when he said this.

"Father, wake up. Somebody is coming." The man leaving the van and coming towards them had a limp, and because of this his approach was slow. Esther could not make out his face as it was obscured by a dark-brimmed hat which was pulled forward.

"Mordechai, I was worried that you had gone! *Shalom Aleichem.*" He held Mordechai in a close embrace.

"*Aleichem Shalom*, Zachary. I am so pleased you came."

"Why would I not come for my dearest friend? Come, let us be on the way."

"Zachary, surely you remember my Esther?"

"Esther, is that really you? A grown woman, no less. *Shalom Aleichem.* Come, come, it's late and you must rest."

Zachary took her father's small suitcase and hurried along. All the while his head moved left and right as if he was checking on something. He swiftly opened the back door and placed their possessions inside, then locked it and walked to the driver's side.

"Come, Mordechai, sit in the middle. There be enough room for the three of us if young Esther does not mind squeezing in. It is not that far."

"Zachary…" Esther's father was saying as soon as they started moving.

"Wait, Mordechai. Ruth is waiting up for us – we can talk when we are inside. We might even have a glass of the finest Tokaji."

Esther knew that she was not supposed to contribute to the conversation until she was officially welcomed into their household, so she tried to take in her surroundings as best she could. The deserted streets were dark, almost black; only the dimly lit headlights made it possible to make out some shapes. Esther hoped she would have time to explore Amsterdam before they had to leave again. She had not outlined her plan to her father, and feared that now he was with his old friend, he would not be prepared to come along. They had reached relative safety, but for how long?

In the darkness, Esther felt rather than saw a building on her left, towering over everything else around it.

"What is that building?" She felt her father push against her leg, and kept her face turned away from him.

"Young Esther, still so inquisitive. That is the Portuguese Synagogue, and since it is so close to where we live, it is where we worship on the Sabbath."

The vehicle stopped outside an apartment block. A young man, who had waited for them in the shadows of the door, stepped forward. Zachary wordlessly handed him the keys. The man walked around the back and unloaded their belongings.

"I'll take that," said Mordechai, and took his rucksack and his case. Esther took hers, and they followed Zachary inside.

"It is only three flights of stairs."

Esther heard movements inside apartments they passed on the staircase on the way up. One of the front doors opened; an elderly woman stared at Esther and quickly retreated.

Zachary's front door was unlocked, and as soon as he pushed it to let them enter, a woman rushed forward.

"Mordechai, is it really you?" Her hands flew to her mouth in disbelief. "And is this your Esther?"

"Let us come inside first, woman." Zachary seemed to scold her, but Esther could see the love for her in his eyes from where she stood.

"Mordechai, Esther, come and sit down at the table, you must be hungry. Jacob will be back soon."

"Jacob, your son, was he the young man we met downstairs?"

Esther felt the time had come for her to join in with the others. She pulled a chair out for her father, but decided to remain standing until she had worked out the seating order.

"Yes. Come, sit next to your father," said Zachary to Esther, then put five empty wineglasses on the table. He went back to the large sideboard which was covering the wall where Esther now sat and got a bottle of wine from a locked cabinet.

There was a sound from the front door, and after a few seconds the young man entered. "Father, I'll help Mother carry the food from the kitchen."

"I have such a good boy," said Ruth with pride, carrying a large wooden board with cold sliced pastrami and a jar of pickled gherkins. She went back one more time, and returned with a basket of rye bread. "I asked Jacob to make sweet black tea."

"But first let's toast the safe arrival of my dearest friend and his lovely daughter." The four of them raised their glasses. "*Mazel Tov.*"

Chapter 5

Pankow Orphanage, Berlin, 9 November 1938

Kurt Crohn was woken by noises drifting from below his window. He liked to sleep with it slightly open, although the damp November days did not favour his stiff limbs. Arthritis, the doctor had called it.

"Susanne, are you awake?" He shook her shoulder when she did not reply. Susanne would never get used to the cold, and almost disappeared under the large duvet each night. "Why can't we light the stove in the bedroom?" she pleaded with him as soon as the last day of October had past.

"Susanne, can you smell smoke?"

Susanne let out a deep sigh, moved the top of her cover and turned around to face him. "Kurt, I can't smell anything. Go back to sleep."

"No, I have to check on the children. Did you hear that? It sounds like somebody is breaking glass. And the shouting is coming nearer." Kurt swung his legs over the side of the bed. The shifting of his body made the metal frame of the bed creak and the mattress move. It had become much worn over the years and hardly gave any protection from the springs below. Recently he'd had to take his tools and try to bend back a few of the springs, only succeeding in breaking them altogether. Now he had to sleep in such a way that he would not create an even bigger hole.

He tried to pull the slippers from underneath the bed with his toes, and reached for his dressing gown which lay perfectly folded on a chair next to the bed. Giving up on his slippers, he stood up and waited until the sharp pain had eased slightly. From where he stood, he saw an orange glow in the distance through the window.

"I am going downstairs to check on the children before I go into the kitchen. Shall I make you a cup of coffee?" He did not wait for a reply, and barefoot he descended the wooden staircase leading from their bedroom in the attic down to the main corridor. He opened the first door on his left and made out the shape of his daughter's body, sound asleep. He smiled; she was like him, her window slightly open. She loved the fresh air, and surely her mother would have scolded her about it again in the morning, but since Kurt had changed their bedroom to the one on the top floor, Susanne only saw their daughter when she was already up and dressed, ready for school.

Opposite, on the other side of the corridor, was his old bedroom. In it were eight new arrivals, among them two brothers, the younger being only four years old. He had not spoken one word since he came in. Their sister slept in one of the downstairs rooms.

Kurt's feet were getting cold, so he decided to check on the dormitories quickly, and if everything was quiet, leave it at that. The cook should be arriving soon; maybe she would know something about the noises he had heard. Or had he just imagined them?

He was going to go back upstairs when he heard a commotion outside. He grabbed a heavy hockey stick; the children must have used it for practice in the back, and somebody had forgotten to put it away. I will have to have a word, he thought, but in reality he knew he would do nothing about it.

He fumbled for the key which hung a little bit too high to the right-hand side of the door. "Alright, alright, I am coming," he called, thinking it must be time for the cook to arrive and she had forgotten her keys again. "Not for the first time," he mumbled to himself, conscious that he was not fully dressed and it did not seem right to greet a woman in such attire. He turned the large iron key twice and pushed the handle down. Normally he needed all his strength to pull the door open; it always stuck in this weather as the hinges should have been oiled long ago.

Somebody pushed against the door from the outside. "What do you think..." but the rest was left unspoken. Outside stood Ivone Kirkpatrick from the British High Commission. He quickly entered, looked around to make sure nobody had followed him, closed the door behind him and leaned his back against it, breathing in and out heavily.

"I did not see your car. Sorry, I did not know we were expecting you today, I must apologise."

Kirkpatrick shook his head, indicating he was out of breath and could not immediately reply. His hands rested on his knees while he tried to calm himself.

"Come into the kitchen, I'll make us some tea."

"I came as quickly as I could, and I can't stay very long," Kirkpatrick finally managed to say. "I have to attend a meeting," he added apologetically.

Kurt had not yet asked him why he was here. In any case, he knew Kirkpatrick would explain himself in a minute; he always did.

"How many children have you here at this precise moment?"

"You know we can never be very precise. Only a few days ago I presumed we were full, and now I am not so sure. Why do you ask?"

"You have got to pack their belongings. They have to leave."

"Why do they have to leave, and where shall they go? This is now their home – most of them don't have anybody else. No, we are not leaving. Why do you ask such a thing of me?"

"Kurt, they are burning the synagogues. They are breaking into stores and homes. They destroy anything in their way, and this will only be the beginning."

"Who?"

"I witnessed SA and Hitler Youth, but I did not wait around. I have just come past the Rykestrasse Synagogue. It has not burned down, but I saw all the windows were broken and the furnishings destroyed. I have heard that the Torah Scrolls were set alight, and the Rabbis and male congregation have been arrested and taken away."

"You walked all the way past the Rykestrasse?" Kurt filled the teapot with the water from the kettle, which had just boiled, and pulled himself a seat on the opposite side of the table from where Kirkpatrick, who was still not breathing normally, sat.

"Kurt, the children have to leave."

"Tell me where and how."

Chapter 6

Amsterdam

Esther walked through the Judenbreestraat. She made sure to pass the house where Rembrandt once lived. There she paused for a few minutes. The area around this street on most days felt alive, with open cafés, storefronts and street vendors. She could get used to the vibrant atmosphere here, she thought, but they could not stay. Living in Amsterdam was not the plan; she just could not bring herself to talk to her father about it. She would have to do this soon, before he became too settled, but first she needed to send a message to Maria's brother in Brussels. She was glad she had insisted on walking on her own today, without being accompanied by Jacob every time she went anywhere. She even managed to ask for the fresh bagels in Yiddish, something her father had insisted she had to do, in the only area in Amsterdam where you could buy fresh bread on a Sunday.

She had offered to do the cooking, but Ruth would not let her into the kitchen.

"You can cook for us when your father has found his own place to live. You will be moving in with him, is that not correct?" Luckily for Esther, Jacob had entered before a reply was expected.

"Esther, Esther!" Her father was waiting for her at the window, and he waved and shouted. She detected great excitement in his voice, and dreaded what would happen next.

Her father and Zachary had heard of an empty apartment not far from Zachary's home, and there would even be enough space for Mordechai's workshop. Esther had secretly hoped they would not be able to see it today – she should have said something earlier.

"Esther, I found it. It is perfect for us! There is so much room. Ever bigger than our home. Yes, you were right, we had to leave. It is safe here. Everybody says so, and we can move in at the end of this month. Oh Esther, we have a future again. I must thank you for bringing me here."

Esther was still standing in the hallway, the shopping basket tightly held in her gloved hand, a woollen scarf wrapped round her head and her boots making puddles on the clean linoleum from the melting ice she had trotted upstairs.

"Father, we are not staying in Amsterdam. We are moving on, the sooner the better."

"Esther, what are you talking about? We will live here in Amsterdam, near our trusted friends."

Esther had her back to him, hanging up her heavy coat. Then she bent down to unfasten her boots.

"Esther, turn around. Don't have your back to me. Explain yourself."

Esther turned slowly to face him, and noticed Zachary, Ruth and Jacob behind him. Ruth was drying her hands on a towel, and her mouth was open with astonishment. She stared at Esther and noticed the anguish in her face.

"Jacob, you go and set the table. Zachary, come with me."

Zachary was going to reply, but thought better of it. Before he entered the kitchen, he turned round and said: "You two must speak together, but do not reach any hasty decisions."

Mordechai, Esther, Zachary, Ruth and Jacob said their prayers before they shared their meal. The normally quite noisy evening event was silent on this occasion. When Ruth and Esther had cleared away the dishes and returned to sit with the others, Zachary could not wait any longer.

"Is anybody going to tell us what is happening?"

"Esther informed me that we are going to England."

Immediately Jacob perked up. "England? But how? They will not let anybody in. I know some friends who wanted to leave for England, but were turned away."

"You have friends who wanted to go and live in England?"

"Why is that so surprising? I think Esther is right, we should *all* go."

"Jacob, what's got into you? See what you have done, Esther? Now my good boy wants to leave his mother."

"Esther, have you thought this through?"

"No. They came for him just before midnight. First we thought it was the neighbours trying to get in. We had seen them a few moments before, running in the opposite direction. Ibrahim was in the bedroom, getting Father up and begging him to keep silent – begging him to pretend we were not at home. But I did not know anything about it. I thought it was the neighbours, don't you see? I let them in. They stormed upstairs. Six of them, all in SA uniform. They grabbed Ibrahim by the hair and pulled him down the stairs, past me, out of the front door. I was still standing there, holding it open. I heard him whisper through his pain. 'Go to England,' he said. I promised him, don't you see?"

Chapter 7

"Let's go over it again."

"Jacob should be in Brussels by now with your note. Are you sure Maria's brother will agree to becoming the contact for everybody to pass messages back and forth whenever possible? It could become a dangerous task, Esther."

"I have been given his address. That is all I know."

"I will get the train tickets as we agreed. Remember, I can only come with you as far as Rotterdam. There I will help you on to the train to the Hook of Holland, but after that you are on your own."

Zachary was sitting opposite Esther at the dining table. They had made some plans earlier in the week. Mordechai and Ruth were sitting side by side on the settee in front of the hot stove. He was only half listening to what was being said, but now he turned his head to face his old friend.

"Will it be safe?" Mordechai said.

"Yes, of course. We can still move around freely."

"And why should we not?" added Ruth. "I do not understand why you insist on leaving. Surely Ibrahim would understand that you are better off here in Holland. What can happen to us here? We do not have Nazis or the SA patrolling the streets. We live in Holland."

"How will you arrange to get a boat to England? This is something we have not discussed."

"I do not know, but I will find a way. First we will go to the place you told us about for food and lodgings. From the map you drew, it is halfway between the station and the dock. There my father can rest while I make some enquiries."

"Esther, it was only you who promised your husband. It was not me. Why can I not remain here? Zachary said I could stay. He could make space for my work. Two of his sewing machines are idle anyway and can be stored. We have it all figured out. Yes, I should stay."

"Father, I am not leaving without you. We have gone over this many times. We are leaving the day after tomorrow."

In Rotterdam, Mordechai hugged his friend for one last time.

"Thank you, my friend. You will be in my prayers. I will try and get word to you and tell you where we are. Please thank Ruth again." The whistle blew, and they heard some of the doors slamming shut.

"*Shalom Aleichem*, Mordechai." Zachary turned around and walked out of the carriage. Before he closed the door behind him, he whispered almost to himself, "I hope you know what you are doing, Esther."

Esther had had very little time to contemplate what she was going to do when they got to the Hook of Holland, but had not admitted to anyone that, in fact, she had not come up with a plan at all. Thankfully her father thought it was best to ignore her and looked solemnly out of the window, not turning round once in the hour it took them to reach their destination. Wordlessly Esther gathered their cases. Mordechai again insisted on carrying his by himself and refused any help with his rucksack.

"Here it is, Father, I told you it was not far. Heenweg: there is the house. Let's knock." Esther climbed the few steps to the front door of a tall house with a small front garden, iron railings on both sides of the steps. The roof seemed more round than pointed, its sides covering the whole of the second storey. Esther smiled; it looked like the bow of a ship. This is a good sign, she thought, and confidently pulled on the string outside the front door. She heard the sound of the bell inside, followed by clonking footsteps. A key turned in the lock, and the door opened a fraction. A little girl, not much older than seven, said, "*Mijn moeder is niet thuis.*"

Esther stared at her. "*Mijn moeder is niet thuis,*" the little girl repeated in case she had not been heard.

"*Laura, wie is het?*" A male voice. "*Ik weet het niet.*"

Laura replied, and decided to leave the door as it was and go back inside.

Esther turned towards her father and waved him to come and join her. Begrudgingly, he picked up his suitcase, which had been standing on the ground, and went up the steps.

Esther had already entered into the hall. An elderly man came out of a room to her left.

"*Wie zijn jullie en wat komen jullie hier doen?*"

To Esther's surprise, Mordechai stepped forward, passed her by, stretched out his hand and said, "I am Mordechai Goldstein, and this is my daughter, Esther Rosenthal, a doctor. We are friends of Zachary, the tailor in Amsterdam, on our way to England. He told us we would be welcome in your home for food and lodgings."

Their host seemed stunned for a few seconds, then said, "*Shalom Aleichem.*"

"*Aleichem Shalom.*"

"Come, come, you must be tired."

Chapter 8

Esther was glad her father did not object when she left him at the lodgings the following morning. The family there had been so kind the previous evening, but Esther did not want to impose on their hospitality for too long. She already felt guilty that they'd had to accept money from Zachary; he had insisted because he did not want them to have to go and look for a bank that could be persuaded to change Reichsmarks into Dutch guilders. Secretly Esther had left a pair of earrings in the bathroom with a short thank you note. She feared that Zachary and Ruth might be offended by her gesture, but she had left them anyway as it made her feel better.

She had no idea how to purchase tickets for a crossing to England, or whether there would be a boat leaving within the next few days. What if they were not allowed to travel on one of them? Or would they be returned once they arrived? What paperwork was required, she did not know.

She decided to go and ask at the station. The station door flew open when she got there, and a little boy shot out, almost knocking Esther over. "*Houd die jongen tegen,*" Esther heard, and instinctively she grabbed his arm, almost making him spin round. She quickly kneeled in front of him to make sure he was alright. His teeth were chattering, tears rolling down his face. His short trousers were wet and his knees bleeding, maybe from an earlier fall.

"Come back, Benjamin. Thank you." A girl who had come looking for him took his hand and pulled him back.

"Is he alright?" Esther asked and followed the girl. Inside the station, she saw a sea of children. There must be nearly

200, she thought. Although the station was totally crowded, it had an eerie silence. The only voices Esther could make out were Dutch adults, shouting back and forth and running up and down, trying to push the children in some sort of line, which seemed totally pointless to Esther. Out of the corner of her eye, she noticed one of the children being sick and rushed to her aid. She took her handkerchief out of her coat pocket and wiped the girl's face. She felt the child's forehead, which was hot.

"*Wie ben jij?*"

"I am a doctor and this child has a fever," Esther replied in German, not caring whether the man who had spoken to her understood her or not.

"You are a German doctor?"

"Yes."

"Are you travelling with these children?"

Esther looked at dozens of frightened faces now forming a circle around her. Some held on to small cases, others clutched only a brown paper bag. Every one of them seemed to have a label either attached or hanging by a string from their neck. All of the children had a number.

"Yes, I am travelling with these children."

"Good, good, their boat leaves in two hours."

"Their boat to where?"

"I thought you were travelling with the children."

"I am, but I was not given their final destination."

"Harwich. Now gather your children in an orderly fashion."

"Wait! I have to get my luggage." When the man looked at her puzzled, she quickly added, "I have been waiting for them at a house in Heenweg."

"Then be quick, the boat cannot wait. You go and help the doctor," he said to a lanky boy standing next to the little one Esther had stopped from running away.

Esther and the boy hurried out of the station and back

to Esther's lodging. On the way, she managed to ask, "Who are you all and where are you going?"

The boy replied, "Most of us are from an orphanage in Berlin."

"Stay here while I get my father," Esther told him when they got to the house. She almost pulled the bell string too hard, then rushed past Laura, who opened the door.

"Father, come and get your things, I have found us a crossing."

"You have a what?"

"Father, please hurry. The boat leaves in two hours, and we first have to gather the children from the station."

"Esther, have you been drinking?"

Esther felt she had no other option. She pulled her father out of his bed, took his case and gave him his rucksack, which still seemed far too heavy. She rushed to her room, then ushered her father down the stairs. Putting her head round the open dining room door, she said, "We have a crossing. Thank you for your help, but we have to hurry."

"Esther, we have to say goodbye properly."

Finally, Esther had her father outside. The boy picked up the two cases and ran ahead.

"Who is that boy?"

"I will explain later. Please come along." Twenty-five minutes after Esther had left the station, she was back. All the children had lined up two by two. The bigger children had smaller ones by the hand, and a few older children carried the youngest.

Mordechai was bewildered, but it took him only a few seconds to realise that all the children here were Jewish. He went over to the little boy who was at the front, holding on to the bigger one who had carried their suitcases, and started to speak with them.

"Are you ready, Doctor? We have to start walking if we

want to ensure everybody gets on board. Who is that man?"

"He is my father."

"He cannot come."

"He has to come, I am not going without him."

"We were only sent word that a doctor would be accompanying the children, just *one* doctor."

"My father is a doctor. Yes, he is a psychiatrist." When that did not get a reaction, she added, "His specialist work is with traumatised children."

"I see. Let's go."

The group started to move, and Esther noticed that the three children whom she had met already never left her side.

"Esther, I am a clockmaker," Mordechai whispered.

"Father, at this moment you are Dr Goldstein, the child psychiatrist."

"But what do I know about psychiatry?"

"Look at me, I am your best example." Esther actually managed a smile.

Chapter 9

"What is your name?" Esther managed to ask, out of breath, trying to get her father moving quicker while keeping an eye on all the children. The bunch of paperwork had dropped on the ground once already. She was glad that at least it had a string tied around it, preventing the pages escaping into the distance as the boy retrieved it and gave it back to her.

"Joshua." Then he stopped briefly and looked at Esther. "Over there, that is my brother Benjamin and my sister Rebecca."

"Joshua, will you help me to get my father on board?"

"Yes, what should I do?"

"When we get there, can you get your little brother to hold my father by the hand and shout or cry, kick, make a commotion?"

"Benjamin does not speak." Esther saw the main gate of the docks about 100 metres away in the distance; she stopped and stared at Joshua.

"He can speak, he just has not spoken since we arrived at the orphanage. He does understand when I speak to him and will do as he is told – besides the shouting, that is."

Joshua rushed over and spoke to Rebecca and Benjamin, nodding towards Esther and then in the direction of her father. The look on Benjamin's face reminded her of a frightened deer. He went over to Mordechai and placed his small hand into her father's. Mordechai nodded that he understood.

"He will do as he is told. They are opening the big gate for us, are we going on the boat now?"

Instead of replying, Esther asked, "How many children are here?"

"Altogether, or just from the orphanage?"

"Altogether."

"196."

"So many?"

"It says so, see, there on top of the papers."

Esther had not even bothered to check. The man at the station had almost thrown them at her. He could not get rid of everybody quickly enough. Esther knew if the boy did not trust her, she and her father would not travel on this boat.

Just minutes before they reached the gate, she took a risk and asked him, "Joshua, do you know who we are?"

His smile could have lightened the darkest corner. "Yes, you are Dr Rosenthal, and your father is Dr Goldstein, a head doctor."

"*Wacht even*! *Bent u de dokter?*"

At that precise second, Benjamin started wailing and pulling on Esther's father's coat, kicking with his foot against Mordechai's shin. Esther saw her father wince in pain, then Rebecca joined in.

"Stop it, stop it, Benjamin. Dr Rosenthal, help."

"*Wat is er met die jongen?*" asked the guard, his concentration directed towards them.

Joshua stepped between him and Mordechai. "My little brother is having a fit, he needs to lie down. These soldiers frightened him. His doctor is with him."

Esther hoped that the guard understood some of what Joshua had said, and waited.

"*Breng dat kind aan boord, haast je, haast je.*"

The same two men Joshua had referred to as soldiers picked up Benjamin. One of them carried the small boy while the other rushed ahead to make space, and Mordechai was right behind them. The other children took this as a sign to follow two by two, not once looking back. Benjamin was by now swinging his head and arms around so much that Esther wondered whether he really was having a fit. She would look at him as soon as they were all settled on board.

Esther handed the guard her paperwork. He did not even look at it before giving it back.

"*Deze zijn voor de autoriteiten in Engeland.*"

Esther found no time during the journey across to contemplate her future. It no longer mattered whether she and her father would gain entry; what mattered were the children. The wind throughout the journey was ferocious and the crossing was on very rough waters. Many of the children were seasick, and Esther was rushing from one child to another.

Meanwhile, her father tried to locate everybody in the group, but he lost count on several occasions. Joshua became invaluable, making sure that the children from the orphanage were gathered on one side in a large corridor. He told them to sit on the floor; this would help to prevent further seasickness. None of the children had received any food during the long journey, and only had what had been provided by the orphanage for them to carry along. Most of it had been eaten only a few moments after they left Berlin. Although he had earlier complained of being hungry, Joshua was now thankful that he had nothing inside him.

The crossing seemed endless, but the children's spirits rose when one of them shouted he could see lights. That almost started a stampede; all thoughts of not being well seemed forgotten. Esther started to panic that a child would fall overboard or get crushed in the rush forward, and her father had to pull her back, preventing her from rushing after them outside.

"Listen to your psychiatrist, Esther. Look at them, they look happy. Something they have not been for a long time, I reckon."

Esther relaxed a little and went to find their belongings and the paperwork. She could not remember where she had put it down and frantically looked round, spotting it on the floor covered by a soggy mess. She bent down and retrieved it with the corner of her scarf, feeling unwell herself at the stench around her, then fumbled to find her left hand glove and put it on. Her father was outside with the children; she saw him speaking to them and pointing to the dim light on land.

There was a loud rattle and bump, and Esther knew the boat had docked. She took a deep breath and opened the door to the outside.

"Come on, everybody, it is time to go to England."

The excitement on the children's faces made it all worthwhile. She believed that most were orphans, leaving nothing behind, and in front of them was a new life. She heard the big doors open and a gangplank being attached. Several officials entered the boat, almost taking a step backwards, overcome by the smell, then they spotted her and walked over.

"Are you the doctor with the children?"

"Yes, I am Dr Rosenthal."

"Welcome to Britain, Doctor. Do you have the paperwork?"

Esther held her gloved hand forward and handed him the soggy paperwork. He looked at it once without taking it, turned round and said, "Smith, come over here. Take the papers down to the office." To Esther, he said, "We can check those later. Can you get the children lined up and start moving? The coaches are waiting outside."

Chapter 10

There was no stopping them. All the discipline the children had shown until now disappeared. Her father was right; even if not all of them looked happy, they looked relieved. Esther counted five coaches and hoped everybody would find a seat.

Joshua, Rebecca and Benjamin remained with Esther and Mordechai. Esther saw that Joshua had removed the labels giving the children a number, and heard him say, "You are not a number any more, you hear? You have a name."

"Come on, children, let's find a seat on the bus."

Joshua was back a few minutes later. "All the seats are gone, Dr Rosenthal." Esther looked around and realised that, besides them, there were still about a dozen children standing outside, and the first of the buses had started to move. To her relief, she noticed another vehicle arriving. At last everybody was on board and the driver climbed back in.

Rebecca was sitting behind Esther, and she whispered, "Dr Rosenthal, the bus is driving on the wrong side of the road. Will we have an accident?"

Before Esther could reply, Joshua said, "Don't you remember? Herr Crohn told us that in England cars drive on the left side of the road."

Benjamin, who had been sitting on Joshua's lap on a seat right behind Mordechai, tapped Mordechai on the shoulder. Mordechai turned around, and Benjamin stretched his arms out towards him. Joshua lifted Benjamin off and handed him over, and Benjamin settled immediately, sucking his thumb and resting his head against Mordechai's coat.

"Who said you are not a child psychiatrist specialising

in traumatised children?" Esther said softly. She could see how content her father had become during the last hours. I wonder whether he still thinks it was a bad idea to come, she thought.

It had started to rain mixed with sleet by the time their coach drove through a large entry gate and down a small gravel road. The vehicle stopped in front of a long one-storey building. Through the coach window, Esther spotted a woman standing outside, ushering the last of the children who had arrived before them inside. She then walked over and knocked on the coach door. Esther had left her seat already and was directing the children, while Mordechai took Benjamin's hand.

Esther was the last to leave.

"Welcome to Britain, I am Anna Essinger. You are Dr Rosenthal?"

Esther took the woman's outstretched hand. "Thank you, Frau Essinger, what is this place?"

"It is a holiday camp," she said, starting to walk towards the door. Esther stopped for a minute and looked around, puzzled.

"You must be exhausted. Please come. First you must eat, and then I will show you where you will be staying. Who is that gentleman with the little boy?"

Esther immediately felt drawn to this woman and felt she deserved the truth.

"He is my father."

The noise from the room Esther entered was deafening. It made her almost step backwards. The room was very long, with rows and rows of tables. In front of each sat the children, still in their coats, their belongings piled up against the wall on one side. At the delicious smell of freshly baked bread and hot drinks, Esther dropped her case where she stood and joined them.

Chapter 11

Esther was the first to rise. Rebecca was in the bunk directly above her, and Benjamin was in the bottom bunk across from hers. He had cried most of the night, and Esther wondered whether she should have agreed to let him sleep in the other chalet with Joshua and Mordechai, but Joshua had been quite firm with him and insisted the little boy should be with his sister. All this was after Anna Essinger had apologised profusely for not having better accommodation for Esther and Mordechai.

Esther wet her face with cold water from the sink at the end of the chalet and found a towel on the little shelf unit to the left. She picked up her coat from the chair to go and find the bathrooms, hoping she would remember the way. It had been after midnight before all the children had settled, and Esther was not familiar with the layout of a holiday camp. Until now she had never known they existed. She would have to do some exploring today, and she wondered where she and her father would go from here.

Esther put her shoes on and slowly opened her door, looking round to make sure she did not disturb the children. Rebecca stirred and sat up on her bunk.

"Watch Benjamin. I don't want him wandering about. I am just going to the bathroom," Esther whispered. Rebecca nodded and settled back down.

Cold air stung Esther's face. The rain had stopped and there was a slight frost on the ground. She saw footprints from her father's chalet going in the direction of the long dining hall they had sat in the evening before, and she saw light flickering to her right. There she found the toilet block and the showers.

On the way back she decided to follow her father's footsteps to the hall. He was sitting across the table from Anna Essinger, holding a hot drink.

"Good morning, Dr Rosenthal. I see you are an early riser like your father."

"Good morning, Frau Essinger. Good morning, Father." Esther pulled up a chair and joined them. As soon as she sat down a hot drink appeared. "That smells wonderful, thank you," she said to an elderly lady wearing an apron which seemed to swamp her tiny frame.

"Meet Doreen, one of my many helpers."

"Good morning, Doreen. Thank you for my drink."

"Your father tells me you have made no plans where to go from here. Why don't you tell me what you have in mind?"

Esther felt all the tension leave her body. Whether it was because of the hot, sweet tea or the welcoming of this lovely woman sitting opposite her, she did not know. She took a deep breath and told Anna Essinger the whole story. Anna listened without interrupting, just waving at Doreen to bring more tea and some bread.

When Esther had finished, Anna Essinger said, "I for one am glad you are here. And for once the authorities have done the right thing by waiving all the formality and letting the children enter the country. Let's say a prayer of thanks."

"Is there a synagogue nearby?" Mordechai wanted to know.

"I have the Rabbi coming over to my school, and now the children are starting to arrive I will ask him to come here."

"You don't work here?"

"No. I used to have a boarding school in Germany, in Herrlingen, but about five years ago, like you, I no longer felt safe over there. I spoke to the parents of the children I taught and suggested I open a school here in England.

48

I had contacts here, you see."

Esther nodded, and Anna Essinger continued, "They readily agreed, so I went first to find the right location and building. I found a good school which I could take over. It is the Bunce Court School in Otterden, and I intend to teach some of the children who are arriving here at my school. I don't know how many places I can make available, but then again, not many of the children will remain here."

"Where will they go, the children who don't stay?"

"Some of them have families who will come and collect them. Some have sponsors who will take them in. Others will go to their relatives in the USA, Canada or Australia."

"Aren't all the children orphans?"

"Yes, you are right, most of the children who arrived with you are orphans from Berlin, but many children who will come here will be sent by their parents to keep them safe, away from Hitler's reach. Last night the first of many children arrived. We will have new ones coming every day from now."

"Your school, is it nearby?"

"Unfortunately, Otterden is about 95 miles from here, but when we had the idea to bring children from Germany over to England, we needed a place as soon as possible. This holiday camp is not used in the winter, and was an obvious choice as it is in close proximity to Harwich Harbour."

"What about the school?"

"It is a boarding school and I have excellent staff. I have got to go back after the Sabbath, and will return in about ten days."

"Who will be in charge here?"

"We have a wonderful team of volunteers, plus the local council will assist if they can. John Green is the manager here. He has many years of experience of running holiday camps throughout England. His German is very limited, mind you, and this is where you come in, Dr Rosenthal." Anna Essinger looked first at Esther and then Mordechai. "I would like you to stay here if at all possible."

Esther was going to reply, but Anna Essinger continued, "Please, hear me out. After that, give it some thought. We have a good first aid room for which we could get more equipment. The children know you already, none of them speak any English, and the volunteers do not speak German. We can find you more comfortable chalets, but I am sorry, I would not be able to pay you. However, you would have free lodgings and food until you have sorted yourselves out. What do you say, Dr Rosenthal?"

"Frau Essinger, I was going to say five minutes ago that yes, we would love to stay." Mordechai shot Esther a thankful look.

"That is settled then," continued Anna Essinger. "Besides a good doctor, we could do with a psychiatrist specialising in traumatised children."

"Frau Essinger, I am a…"

"I know, Herr Goldstein, but don't forget I saw you calming the children yesterday."

Chapter 12

Esther decided to stay in the chalet together with Rebecca and Benjamin. Joshua was happy to move into one further down, so Mordechai kept the one next to Esther, and most of their belongings were placed in there. Esther planned to check out the first aid room as soon as she could, before Frau Essinger had to leave. John Green had arrived first thing in the morning, together with at least half a dozen helpers, among them two young teachers who would take it in turns to teach English to the children. The lessons were to start before lunch in one of the entertainment halls which John was turning into a classroom. There were rows of desk with pencils and books to write in, and a larger desk for the teacher was placed at the front. Esther was surprised about how well everything was already organised; after all, the first children had only just arrived, but Anna Essinger explained the equipment had been given to them by local schools.

It took John Green most of the morning to show Esther and her father around. The first aid room was at the other end of the holiday camp, where the chalets seemed a little larger than the one Esther was staying in. There were also games rooms with table tennis tables.

"What is that over there on the wall?" Mordechai asked John, pointing towards a dartboard.

"A dartboard." When John realised that this meant nothing to them he started to explain the rules, but noticed he had lost them halfway through and laughed.

"Herr Goldstein, I will make a master player out of you, don't worry."

Outside they passed a small football field, where some older boys were already kicking a ball around. John beckoned them to come over, smiled, and said, "Dr Rosenthal, would you mind asking them whether they have been to the shower block?"

The answer seemed obvious. The smallest boy had dirty smudges all over his face, and dirty hands and knees. Esther looked at him with some concern.

"Mr Green, some of the children came only clutching a paper bag."

"Yes, we had a discussion about it when we knew the first children would arrive soon. We have a selection of clothes for some of them, and hope to have more soon. The problem is most families pass the clothes down to the youngest child, and if there are no younger ones in the household they go to cousins or friends. Money is tight everywhere. Sorry, but I have got to go back now. You are welcome to have a look around on your own."

"I will come with you," said Mordechai to John.

Esther was pleased to be left alone for a while; she needed to use the time to have a better look at the first aid room and find a way to make it into a clinic, but first she wanted to see inside the chalets on either side and hoped they were unlocked. She walked over, trying not to slip on the icy ground, and pulled on the door handle of the one nearest to her. It opened with a slight squeak, and she remained where she was to take it all in. Yes, that would be perfect, she thought. Closing the door, she went to the first aid room. It was light and airy; the wall was a brilliant white, and a desk stood on the opposite side, facing the door, one chair behind it and one in front. To the right stood a red leather examination couch, and Esther went over to inspect it. It seemed in excellent condition, with wooden legs and a back that lifted up, a wooden latch keeping it in the upright position.

On the opposite side of the room was a tall cabinet with glass doors. Esther tried to open it, but it was locked. Through the glass she could see several bottles of all shapes and sizes; she would have to check those later. She sat on one of the chairs, retrieved a piece of paper and a pencil out of her coat pocket and started making a few notes.

Satisfied, she had another look and left. Before she returned to see Anna Essinger, she checked the other chalet again.

Anna Essinger came to greet her halfway. "Dr Rosenthal, I have been looking for you. I received a phone call from the school, and I have to leave sooner than I hoped. Tell me, do you think the first aid chalet would be useful?"

"It will be lovely. I have a few ideas – do you have time to go over them?"

"Let's sit in the dining hall."

"I made a list of items I would need and medicines we should carry, plus towels, soaps and disinfectants. Whom do you think I should go and see?"

"I will arrange for John to take you first to the town hall, and from there to the local hospital. It would be a good idea if you got to know the doctors in charge. Would there be anything else?"

Esther knew this woman was already stretched to her limit, but she needed to discuss as much as she could now. "I checked the chalets on either side of the first aid station and they would be ideal for little recuperation rooms."

Anna Essinger gave her a questioning look.

"What I am trying to say is: children will fall ill while here, about that I have no doubt, with measles and chickenpox, for example. You saw for yourself how thin some of the orphans are. Their immune systems will be compromised at this stage, and I also assume they will be the ones to stay the longest before arrangements can be made."

"Dr Rosenthal, it is a very good idea. I trust your judgement completely. I will have a word with John. He is very resourceful. If he is in any doubt about something, he will be the first one to say so. Go ahead and have your unit. The only condition I am going to make is you will have to move into the chalet next to it. If we have really ill children in there, you have to be close by."

"Thank you, Frau Essinger."

"There is no need to thank me. You have no idea how grateful I am that you are here. The bigger boys can help you to move your things."

"What about the children?"

"Rebecca and Benjamin?"

"Yes."

"I think it would be best if the children do not get too attached to you. We will have to find a family to take them in."

"I am sorry, Frau Essinger, I have to disagree. Benjamin is just learning to trust people again, so we cannot send them to total strangers at this moment."

Anna Essinger let out a deep sigh. "Dr Rosenthal, the children can go with you if you feel that is the right thing to do at the moment, but I am concerned how they will react when they do have to leave."

Both women got up from their chairs and shook hands.

"Good luck, Dr Rosenthal. I will see you in about ten days' time."

"Goodbye, Frau Essinger, and thank you again."

Mordechai entered the room just as Esther was leaving. "Where are you going, Father?"

"I am going to improve my English."

Later, Mordechai left the hall together with John to go and look for Esther. They spotted her directing two boys pushing a wooden cart towards her new chalet. Benjamin was holding her hand. When Benjamin noticed Mordechai, he left Esther and ran towards him. Mordechai picked him up and spun him round, immediately regretting such a move, and quickly put him down and held his back.

"I told you, Father, you are not getting any younger." Esther laughed. Mordechai was pleased and relieved that Esther seemed in such high spirits.

"I see you are moving."

"Yes, you can have the chalet on the other side."

"No, thank you, I think I'd like to stay where I am. Esther, I need to talk to you."

She stopped. "What is it, Father?"

"We need money. I know we don't need anything here, but we cannot live off these kind people forever. We need to have our own funds. Tomorrow John will take me to a pawnbroker. I want to take some of your mother's jewellery, if you agree."

"John?"

"Yes. England is far less formal, and he feels awkward if I keep calling him Mr Green. Anyway, Esther, what do you think I should take?"

Esther looked down at her coat, and then at the coat her father was wearing over his jacket. No wonder their clothes felt heavy; it was time to put them back as they should be.

"Can you leave your jacket and coat with me for the rest of the afternoon?"

Mordechai took them off and handed them to one of the boys.

Chapter 13

The honour befell Mordechai: he lit the first of the Hanukkah candles. There had been great excitement and anticipation when it was announced that this year they were allowed to celebrate Hanukkah openly again. It had been especially hard on the children in recent years. They had failed to understand that candles, which were supposed to be seen by the outside, had to be hidden instead, so the Menorah was placed as close to the window as possible without endangering the children. Mordechai had said the three blessings before the first candle was lit, and while lighting it he sang the 'Halalu'. He had followed this routine since boyhood, although in some households the hymn would be recited at the end.

The children were served the traditional latke, potato pancakes and apple sauce, followed by jelly doughnuts. After the blessing and the singing of 'Ma'oz Tzur', each child was presented with a small gift. Rebecca joined her new-found friends, and for the first time Benjamin left the table where Joshua sat with the larger boys. He ventured to one nearby where five other boys of a similar age were eating their doughnuts, holding on to his grey socks and sweater in case they got mixed up with the ones the other boys had been given. Some of the jam from the doughnuts had left smudges across his face.

Esther smiled as she watched him. She sat at a table not far away, just her and her father sitting together. She knew her father had treated them to a bottle of wine, which they would share at his chalet later. None of the volunteers or John had joined them for the celebration. They had left after the food had been served, and Esther appreciated their gesture.

The remaining seven days of Hanukkah would be celebrated by everybody. Anna Essinger split her time between her school and the children here. Some of the children were lucky enough to go and live with their relatives or temporary foster parents. During the last three weeks, most of the children from the Berlin orphanage had moved out, thanks to the tireless efforts of Anna Essinger. Esther was a little bit surprised that Frau Essinger never mentioned the fate of Rebecca and Benjamin during her visits. However, a few days ago she had raised the question about Joshua. She would arrive on Tuesday and had to return on Friday, which was when she required an answer.

Esther looked over to Joshua, who was laughing at something one of the other boys had said. His confidence and the way he so easily made friends amazed her. She doubted whether it was right to unsettle him again so soon. Across from her, she spotted Rebecca and the group of girls clearly having a good time. At the beginning, Rebecca had been disturbed at the constant coming and going of new children. No sooner had she made a friend than the girl moved on, but slowly Rebecca learned to understand that this was not a permanent home.

"Are you going to tell him today?" Mordechai had carried two big cups of tea to their table and sat down again.

"I don't know, Father. Maybe not today."

"You will have to give him some time to think about it. Also you might have to approach Rebecca and Benjamin together. Either way, you have to have a reply this week."

"A reply about what?" They had not noticed that Joshua was standing next to them, and had overheard what Mordechai had just said.

"Come and sit down, Joshua, there is something we need to discuss."

Joshua did what was asked of him: he pulled up a chair

and sat next to Mordechai and opposite Esther.

"Are you going to send us away?"

"No, Joshua, I would never send you away." Joshua visibly relaxed.

"Joshua, you do know that Frau Essinger has a big boarding school?" Joshua nodded. Esther looked at her father, sighed and said, "Frau Essinger would like you to go there."

"I have to leave?"

"No, no, no, let me explain it better. Frau Essinger has noticed how well you are doing at your English classes. Also she has heard nothing but praise about you from the other teachers who recently arrived: how bright you are and how awful it would be if you were not given a chance. She wants you to go to her school as one of her boarding students and learn."

Joshua tilted his head to the side and raised his eyebrow, as if to say, you are trying to send me away, aren't you.

"Joshua, Frau Essinger believes it would be very good for you if you go with her in January."

"But what about Rebecca and Benjamin? Are they coming as well? I cannot leave them behind, I promised to take care of them."

"Joshua, listen to Dr Rosenthal. Take this chance which is offered to you. We will make sure your sister and brother are safe here with us. You do trust us, don't you?"

Joshua nodded. "At the beginning of January, you say? I would be able to visit you, do you think?"

"Yes, yes, definitely."

"And you will make sure nobody takes Rebecca and Benjamin?"

"You have our word on that."

"Can we wait until after Hanukkah to tell them?"

Chapter 14

"Joshua, it is time to leave. Have you seen my daughter?" Mordechai hesitated in the doorway for a moment and saw that some of Joshua's belongings were still on the floor.

"Herr Goldstein, Rebecca is still very upset. I think I would prefer to stay here."

"No, you must go and learn. You said you wanted to become a doctor, just like my Esther."

"I can't, I am sorry. I will not leave them behind." Joshua continued to unpack his small case and put everything back on the bottom bunk.

He had said goodbye to the three new boys now sharing his chalet who had only arrived the previous week. All three wrote letters to their parents each night, taking it in turns to use the chair like a desk, kneeling or sitting on the floor. The first night they had asked how often Joshua received word from home, but after he had explained that he had no family other than Rebecca and Benjamin, they decided not to press him any further.

Instead, he heard them whisper together at night when they thought he was asleep.

"What do you think happened to his mother and father?"

"Some of our neighbours disappeared when our synagogue burned, maybe that is what happened."

"No, Rebecca told me they were in an orphanage in Berlin when that happened."

"I first thought that Rebecca was Dr Rosenthal's daughter, they seem so close."

"That Benjamin is weird. Some boy on the football field

told me he has not said a word since he arrived."

"Yes, the tall boy said it. He arrived with them. They met on the train."

Joshua had tried to cover his ears with the blanket.

"I can't believe Joshua is going off to a boarding school and leaving them behind. I would never do that to my brother and sister."

"You don't have a brother and sister."

"No, but if I had, I mean."

"Psst, I think Joshua has just woken."

"Joshua, stop unpacking. Sit next to me. Come and talk to me."

Mordechai sat on the bunk opposite and indicated with his hand to the place right next to him where Joshua should sit.

Joshua did what was asked of him. Looking at Mordechai, he said, "I promised my mother I would look after them."

Mordechai's heart missed a beat. This was the first time Joshua had mentioned his mother. He kept as still as he could; he did not want to stop the boy now, but Joshua said nothing further.

"Your mother and father, are they still alive?"

Joshua shook his head. "No."

"You do not have any other relatives, like an aunt and uncle?"

"I don't know."

"You never met a member of your mother's or father's family?"

"Only my grandparents, but they are gone as well."

"So you promised your mother, you said?"

"Yes. Herr Goldstein, what will happen to us?"

"Joshua, Esther and I – we have no other family besides Dr Rosenthal's husband. What would you say if we were to become a family now? You, me, Dr Rosenthal, Rebecca and Benjamin. What do you think?"

"I would like that very much. Thank you, Herr Goldstein."

"Don't thank me, Joshua, I am your granddad. Now let us tell Esther and my new grandchildren."

Chapter 15

"What paperwork do we need to go ahead?"

Anna Essinger had not questioned their decision when she arrived the Sunday afternoon after New Year's Eve. She had half expected it. It did surprise her, however, when Esther said that it was Mordechai who first raised it.

"You are aware we only have our own identification, and nothing for the children to explain how we know them."

"I am sure we can convince the board on the local council here that it has always been your intention to adopt the children. Nobody will have any proof that this was not the case when you were in Germany. They will not question the children, other than to ask whether this is what they really want and are there no other relatives to take them in. I will have to do the translation, and we will have to sit together with Joshua, Rebecca and Benjamin to go over and over it again. Benjamin is my greatest concern."

"How long do you think it will all take?" asked Esther.

"To be honest, Dr Rosenthal, I think the council will be relieved that another group of children is no longer their concern."

Esther looked shocked at what Anna Essinger had just said, but Frau Essinger continued, "Please remember more children arrive every day. Not all of them have funds from their family back home to make sure they are taken in and cared for. You know as well as I do that some of the children arrive with nothing at all. The authorities here are feeling the strain, and I am beginning to worry about how we will cope. No, believe me, it will not be long until you have the official papers."

"What happens after that? Do we leave?"

"No. Right now we cannot do without a good doctor and a 'psychiatrist' on site." At the mention of Mordechai's new-found profession, Frau Essinger smiled. "But we will have to look beyond that. News from Germany is that the situation there is getting more unstable every day. I fear there will be a war after all."

"Yes, my father agrees. Hitler will not give up. I am still shocked that he was allowed to take over the Sudetenland the way he did. You are right, it will not end there."

"Dr Rosenthal, you and your father will have to talk about your future and the future of the children. Joshua is coming with me as a boarder exactly as planned. I really don't like raising this again, but as soon as he is officially your son, the school will have to charge fees just like they do for every other child. Any spare places I have I must keep open for a child without means. You do understand that, don't you?"

"Please, Frau Essinger, you have done so much for us already. My father will be giving you the fees for Joshua immediately."

"That is really not necessary."

"It is what my father wants. It is important to him that Joshua has a family when he goes with you. He also insists we no longer live here for free."

"I have got to stop you there. You are not living here for free. You are an excellent doctor and we really need you. It should be us paying you."

"There will, of course, come a time when we have to move on. As you say, my father and I have to decide where we will go from here. I have already spoken to some of the doctors at the local hospital, and will speak to them again. My English is good, and I have left the paperwork showing my qualifications with them. Also I am really friendly with a young nurse in the Casualty Department. You are aware there have been a few broken bones and Miriam had a burst appendix last month?"

"Yes, how is Miriam doing? Is she still there or have her foster parents collected her? Unfortunately the family she was going to move in with wanted a strong boy to work on their farm. They only said yes to a girl because Miriam's father has a big department store in Hamburg and they imagined they would be paid well to look after his only child."

"It saddens me. There have been two further cases identical to this one. Two more children whose parents believed they were safe only to be taken advantage of."

Anna Essinger picked up her cup of tea, which had long gone cold. "Have all the children with Rubella recovered?"

"Yes – besides Rebecca, that is. All the others can continue with their lessons at the end of the week."

"And no other cases reported?"

"None so far. I would like to enrol Rebecca in the local school here after the holiday. The young nurse I told you about, her brother goes to one not far from here. She has given me the name of the headmaster."

"Yes, that sounds a good idea. Are you going to enrol her using her new family name?"

"I had not thought about it, but yes, I will do just that."

Chapter 16

"Stop fidgeting."

"Is that a new word you have just learned? It's the third time you have told me that."

"Rebecca, don't tease your brother."

"Well, Dr Rosenthal, you already sound like their doting mother."

All six of them were sharing a wooden bench outside a closed ornamental door in a corridor on the second floor. 'Courtroom' said the polished brass sign to the right of the door. The group had arrived far too early, and Esther was regretting that she had made them set off over an hour ago. She had forgotten how impatient children could get when they were excited. The woman coordinator who had been assigned to their case was nowhere to be seen; they had only met her once, and even then she was in a hurry to go elsewhere.

"Will Benjamin start at the same school I am in?" Rebecca sat next to Esther. On Rebecca's other side was Joshua, who had now started pushing her with his knee. "Stop that. Mama, will you tell him to stop it? He is creasing my school skirt."

Rebecca had starting calling Esther 'mama' as soon as she was told about the possible adoption. She wanted to make sure Dr Rosenthal would not change her mind. The first time they had talked about being a family was just before Joshua went off with Aunty Anna, as they were allowed to call her. They had sat in the great dining room, just the five of them. As a special treat, the children had each been holding a hot chocolate which made their hands lovely and warm. They had listened to Esther when she explained what an adoption meant and how it would affect all their lives together. Esther needed to know that they understood, she had said, and whether there really was no other family they could go to. She also suggested they could call her Mama Esther, because they did have a mother already. Nobody had ever talked to them like this before.

Rebecca now went to the local primary school, which she insisted she could walk to on her own. For the first few weeks, when the attendance list was read out she would not automatically reply when her name was called. Rebecca Rosenthal. She loved how that sounded. The teacher had thought she did not reply because of a lack of understanding of the language, but she understood far more than she let on. She just wanted to hear her name again – instead of introducing herself on the first day, she had said, "My mother is a doctor."

"Yes, Rebecca, Benjamin will be starting there in September, just after the summer holiday."

"Did you hear that, Benjamin? You can come to school with me." Rebecca bent slightly forward so she could look past Aunty Anna and her new grandpa. Benjamin, as always, was holding Mordechai's hand.

"I am going to go downstairs to see whether that dreadful woman has turned up." Anna Essinger got up, and Joshua quickly moved into her vacated space.

The courtroom door opened. The man opening it studied them for a brief moment; as the glasses on his face slid down, he looked over the rim. His dark grey suit was creased and swamping his tiny frame, which made him look really uncomfortable and stern. Benjamin immediately moved closer to Mordechai and hid his face in Mordechai's jacket. The man looked down the corridor, went back inside and closed the door behind him again.

They heard voices and footsteps coming from the right, and Frau Essinger reappeared with a red-faced female in tow.

"Has anybody come to get you?" was all the woman said.

Esther was momentarily lost for words. She was still very concerned whether the adoption would actually go ahead today; the date had been changed twice before.

"Yes, and I think we should get inside."

Rebecca stood up. She did not like this woman. When she had questioned the children, she had made it sound as if it was all Aunty Anna's idea to 'get rid of them', as she had put it. She did not even let Frau Essinger or Esther sit in with the children. A translator had to come from another town, and Benjamin had immediately wet himself when he was faced with a man in a dark uniform.

Rebecca went to the door and touched its large metal handle, but the woman pushed past her, opened it instead and disappeared inside. After what seemed like a long time, but must have only been a few minutes, she came out again with the sweetest smile she could muster.

"They are ready for you now."

"Come along, Benjamin, we are going to be a real family now." Mordechai bent down as far as his back would allow him and looked into Benjamin's eyes.

"Yes, Grandpa," replied Benjamin.

Thud! The *Rupert Annual*, the book Rebecca had chosen as her present and to which she had clung like it would be her last book ever, landed on the polished floor.

"Let us celebrate."

"Yes, Grandpa. We can go out. Where shall we go to?" Rebecca had totally accepted her new position as daughter and granddaughter. After all, it was official now. The judge had said so. He had even said it was a very sensible solution. She did not fully understand what that meant, and she was sure neither did her grandpa, but they had all nodded and shaken hands, even with the red-faced woman. Rebecca only agreed to this after Joshua had whispered, "If we do not say goodbye to her now, she might come along with us."

"There is a Lyons Corner House not far from here," suggested Anna Essinger.

If the children had thought that their dining hall at Dovercourt Holiday Camp was large, the Lyons Corner House was enormous, and busier than Rotterdam Railway Station. At first the whole group seemed a bit overwhelmed and just stood in the doorway, not moving until more people started to form a line behind them. A young waiter carrying a large tray spotted them and waved to them to come inside. He pointed to a large table in the middle which had just become vacant.

Esther explained the menu and suggested what the children should order. They were even allowed a chocolate pudding afterwards.

"Grandpa, your watch is a different colour." Benjamin pointed to Mordechai's breast pocket with his chocolate covered spoon, wiping the remaining chocolate off his face with the other hand. Mordechai got his watch out and checked the time.

"Yes, Benjamin, the gold one has stopped working."

Back at the holiday camp, the children went off to play with their own group of friends. Esther wanted to check whether the delivery of the medicine she had requested had arrived, so went to her office. Several parcels were stacked on top of her desk. She lifted them off to check the labels, and beneath the last one she saw a brown envelope which had her name and address on it. She turned it over to see where it had come from, but there was no return address.

She looked at the envelope again, and then all colour drained from her face. It had a Belgian stamp on it.

Chapter 17

"Mama, is it wrong to lie?"

"Yes, it is very wrong to lie. Why do you ask?"

"Is it always wrong to lie or can you lie just a little to help somebody understand?"

"Rebecca, do you want to talk about it?"

Rebecca was in the chalet with Esther. She had climbed on to Esther's bunk, swinging her legs forth and back, wiping the sweat off her face, looking nervously towards the door. She was not supposed to hide inside: those were the rules when you played hide and seek.

"I told Benjamin that you have to stay at the hospital overnight because there are some ill people who need you."

"Rebecca!"

"But Liverpool is really far away and you will not be able to come back on the same day, will you? So I told him you have to stay overnight. What else could I do?"

"We will have to talk to him together."

"Mama, when he sees you leaving with the children and their cases, he will think you are not coming back."

"Surely he would not."

"I know my brother. He would, especially with Joshua still being at school. He is quite bright. He knows all the schools are on holiday, but Joshua is not back."

"I will only be away one night."

"Mama, when are we going to tell him that Joshua is not coming with us?"

Only a few days ago, Frau Essinger had been urged to

69

come to the camp immediately. Two brothers had arrived from Germany with their cousin and were supposed to travel on to New York, but there had been a misunderstanding. Their family back home wrongly believed that Dovercourt Bay Holiday Camp had confirmed passages on crossings to America. None of them could speak a word of English, so Esther had been called to the reception office when the children had refused to follow one of the volunteers to a chalet.

When Esther had got there, John was wrestling with the elder one, trying to remove a pocketknife the child had taken from inside his boots. As it turned out, all he wanted to do was to cut the lining in his jacket to show their paperwork and the money for the fare. Esther calmed the situation and moved the children to chalets close to her own. After that she spoke to Anna Essinger on the phone.

When Frau Essinger arrived three days later she had already spoken to the Cunard Line and been promised some passages on the *Queen Mary*, which was due to leave on 1 September 1939, only three weeks away.

"Dr Rosenthal, we have a problem," she had said when she sat with Esther and Mordechai at their usual table in the dining hall. Mordechai thought it best to listen and concentrated on his black tea and freshly baked scones. He preferred them as they were and declined the jam every time, but he did not say no to the occasional shot of dark rum which Doreen, one of the volunteers, slipped in.

"For medicinal purposes," she would whisper, brushing her cheek lightly on his face. Esther had witnessed him blushing once or twice.

"We cannot send the children unaccompanied. That was one of the conditions made by the Cunard Line."

"How will we tell their mother and father that we have to look for foster parents here in England?"

"Dr Rosenthal, somebody will have to accompany them

– somebody who will be welcomed into America because of their skills. That person has to speak good English and German."

"Surely you are not considering you go yourself? It will be weeks before you can return."

Mordechai sighed, put his tea down, swallowed the last of his scone and shook his head. "Esther, Frau Essinger is saying that you will be going."

"Me? But I can't. I am taking a brother and sister to Liverpool to hand them over to their grandparents. I cannot go to America. No, I cannot be away from Rebecca and Benjamin for longer than necessary. Plus what if there really is a war? You have heard the rumours, haven't you? No, I cannot go. No, Frau Essinger. If that is what you wanted to tell me, then no. I am really sorry."

"Dr Rosenthal, what did the letter from Belgium say?"

Besides Mordechai, nobody had been told about the letter she had received. Esther, however, was not surprised that Frau Essinger knew about it anyway.

"Nothing good."

"Did you get word about your husband?"

"Yes. They took him to Dachau in the south of Germany, apparently to work in a munitions factory there, but everybody knows it was turned into a forced labour camp by the SS in 1933." Esther wanted to add "You obviously know what was in the letter already," but stopped herself just in time.

"Dr Rosenthal, I hope I can persuade you to take up this offer for you two and your children to have a new beginning in America. I have booked the passages, and we will have to confirm them within two days. We have friends in the American Embassy in London who will issue you the visas."

Esther did not reply, but Mordechai got really excited. "Esther, we are going to America. We can make ourselves a new life. The children will have a future. A future you hoped they would have. Why are you even hesitating?"

"Father, what are we going to live off? Where are we going to go? Where are we going to live?"

"Esther, maybe it is time you started relying on your old father."

Chapter 18

The stop was a request stop. Esther hoped they had not missed their bus to the railway station; if they could not get on to the 9.15 to Manningtree, there would be no connection to London today. She was not looking forward to this long journey and hoped they would actually reach Liverpool in one day. Just as Esther had been ready to leave, Benjamin had run away and was nowhere to be found. Mordechai had explained to him that his new mother would be back the next morning, but still he did not believe it.

"Father, I have to stay. Somebody else will have to go instead."

"There is nobody else. We will find him. Besides, he has to learn to trust what we say is true."

Esther was annoyed with herself for not handling it better. Rebecca was right: it was she who knew her brother.

"Dr Rosenthal, here comes a bus. Is that the one we are taking?"

"It has to say 'railway station' on it. Have a good look." Esther had already seen the words were clearly visible on the front in a little window above the driver, but she wanted to teach the children as much as she could, making them look out for names and signs in a country they might be living in for some time.

"It is, it is." Gabriela immediately stretched her hand out to make it stop, just as she had been told to do, and they reached the station in no time. There were only two platforms, and their train would arrive at 9.12 on platform one. Samuel was a real gentleman despite his young age. He asked Esther to board the train before him, handed the cases up and told Gabriela to take them. The whistle had blown and the train was starting to move before Samuel got on himself and shut the heavy door behind him. The journey to Manningtree was less than one hour, and there Samuel did the whole procedure in reverse.

Esther could not spot any signs which pointed them to where they had to go next, but saw a guard and walked over to ask him. When he heard her strong accent and noticed the children were speaking German together, he viewed them with suspicion.

A fellow passenger right behind her overheard what she had said. "I am on the same train as you, just follow me." He lifted his bowler hat.

They sat together in the same carriage all the way to London, and he kindly explained to her how to get to St Pancras station.

"I am sorry, I have not introduced myself. Alexander Borstein."

"Dr Esther Rosenthal."

He stood up and shook her hand. "Where are you going from here?"

Esther felt strangely comfortable with the man sitting opposite her and explained a little bit about their situation. He was silent when she finished. Eventually, he said, "I am an editor of a national newspaper in London. Would it be possible for me to send a reporter to Dovercourt next week? I would very much like to report on the children's story. What was it you called it?"

"*Kindertransport.*"

"This might highlight their plight and educate some of our citizens, who are largely ignorant about what is really happening in Germany. Like the guard at the railway station you just encountered," he added.

"I don't know, maybe Frau Essinger would not like it."

"Would you mind if I made some notes?" He put his hand into the inside of his coat and retrieved a little notepad and a small pencil.

"Do you always carry those with you?"

"Old habits don't die. I am still a young reporter at heart."

Both laughed. Esther had almost forgotten the children, but now she turned towards them and translated most of what she and Alexander Borstein had been saying, and they started to relax as well.

"Can we get our bread out to eat?"

"Please tell me everything again, from the beginning."

When Esther had finished her story, he was quiet for several minutes. He then looked at her and said, "You are a remarkable woman, Dr Rosenthal, and as for Frau Essinger, I had no idea what some people would do for their fellow human beings. I must speak with her. Do you have the telephone number at her school?"

"Frau Essinger is a very private person. I am sure she would not appreciate a phone call from a newspaper without me telling her about it first."

"Dr Rosenthal, there is very little time. You are travelling to New York soon, you said. May I ask whether you have your tickets? I am sorry, I don't want to be rude, but your tickets – do you know what class it says on them?"

"Why are you asking me that?"

"You should make sure you travel at least second class."

"Why would that matter?"

"It matters greatly, Dr Rosenthal. The immigration process would not be on Ellis Island, but the authorities would come on board and check your paperwork there and then. You are getting a visa, you said?"

"Yes. Frau Essinger said she would get in contact with the American High Commission."

"I really must speak with Frau Essinger today."

Esther was not convinced that this was necessary, but gave him the number anyway. "I have good friends in New York. I will write to them. Maybe they can be of help. With your qualifications it should be easy to find work in one of the hospitals."

"Why are you helping us?"

"As I said, my name is Alexander Borstein. My parents came over from Germany before I was born."

Chapter 19

It had been a long journey to Liverpool, and Esther was glad for all the help Alexander Borstein had given them. When they arrived in London, to the excitement of the children, he hailed a taxi for them, one of the black ones they had seen in the English book at the camp, accompanied them to St Pancras station and found their platform. Their train would not leave for over one hour, so he had insisted they should eat together before they left.

There was a large eating room at the station, and he ordered pastrami sandwiches on rye bread served with pickles. Esther had not believed they would have such food here in London, and silently hoped the children would not be sick on the train when she saw how much mustard Gabriela had put on.

Fifteen minutes before their train was due to leave, Esther got nervous. She did not want to miss it. Alexander Borstein paid the bill and found them an empty carriage, a single one, the doors on each side giving entry to this carriage only. Esther wondered how anybody could come and check their ticket.

Until they reached Leicester nobody joined them, although the train stopped many times before that. Both Gabriela and Samuel slept most of the way, and Esther pondered on her future while letting the countryside go past. She would not live here after all, but was still unsure that emigrating to America was the right thing to do.

There was one more train change in Nuneaton before they reached Liverpool, and it was getting dark when they stepped on to the platform at Lime Street Station. Esther followed the instructions and found the place where the number 63 tram would be leaving from.

"Dr Rosenthal, it is over there. Look."

Both children had been very careful not to speak unless it was just the three of them. At the last station, a group of boys, one selling the latest edition of a newspaper, had spat at them and shouted, "Bloody Germans." Gabriela had started to cry and wiped the spit off her coat; she had felt safe until then, and all Esther wanted to do now was deliver them as promised to their grandparents in Garston.

In the drizzle, which had started to fall persistently, she spotted the sign: the three gold coloured balls hanging above a shop door. A woman was trying to open it, but it seemed locked. The children had also seen the sign and started to run, racing each other, keen to be the first to get there. Samuel beat his sister, ignored the woman, and started to bang on the door. The woman stepped away, and Esther saw she was heavily pregnant, with another child in a pram, fast asleep despite his face being soaking wet by now.

"Grandfather, Grandfather, open up, we are here."

Lights came on at the back of the shop and they heard the rattling of keys. The door opened with a little 'ding' of the bell.

"I was expecting you tomorrow," said the elderly man.

Esther only half listened to what he said. She had heard a groan coming from the pregnant woman, who looked like she was just about to faint. Before she could fall to the ground, Esther was by her side.

"Come, let's get you inside."

"We are closed," the elderly man said.

Esther was in no mood to argue. "Samuel, get the pram and push it inside." He looked at his grandfather and then at Dr Rosenthal. His grandfather shook his head as if to say no, but Samuel sighed and did as Dr Rosenthal asked, hoping his grandfather would not scold him later.

"You are here!" Their grandmother had entered without being noticed. She took one look at Esther trying to keep the woman upright and pulled a chair towards them. The woman accepted it thankfully.

"Get some water, Frank, don't just stand there."

Esther was kneeling on the floor, and brushed the woman's damp hair away with her hand. She felt hot.

"I am Dr Rosenthal, can you give me your name?"

"Annie."

"You gave us quite a fright, Annie. What are you doing here?" The grandmother had returned and handed Esther a glass of water, which Esther put to Annie's lips. Annie got up, walked over to the pram and retrieved something from below the still sleeping child. She held out a gold pocket watch.

"Annie, you know we are closed. I cannot take your watch now. Where is that husband of yours?"

"My George is ill, you see. We need some money so I can get him his medicine and pay for the doctor." Annie now pleaded with Esther.

"Frank, take the watch from Annie and give her what she needs. We know she is good for it. George will collect it as usual on payday."

Another knock on the door.

"See what you have done, Marge? Now everybody believes we are open."

"Mr Kett, have you seen Annie? George told me she would come here."

With a loud tut, Frank Kett went past Esther and Annie to the shop door and opened it wide. "Hello, Flo, why don't you come in and join us?"

"Annie, are you alright?" Flo ignored him and was at Annie's side. Frank Kett took the watch, went behind the counter and locked it into a cupboard. Then he went through the door into the house and came back with the money.

"I cannot give you a receipt today. Legally I cannot accept anything after closing. If you don't mind, can you go home now and let us have some time to greet our grandchildren properly?" He held the front door open for them.

"I hope your husband gets better soon," said Esther just before the door closed behind them.

Chapter 20

Alexander Borstein had kept his word. The arrival of a reporter together with a photographer was expected the following week. At first Anna Essinger had had her reservations about exposing the children in a national newspaper, but there had already been a two-page spread in a paper produced locally, and he had pointed this out to her over the phone. Alexander had made sure he had a copy of that article before he approached Frau Essinger, but he wanted to portray the story more powerfully, he said.

Anna Essinger was not sure that this was the right approach. How would people react to having a German school and German refugees right on their doorsteps? However, the news from Germany was getting worse. She desperately needed to raise more funds and find foster homes for the many children who had arrived, as most of them had no contacts at all, and all the places nearby had been taken so she would have to look for homes further afield. When Alexander Borstein had told her he himself and two of his friends would be happy to look after some of the children and he would spread the word, she felt she had no choice. A day for the newspaper people was arranged.

As an afterthought, or so he said, Alexander took time off from his busy schedule and came down as well. He felt he should meet Anna Essinger and see the place for himself, but secretly he hoped he would see Dr Rosenthal.

Frau Essinger, together with Esther and Mordechai, waited for the arrival of the newspaper people in the dining hall.

On the table in front of them was a spread of documents: the visas, the tickets for the passage across, letters to the children's relatives, a list of addresses, a book about New York in German. Frau Essinger had taken it from the library at the school and handed it to Mordechai.

"You might find this useful," was all she said.

Mordechai picked it up immediately. It had a comfortable feel to it, and was large enough for him to read the writing, but not too large and it would fit into his rucksack. He tried to guess the weight. About one kilogramme, he thought, so yes, his rucksack would be extra heavy. He still had not unpacked it fully since the day he arrived.

He opened the book. To his delight there was a map at the back of it. Unfolded, it almost covered half the table.

"This is a wonderful book. Thank you for your kindness. Are you really sure I can take it, Frau Essinger?"

"Herr Goldstein, I would really like you to have it. I brought it all the way from Herrlingen. I am really happy it has now found its rightful owner. Please think about us sometimes."

"How could we ever forget you?" He put his hand on top of hers, a gesture you would only do to your dearest friends. She did not pull it away.

Esther watched him in amazement. He cleared his throat and said, "Frau Essinger, did you manage to get us the money?"

"What money?" asked Esther.

Frau Essinger bent down and reached into her bag. She put a brown envelope on top of the now closed book.

"It's all there. Seven hundred dollars, just as you asked."

"Seven hundred dollars?" Esther picked up the envelope and looked inside. She took the money out and held it to her father. "Father?"

"Esther, we do not need the English money any more, plus I sold two of your mother's brooches and the ruby necklace."

Esther gasped. "We got all this money for that?"

"The matching bracelet. That went with the necklace."

They heard the car arriving, and Mordechai placed the envelope with the money into the inside of his jacket pocket. Esther started gathering the paperwork. The letter from Joshua addressed to Rebecca and Benjamin she slipped into her father's book.

Chapter 21

Southampton, 1 September 1939

"Look, Benjamin, look how big it is."

They had joined a long queue of other passengers ready to board the *Queen Mary*. Mordechai had insisted that he would be in charge of their papers, and held on to Benjamin, who now had a rucksack of his own. In it were a few American coins, an English picture book, a colouring book with crayons, plus a small paper bag with chocolate money covered with gold and copper coloured paper. Alexander Borstein had presented Rebecca and Benjamin with their presents when he said goodbye to them on his second visit to Dovercourt.

They went to Southampton in a small bus organised by the newspaper. When Esther protested that he had done enough already, Alexander explained that the reporter and photographer would accompany them. He needed more material for his article, he reasoned.

"Grandpa, how many people will be on the same ship as us?" Benjamin had a tight grip on Mordechai's hand and looked up when he asked.

"Over 2,000, I believe."

"Is that many? Will there be space for us?"

"We have got cabins, remember? I told you," replied Rebecca before Mordechai got his chance. "Grandpa, have you got our tickets?"

It was their turn to step on to the gangway. First in line was Mordechai, followed by the cousins they had promised to accompany. Rebecca was behind them, and last in line was Esther. They stopped in front of the officer. Mordechai let go of Benjamin for a minute, but Benjamin immediately held on to his grandpa's coat, making an already unsteady Mordechai sway. He tried to regain his balance by holding on to the railing, and a large envelope fell to the floor, the open end facing downwards. Its content began to slide down the slope.

"Our tickets!" Rebecca quickly bent down to retrieve everything, but the man behind the group had become impatient and wanted to overtake. A hand appeared out of nowhere and pulled him back.

"Not so quickly," intervened the photographer, and placed his press card under the surprised passenger's nose. "We are doing a feature, and you have to give us some space here, mate." To emphasise what he had said, he lifted his camera and turned round. "Hold it! All stand back a little way." He took a photo of the remaining passengers waiting on the quay.

"Have you got everything?" The officer took the papers from Rebecca's shaking hands. She had noticed something slip into the water before she could reach it; it looked like a letter, and she hoped it was not important.

"All in order. Have a pleasant journey. You will be directed to your cabins by the steward. I believe all your luggage has been loaded?" Being aware of the press behind this family, the officer was as polite as he could possibly manage. Esther silently thanked Alexander for the foresight to let the press accompany them this far; she feared they would have never managed otherwise.

"Welcome on board," was the greeting they received once they had reached the top of the gangway.

"Father, let's find our cabins. The boat will leave in forty minutes. I am sure the children would love to watch."

"Can we?"

"I am sorry, Dr Rosenthal, would you mind staying here

on deck until we depart? We need more pictures, and interviews with fellow departing passengers, if you don't mind," the reporter explained, all the while looking nervously over his shoulder to the crowd of accompanying relatives below. How could anybody recognise their family this high up on the ship? The ground just appeared like a blur, people jostling unsuccessfully to get a better position. No, he thought, no chance.

"Benjamin, you hold on tight and don't let go of the railing, you hear?"

Rebecca was standing next to him and stood on the first rail to get a better look. Benjamin wanted to copy her example, but was quickly pulled back by a worried Mordechai. Everybody seemed to have boarded because the gangplank was being removed. A large black car arrived, hooting its horn, which was almost drowned out by the ship's engine noise, but the people below parted to let it pass until it stopped right in front.

"Those passengers are too late, the ship is moving!" shouted Rebecca to where Esther stood.

A boy climbed out first. It looked like he was wearing a school uniform. "It's Joshua, Grandpa, it's Joshua!" Now they had all seen him.

"Joshua, Joshua, we are here!" Joshua was scanning the people on top; then he spotted them and waved. He shouted at them, but they could not hear what he said. Alexander now stepped behind him and put one hand on his shoulder. With the other hand he waved, his eyes desperately searching for Esther.

Chapter 22

"*Einundfuenfzig, zweiundfuenfzig…*"

"No, Benjamin. In English. Do it again."

He looked up at Rebecca. The children had run ahead to search for their cabins.

"Fifty?"

"Yes, that is good. Fifty?" Rebecca showed him a finger.

"Fifty-one."

Esther and Mordechai had caught up. Their cabins were next to each other. Mordechai was going to share his with the cousins. Esther, Rebecca and Benjamin were in the other one. Big keys were already in the locks of the doors with their cabin numbers clearly marked. Rebecca could not contain herself much longer and reached to open the cabin. Her hand still on the door handle, she stopped and looked.

"What is it? Don't we have any beds?" Benjamin ducked under her arm and went inside. "We are going to stay in here? Grandpa, let's see whether yours is the same." He shot into the corridor and opened the other cabin. "Ours has flowers on the table," he proclaimed, and returned to his own quarters.

Esther was now inside and placed her rucksack on the floor. Rebecca was already sitting on the double bed. A single bed was pushed against the wall underneath the portholes. Benjamin was just going to climb on it, but thought again. He looked over to Esther and took his shoes off, then in his socks he stood on the bed and looked out of the first porthole.

"Why has it curtains? Nobody can see us from the outside, can they?" he asked.

"Let me see."

Esther tried to take it all in, and wondered whether all the second class cabins were the same, or whether Alexander had again worked his magic. There was a sink unit next to the double bed and a desk with a cupboard above it which reached the ceiling on her right. A wardrobe was opposite. Rebecca now claimed the large armchair, and Benjamin, not to be outdone, sat on the chair in front of the desk.

"Ouch!" Benjamin withdrew his finger and stuck it into his mouth, took it out again and inspected it until he saw the little bit of blood welling up. "That flower hurt me."

"Teaches you not to touch everything."

Rebecca was the only one to hear the light knock on the door.

"Your luggage, madam."

"When can we go and see the ship? Can I see the big engines?"

Mordechai now appeared in the open doorway. "The reporter said he is going to check on our table. I think we will go with him."

"Me too." Benjamin was already at his side.

"Father, what do you mean? The reporter and photographer have gone, surely."

"No, they are in the cabin next to mine."

Their table was close to the door, and all nine of them fitted around it comfortably. Mordechai kept a close eye on the cousins. Their white serviettes neatly on their laps, they pushed the food back and forth on their plate without touching any of it.

The reporter arrived just in time for the main course to be served. "I have been to the bridge," he explained. "The captain will show us around the ship tomorrow. Maybe the boys would like to come along?"

"Is everything alright?" A waiter appeared out of nowhere and inspected the cousins' plates.

"*Wir duerfen das nicht essen.*"

The waiter looked puzzled.

"The boys are of a very strict Jewish faith which does not allow them to mix any milk products with meat."

"We have not been advised of this beforehand, madam."

"You know it now," replied the reporter. "Please go and check with the kitchen what can be done."

Within minutes the waiter was back.

"Would it be possible for the boys to come with me? On the other side there is a table with passengers who have the same restrictions. We can place some extra chairs, and your boys can join them."

"Good," said Rebecca after they had gone.

"Rebecca!"

"Grandpa, honestly, I don't know how you can stand being in the same cabin. Those three have hardly said a word since we left."

"That is enough, Rebecca!"

"Now, when are you going to explain to us why you are here, Thomas?" Esther directed her question to the reporter.

"I am sorry, Dr Rosenthal, I believed you were aware that we would travel to New York. The editorial office received word from the Cunard Line that the *Queen Mary* was going to attempt another record breaking crossing." When that met with blank expressions, he continued, "The *Queen Mary* holds the record set in 1938, when the crossing took just under four days. They are trying to beat that time again, and our newspaper has the exclusive coverage, as far as we know."

"We might get there sooner than we thought?" interrupted Rebecca.

"Can I see the big engines now?" added Benjamin.

"If your mother thinks this is alright, I will check with the bridge."

"What's a bridge?"

"I can see you have a lot to learn about boats, Benjamin. The bridge is right on the top, where the captain stands and makes sure he tells everybody what to do," laughed Thomas.

"Can girls come as well?"

"I can't see why not, but we will also have to ask the young friends you are travelling with."

"They are no friends of mine, and I don't want to see an engine anyway," Rebecca chipped in.

"I think you two are ready for bed."

The news came on the day they attended prayers. The Rabbi announced it himself: Hitler had invaded Poland the day before. The cousins' reaction was Esther's immediate concern. Whereas before they had been quiet, now they were silent, despite the obvious commotions this news caused. Esther thought it prudent to search for the medical deck, where the doctor gave them a slight sedative and told her to keep an eye on them.

Esther and Mordechai took it in turns to sit with the cousins. To make matters worse, the crossing was beginning to get really rough. The storm had started the night before. Only Rebecca seemed to be unaffected; she even agreed to look after Benjamin, letting Esther rest on the bed for a few hours until the reporter came to their rescue once again, proudly presenting a little glass jar full of sea sickness medicine. Esther was just going to enquire where he had got it from, since the doctor on board had apologised that all pills had been distributed to the first class passengers, when she heard noises and passengers running past their cabin, but could not make out any words. Surprisingly she already felt a bit better. She opened her eyes. Rebecca was sitting in the armchair with a book, and Benjamin was on the floor with his colouring pencils. Benjamin forgot all about going to the swimming pool for a moment – he had talked about nothing else; this and his forthcoming visit to the engine room.

"Mama, you are better." He joined her on the bed.

"What time is it?"

"It's very late. I cannot see anything outside the window because it is very dark," volunteered Benjamin.

"Move, let me pass!" The first officer opened the radio control room door. The photographer managed to hold his camera in position and quickly pressed the button.

"Has it been confirmed?"

"Yes, sir!" The door closed, and the sounds from inside were drowned out.

"You could take better pictures when we do the tour." The reporter was pushed from behind.

"I think this might be a historic moment and I needed to capture it. This is why I am the photographer and you are the reporter." The photographer grinned.

"Sorry, mate. Has it been confirmed?"

"We are waiting for an official announcement."

More and more men arrived and started to gather in the gangway.

"Does anybody know what is happening?"

The radio control room door opened and a grim looking first officer appeared. "Gentlemen, please gather your families. Report to your dining rooms. An announcement will be made shortly."

Esther held on to Benjamin. They had not bothered to sit at their table. Other passengers stood in groups, all of them speculating as to what might have happened, a few of them clutching their lifejackets. Confusion was around them; most of the smaller children were crying, but whether that was because they were tired or out of fear, Esther did not know.

"Is the ship sinking?"

Esther shot Rebecca a look, and she immediately became quiet and concentrated on the shoelaces she had forgotten to tie.

"Is the ship sinking?" Benjamin now wanted to know.

"We have to get our lifejackets! You should have told us to bring them!" One of the cousins panicked, ready to run off. Mordechai just managed to grab him by the arm.

"You stay right here."

Rebecca used her chance to push him forward.

"Ouch, watch it!"

"No, you watch it, Reuben. You should be glad we have not thrown you overboard." Rebecca was fuming, looking at her mother out of the corner of her eye.

"Attention, please, passengers and crew." One of the officers had entered, holding a megaphone in front of him. "Passengers and crew, it is with great regret I have to announce that Britain is at war. Britain and France jointly declared war on Germany on 3 September at 11.15 BST. Our Prime Minister, Neville Chamberlain, made the announcement to the nation at that time. We are now in contact with the American authorities to get permission to disembark on arrival."

Chapter 23

Otterden, Kent, 3 September 1939

"We have to tell the children at lunchtime," Anna Essinger advised her secretary, "but before that I must speak to our teachers. Please go and tell them to meet me in the library after they have finished the morning lessons instead of going straight into the dining hall."

Alexander had phoned her from the newspaper office immediately after Neville Chamberlain had made his announcement to the nation. She put the wireless on as soon as she had replaced the receiver; she needed to hear the statement for herself before she told everybody in her care. Then she went to the library, via the kitchen to speak with the cook.

She had expected the shocked reaction of the teachers, but was surprised that one by one they came over to where she stood and put their arms around her.

"I don't know what will happen to the school now. They might close us down altogether." Anna voiced her opinion. "It will be very hard on the children. Some of them have not heard from their families for a few weeks already, and I have to think about the remaining children at Dovercourt Bay. I will have to go there as soon as I possibly can. Alexander has agreed to accompany me. He is worried that it might be difficult to travel there by myself now."

They entered the noisy dining hall as a group, where the children immediately stood up from their seats and fell silent, something they did every mealtime. In the mornings they were greeted by a cheerful "Good morning, children."

"Good morning, Aunty Anna," they would reply, followed by the 'Shema': "Hear, o Israel, the Lord is our God, the Lord is One."

"Please sit down. The news is not good. I have been informed that England is at war with Germany. I do not know how it will affect our life here. I know you all are worried about your families, and I will try to find out as much as possible. Right now it is important that we carry on exactly as before. You need to be extra strong."

A few of the boys left their seats and ran towards the exit, obviously in tears. The English teacher standing next to Anna was going to follow them, but Anna held her back and shook her head.

Joshua had come over to where Anna stood.

"Aunty Anna, has my family reached America?"

Chapter 24

New York, 4 September 1939

Most of the passengers gathered on the outside decks. The arrival and docking of the *Queen Mary* was not something anybody would want to miss. Esther, Mordechai and the children managed to find a spot right by the railings again. Rebecca had insisted she go there as soon as they finished packing; she wanted to be the first one to see the Statue of Liberty. When it came into view, she failed to return and tell the others; she was not going to miss one minute of seeing it. When Reuben arrived, she insisted he go back to fetch them.

"What is the Statue of Liberty, Grandpa?"

"This is a gift from the people of France. They gave it to the people in America so that everybody who comes here can see it and know they no longer have to be afraid."

"I am not afraid anymore, Grandpa."

"What are all the smaller boats for? They seem to be waiting over there, see?" Rebecca pointed in the direction the *Queen Mary* was heading.

"We are going to dock soon, and those boats will take some of the passengers to Ellis Island."

"Have they done something wrong, Grandpa? Will they be taken away?"

"No, Benjamin, they have done nothing wrong. There is just not enough space for everybody to have their immigration papers checked here on the ship."

"What is immigration?"

"Come along now, we have to go to our dining room.

As soon as we have docked, the officers will board."

"But…"

"No more questions today. We are going." Esther rubbed her temples. The splitting headache would not leave her. Mordechai and Esther had sat up most of the night, talking and worrying, the fate of the passengers on the *MS St Louis* foremost in her mind.

"What if they turn us away like the passengers on the *St Louis*? We would have nowhere else to go."

"It was the Cuban authorities who did not keep their word, Esther. We have the right papers and visas. Of course they will let us in."

"Father, so did the passengers on the *St Louis*. They had brought their visas. Alexander told me when I asked him whether he had reported it in his newspaper."

"Esther, they are not going to turn a good doctor and her family away, I am sure about it. Especially one who is accompanied by a newspaper reporter and a photographer," he added, smiling.

It was their turn to be seen. "Do you mind if we take some photographs? British Press."

The immigration officer looked puzzled, and did not notice Mordechai was shaking with anxiety.

"Please, Herr Goldstein, sit down. Children, you go behind your grandpa. Maybe, Officer, you could be on the photograph too?"

"Yes, of course, but you will not be able to use these in your newspaper back in England for a very long time."

"What do you mean?"

"The ship will not be able to return. The *Queen Mary* has been ordered to remain in port until further notice."

"But how are we supposed to get back?"

"No idea," replied the officer. "All your papers are in order. Welcome to the United States of America."

Chapter 25

"Where is your family?" The group was almost the last remaining outside the gates. Two porters had helped them with their luggage, but that was as far as they could go.

Rebecca and Benjamin sat on a suitcase each. They had already taken their coats and cardigans off, but Reuben and his cousins remained fully dressed.

"Are you not sweaty?" Reuben did not reply and looked nervously at the last few passengers now being greeted. "Do you know what your uncle looks like?"

"No," he admitted.

"Mama, Reuben does not know his uncle. We will be stuck with them forever."

Esther, Mordechai, Thomas the reporter and Arthur the photographer had been standing a few paces away, discussing where to go from here and whether they should stay together as a group. Thomas and Arthur's main concern was how quickly they could make contact with the newspaper office back in London.

"Mama, Reuben did say he does not know his uncle." Rebecca had walked over to them.

"Yes. They have never met, that is true, but we can't wait here forever. We will find their addresses," Mordechai suggested. "The porter said there is a small deli around the corner. Maybe we can take our belongings there and discuss it over a cup of coffee."

Before Rebecca went back to get the others, he added, "Rebecca, do not argue with Reuben now. They must be very frightened. They are far away from their mother and father with virtual strangers in a country they have never been to, speaking a language they do not understand."

Rebecca felt the heat rising in her face.

It took Thomas and Arthur two trips to get their luggage together and store it in the corner of the deli. Besides them, there was nobody else who needed serving. The proprietor had greeted them kindly and pushed two tables together. Then, when he realised that some of them spoke hardly any English, he asked the children in German whether they had ever tried a Coca Cola before. Even Reuben decided it best not to ask what was in it and accepted the drink placed in front of them. He looked around for a glass, but the owner placed a straw into each of the open bottles.

Reuben had removed his coat and reached under his sweater. He pulled up a small, flat cloth bag which had hung down by a string from around his neck. Silently he opened it and took out its contents, placing a few dollars and a sheet of paper on to the table in front of him.

"They live in Brooklyn." He pushed the note over to Mordechai.

"I think we should all go there for now. Maybe their uncle can suggest some places we could stay for a while. Once we have rested and freshened up, we can start contacting people from Alexander's list. But we should stay together." Esther looked around the group, and Thomas and Arthur nodded in agreement.

"Dr Rosenthal, we don't have funds available to us. We were supposed to report to the *New York Times* headquarters in Manhattan today, and then return on the *Queen Mary* to England," the normally reserved Arthur volunteered.

"We have enough, please don't worry about it at the moment. Father, what are you looking for?" Esther turned towards Mordechai, who was rummaging in his rucksack, his face as white as a sheet. The large brown envelope was in his hand.

"Esther, it has gone. The envelope with the money and all the addresses, it is not here. I am sure I put it there together with our papers."

Chapter 26

Kent, England

"We have had a visit from a council officer. We will have to leave."

"Surely you don't."

"Yes, Alexander, it's official. The War Office needs the school. The area is classified as a major defence area."

"Where will you go?" Alexander turned around to face her, taking his eyes off the road for a moment.

"Watch out!" He had drifted slightly to the right on the narrow country lane, almost being hit in the rear by an overtaking military lorry. Slipping on the wet road, he only just managed to swing the car back in time, but could not stop it quickly enough to avoid going into a ditch and scraping against a tall hedge. He looked at Anna, but before he had a chance to enquire whether she was hurt, she reached behind her seat and produced a handkerchief from her coat pocket, which she carefully dabbed on his forehead.

"Anna, you are hurt." He noticed the red stain which covered Anna's hand.

"No, Alexander, I am fine. You bumped your head. Will we be able to continue?" He tried to open the door, but it did not move.

"It is stuck, something must have jammed it. What about the door on your side?"

"I can't get out on my side. The car is leaning against the hedge. The lorry did not stop, I presume?"

"No, they have long gone. I will have to climb over to the

back and hope I can open the passenger door." Alexander kneeled on his seat and started to wiggle his body across, then he managed to reach the door handle without having to go across totally. It opened without further problem and he climbed over. Standing outside, he felt the slight drizzle cooling his face. He sighed and cursed the lorry; his new Austin 12 had only been delivered last week, but he was glad he had taken it today instead of the smaller sports car.

He went to the back of the car and realised they would never be able to move it from the ditch on their own. It seemed quite deep, and he could not see the front wheel. Walking around to inspect the damage, he had to crouch down and hold himself steady with his left hand. With his right he felt the tyre. From what he could make out, he had a puncture. He raised himself up and tried to open the driver's door from the outside.

"It is no good, the door does not open. Maybe you should stay here and I will go and get some help." Alexander was sitting on the back seat, feeling a little light headed and dizzy.

"We will both go. Don't look so shocked, I am quite able to climb over the seat."

The rain had changed to a persistent downpour by the time Anna and Alexander had reached a small farm. They had only noticed it at the last moment when Anna heard a dog barking. The farmhouse was hidden from view by a set of large bushes, and the only way to reach it was over a recently ploughed field. At one time Alexander fell, and it took all of Anna's strength to get him back on his feet. It was beginning to get dark when Anna used the large door knocker several times until she heard a key turn in the lock.

"Jesus!" The large farmer's wife covered her mouth in shock as Alexander lost his hold on Anna's shoulder and sank to the ground. Anna was staring at the large Alsatian, fearing that any second now it would break its chain and attack Alexander, who had fallen only a few feet away from it.

"Good evening. I am Anna Essinger…" she started saying.

"Harold, come quickly. There are some Germans at our front door."

Anna had never tasted tea with milk before, and it was comforting when she felt it warming her stiff body. The dry clothes from the farmer's wife were rough on her skin, but she was thankful to be wearing them. She pulled the blanket up towards her chest and sank further into the armchair.

"Doctor came. Me, Bertha." The woman pointed first upstairs and then towards herself. "You stay." With that, she disappeared again. A few minutes later she returned with a tray, on which Anna spotted chunks of white bread, butter and cheese. "You wait." Bertha pulled a small table across and placed it next to where Anna sat.

"Bertha, I don't think I had time to explain. Alexander Borstein is an editor of a London daily newspaper. He was taking me to Dovercourt Bay near Harwich when we were in a near miss with a lorry. They just drove off, although it was they who almost hit us."

"Sorry, I forgot you speak very good English."

"Thank you, Bertha."

"Harold, we will be in the newspapers."

"Bloody unlikely, otherwise we will have them all coming to take refuge here."

"Harold!"

"It is alright, Bertha, I totally understand. We will be on our way as soon as we can."

"You will do nothing of the sort," the doctor exclaimed. "Your friend cannot be moved for a few days. I am afraid he might have concussion. He has explained who you are and where you are heading."

"Is somebody going to tell me what is going on? It is my bloody house, after all."

"Frau Essinger, Harold is not nearly as gruff as he makes himself out to be. Go and get another chair from the kitchen, Harold, and when you do, bring the bottle of that whisky I know you have. I think we could all do with a stiff drink now."

Anna had phoned the school before she sank into the comfortable bed the farmer's daughter had said Anna could use when she had come home from work after dark. The daughter was a newly recruited community nurse, and she checked on Alexander as soon as she heard the instructions the doctor had left.

"I will sleep on the armchair in his room," she insisted. "It is best to keep an eye on him. The doctor said not to let him go into a really deep sleep. I am sure he will not appreciate me waking him up every few minutes, but it is important, you know," she explained to Anna. "My two brothers will share a room for tonight. Please, have a rest. I might not be here by the time you get up."

Anna's dry clothes were on a chair when she awoke the next morning, and a jug of warm water stood next to a basin on a marble top table, while a piece of well used soap lay on a blue towel at the end of her bed. The smell of cooking, which made Anna feel slightly nauseous, was drifting up from the kitchen. She went over to the window to let some fresh air in. The rain had stopped; only a few big raindrops remained on the leaves of the trees outside. How peaceful it was here, she observed.

She knew that Alexander was in the room at the other end of the corridor. She knocked only lightly, and heard a confident, "Come in." He was sitting in his bed, holding a steaming cup of tea.

"Wait until I find out who those soldiers were."

"I can see you have lost none of your fighting spirit," Anna laughed. "You should be able to travel on in a few days."

"I have news for you. We will go to Dovercourt this morning." Anna was just going to protest, but he held out his hand to stop her. "Hear me out, please. I feel fine. I have not been sick, therefore my concussion cannot be that serious. The car was pulled out of the ditch and the tyre has been changed. We have used up enough of these good people's hospitality already. How I can ever repay them, I do not know. What did they say in Dovercourt when you rang them last night?"

"I have not been able to reach them, and to be honest it worries me greatly."

Chapter 27

"I'll be dammed!"

They pulled into the road leading to Dovercourt by mid-morning. A makeshift barrier had been placed across the main entrance, and several military vehicles were parked across from the dining hall. Alexander opened the driver's door and got out. He had managed to find his camera underneath the back seat before the first soldier appeared.

"We have to move you on, you cannot park here!" the soldier shouted from a distance. Calmly Alexander took the first photo. "Oi, you, stop that. Give me that camera. This is a military zone."

"Press," was all Alexander replied and produced his credentials.

"Hold it right there." The young man in charge sounded less confident now. Anna had joined Alexander and was trying to spot some of the staff in the distance, but all she could make out were military personnel.

"And who are you? Press as well?"

"I am Anna Essinger."

"We have been expecting you. Please get back into your car and park it over there on the right." He lifted the barrier and waved them on to the drive, as though glad they were now somebody else's problem.

Doreen spotted them through the dining hall window and came running towards them. "Anna, thank God you are here."

"What is going on?" Anna heard Alexander addressing a soldier who looked like he could be in charge.

"We have orders to move everybody out. The buildings are to be used for training purposes and defence with immediate effect. Please report to the officer inside who will issue you with instructions."

"Aunty Anna, where will we go?" Anna was greeted by worried looking boys and girls as soon as she entered the dining hall. She could see there were several dozen of them who still had not found a place to live.

"Mrs Essinger, please come and sit down."

"No, thank you, I have to speak with my staff and the children. I have to find out what is happening here. Come, children, you sit over there. Doreen and I will get you a hot drink." Anna realised the situation did not look good, but she wanted to have a quiet word with Doreen in the kitchen before she worked out what could be done. She trusted Alexander to find out everything he could from the military personnel.

"I phoned you at the school, but they said you had left yesterday morning. I tried to reassure the children as best I could, but I was already late and the teachers had gone. One of the bigger boys speaks English and was a great help. Him over there." She pointed through the slightly opened door. "They arrived in convoy, shouting orders. John took the bus and went to the police station, but they said there was nothing they could do. 'England is at war with Germany' was all he could get out of them. Useless lot. Anna, the children are so frightened. What shall we do?"

"Where is John now?"

"He has gone back into town. This time he took two of the teachers along. To give him support, he said. They have gone to the town hall and are going to bring a councillor back with them if it takes them all day. Yes, that's what he said."

"Anna?" Alexander appeared in the kitchen. "It would be best if you could come now."

Chapter 28

John had come back and, as promised, he was with a councillor, who had begrudgingly agreed to accompany him and was now sitting across the table from the military officer. Unusually for the normally busy John and the teachers, they had also pulled up chairs and were sitting behind him. The officer beckoned Anna and Alexander to join them, while Doreen enlisted the help of some of the children and distributed the promised drinks. After placing them in front of everybody at the table, Doreen looked at John, and when he nodded at her, she also carried a chair over and sat down.

The councillor introduced himself, and continued, "Frau Essinger, I am very sorry for the distress this is causing to you and the children, but Britain is at war." John was just going to intervene, but Anna's look told him not to. For once, she wanted to hear what the councillor had to say.

"We know it is unsettling for the children here, but as Councillor Hogan says, Britain is at war," the officer contributed.

"Is this all anybody has to say about it? Can somebody actually tell us what is happening here?" It was Alexander who raised these questions, ready to write down everything he heard and saw.

"Are you writing all this down?"

"I certainly am. I have a duty to the good people of Britain to tell them that military personnel can just march into their property without warning."

"Without warning? Councillor?"

Councillor Hogan cleared his throat. "We received notification a few days ago that the holiday camp would be used to house military personnel. We are right in the south of England, and the enemy could soon be across the water," he added apologetically.

When nobody came to his rescue, and not even John commented, Hogan had no choice but to continue. "I did not realise what the plans were for the remaining children."

"And to think I voted for you." John could no longer hold his tongue. "What are the plans for the remaining children?"

"Ah, yes, here is the list." The officer took refuge behind his pile of papers. Anna held her breath, waiting for what would come next. "These will be picked up by relatives later today." He handed her the paper, and Anna quickly checked the names. "We found foster homes for these." Another list. Anna was shocked to see it contained only the names of the youngest.

"Why are these people coming forward now when we have been asking for foster addresses week after week?" She looked at the councillor.

"I have worked tirelessly every day to find them homes, which was not easy under the circumstances."

"I bet you have." John was not going to stop now. "And exactly what circumstances would that be?" The councillor was opening his mouth to reply, but John cut in, "Don't tell me: Britain is at war."

"We can argue all we want, but orders are orders, and we are taking the camp over by this evening at the latest. Here is the list of the children with nowhere to go."

Anna scoured the paper he handed over. It did not contain all the names she had expected to see.

"But there are still some names missing. The bigger boys."

"Ah yes, those." Yet another list appeared. "Here we are: the names of the ones who will be taken to the Isle of Man."

Alexander jumped from his seat, knocking it over, and grabbed the councillor by the top of his jacket, pulling him up.

"And you agreed to that?" He let go, and Hogan slumped back into his chair, unable to hide his shamed face from Anna.

Chapter 29

New York

All the money had been counted and placed on to the surface of the table. Thomas the reporter explained their situation to the deli owner. When he scrutinised them with suspicion, Benjamin emptied his rucksack, found his coins and held his outstretched hand towards the owner.

"You keep those, young man. How far do you have to travel?" he then asked them. He read the address Reuben provided and studied the money still on the table. "I make that twenty-nine dollars, fifty cents. That would be enough money for accommodation and food for a week, at least. The taxis will cost you about one dollar, ten cents. It will not take long to get there."

"What about our drinks?"

"I think you will come back and pay me when you can. I will tell the cab drivers to go over Brooklyn Bridge. That will be the most direct route."

Rebecca, Esther, two of the cousins and Benjamin travelled in the first taxi, followed by the others. "It's all your fault," whispered Reuben at the first opportunity. "Now who is stuck with whom?"

In Kane Street, Brooklyn, the taxi driver slowed down and checked the numbers on the houses.

"Here we go, you have arrived," he announced. Rebecca momentarily forgot about their situation. They stood outside one in a row of red brick houses. She counted the number of floors: three. Steps led to the front door with railings to each side. The tall front door was half glazed, with black wood curved at the top and tall windows to the side of it. There seemed to be another entry at the basement. Rebecca wondered which of the apartments Reuben's family occupied. She had promised Joshua she would write to him with everything she saw, but she had no intention of telling him that because of her they had arrived without any money.

The front door was opened by a young boy.

"Mother, they are here."

"Oi – *elohim*! *Shalom*. Reuben, Ely and Uri, you are so tall." Their aunt came down the stairs to greet them, and to Reuben's embarrassment, she gave him a hug. He could see Rebecca out of the corner of his eye, smirking at his obvious discomfort.

"Reuben, why don't you introduce everybody? But I am forgetting my manners. Please come inside."

Thomas shrugged his shoulders and helped with their cases, but stopped at the front door. "I am sorry, Mrs Benowitz. I am Thomas Harris, a reporter with a newspaper in England. We have been accompanying Dr Rosenthal and your nephews, but I am not sure whether we can come in."

"And why would that be?"

"They are Christians, Aunty," volunteered Reuben. His aunt seemed to hold her breath for a minute.

"What difference would that make? You got my nephews here safely. Please come. I am sure that my husband will not object. He has taken his elderly mother to the hospital. You know, men and their mothers. I am sorry that he could not be here to greet you. You must be very tired." She now addressed Mordechai.

"Frau Benowitz, we will not be staying very long. I am Mordechai Goldstein. This is my daughter, Esther, a very good doctor, and her children, Rebecca and Benjamin. Could you recommend some lodgings nearby?"

"Why don't you all make yourselves comfortable in the living room? Reuben, Uri and Ely, your bedroom is on the top floor. You can take your things upstairs."

"The whole house is yours?"

"Yes, but there is no space for you." Reuben got his own back, but made sure only Rebecca heard him.

"A doctor, you said. What kind of doctor?" Mr Benowitz enquired.

"I am a paediatrician."

"My daughter is an excellent surgeon. Esther, why are you being so modest?"

"Father, we have taken up enough of Mr and Mrs Benowitz's time."

When Mr Benowitz had returned with his mother from the hospital, Esther had overheard him speaking in the kitchen to his wife.

"Christians in my house? What are you thinking?"

She did not wait to hear any more, but returned to the others and stressed to her father that they should leave as soon as they could. Frau Benowitz had sent her son to the synagogue which was just down the road, and Reuben went with him. They were supposed to ask there for addresses of lodgings, but before they rushed out, she told them to make it clear that they also needed accommodation for two Christian men.

Rebecca heard the front door. "They are back," she whispered into Benjamin's ear. "I hope they found us somewhere to live as far away as possible from here."

Benjamin rewarded her with a grin and a nod.

"I see," said Mr Benowitz when he read the piece of paper his son had handed over without saying a word. "Yes, Isabella's husband passed away recently, she would have space. I am surprised at Mrs Braun. I know she lets out some of her rooms, but to Christians? Anyway, these are the addresses we have got. They are not far from here: both are in Clinton Street."

Chapter 30

It was so comfortable at Isabella's that Rebecca hoped they could live there forever. The house was identical in size to the one they had just left, but that was the only similarity. This house was warm and welcoming. It smelled of freshly baked bread, and although it was not cold outside, Isabella had lit a fire in her sitting room. She kindly allocated four rooms instead of two without extra charge. Rebecca and Benjamin both picked a room right under the roof, from where they had a view over a park nearby.

They sat around a long wooden table in the large kitchen while Rebecca and Benjamin wolfed down chicken soup. Isabella had phoned Mrs Braun to ask her new lodgers to come over and join them, but she was told they had left for the newspaper office on Madison Square.

"I like a family with children sharing my house. My husband and I were not blessed with children ourselves, but we are fortunate enough to have many nieces and nephews," Isabella explained in very good German.

"Can I call you Aunty Isabella?"

"Benjamin, that would be lovely. Yes, I would like that very much."

"Can you show me how to speak English properly? I am not very good yet."

"I am sure you will learn it very quickly once you go to school here."

"I will be going to school?"

"Benjamin, of course. We have to go to school. Aunty Isabella, is there a school nearby?" Rebecca had worked out very quickly that if they were to enrol in a school not far away, the chances were they would remain right here.

"The Abraham Lincoln High School has an excellent reputation, but you are both still too young to attend there. My nieces and nephews go to separate private schools, so maybe I can make some enquiries."

"Does that mean Benjamin and I would go to different schools?"

"We might not be able to stay with you for long." Esther and Isabella were the only ones still up late into the night, after it had taken all their efforts to settle the children. Rebecca was too excited to sleep; this was her 'first sleep' in her new home, after all, and Benjamin had never slept in a room on his own. He told his grandpa he was afraid – but not afraid to be here, he quickly explained, just to sleep on his own.

"Grandpa, could you sleep the first night in my room?"

"Benjamin, Grandpa is really tired today," Esther explained. "What about if Rebecca and you leave your doors open so you can see a little light coming from downstairs? What do you think?"

"Grandpa, will you leave your door open as well?"

"Dr Rosenthal…"

"Call me Esther, please."

"Esther, you could stay here, you know. I mean, really live here. The house is big enough, as you can see. What do you think?"

"If only we could, but I fear Brooklyn might be too expensive for us right now."

"You and your family belong in Brooklyn, I just know it. Tomorrow we will go first to the synagogue. It is a good idea for you to meet the local Rabbi." When Esther did not immediately respond, Isabella smiled and added, "His eldest son is a surgeon at the hospital. I know for sure, even before we tell him that you are a doctor too, he will have sung his son's praises for at least twenty minutes." Esther laughed out loud. This was the first time she had really laughed since that fateful night back in Hildesheim.

"You two seemed to have a good time," Mordechai said when Esther opened her bedroom door, which was across from his own.

"Father, did I wake you?"

"No, no, come in. Come and sit with me. What did you two talk about?"

"Isabella suggested we live here in her house."

"It is a wonderful idea. What else did she say?"

"Father, I know you. You listened to every word."

"True enough. I also know you told her nothing about the money which we lost. That is good."

"I will have to tell her, Father. We have no funds right now, and we are not going to ask Alexander's publishing friends for any help. I hope I can find work quickly and we can pay Isabella at the end of the month. The schooling for the children will have to wait."

"Have faith, Esther. Hand me my rucksack, please."

Esther handed the rucksack over, and Mordechai slowly emptied its contents on to the bed. Finally he reached down to the bottom.

"Hold it so I can pull it up."

Esther did what her father told her, and even in the dark of the room she could see his smile.

"There it is." He held it up for her to see.

"The cuckoo clock! Father, you brought the cuckoo clock?"

"Yes, my child. Watch very closely." He reached for his cardigan and held one of the metal buttons between his fingers, then he rubbed it against one of the weights. Esther opened her mouth in wonder. His button left a scratch, and she could clearly see gold underneath.

Chapter 31

Dachau, Germany, December 1939

Ibrahim pulled his arms around his body in a futile attempt to retain some of his body heat. He had stopped shivering a few hours before. Maybe I will die today, he thought. There were only five of them still standing; one of the others had fallen hours ago, and had been left there for them to witness. Another one had run across the ten-foot wide strip of no man's land. The guards waited until he had manoeuvred through the four-foot deep creek and on to the land behind before they killed him. Ibrahim had witnessed others getting as far as the electric barbed wire fence before getting shot in the back. He could hear the guards laughing on top of the watchtower and discussing whose turn it was and how many shots would be needed. On other days, the guards would entertain themselves by taking away one of the men's caps and throwing it on to the forbidden strip of land. Trying to retrieve it would cost you your life, but if it was missing at morning count, that carried a similar punishment. Either way, you lost. It was best to keep yourself to yourself, he thought. Bend your head to the ground at all times. Do not make eye contact.

It was only today that they had called him over to help with the new arrivals. He had watched them entering through the *jourhouse* building, wondering what their thoughts were as they read '*Arbeit macht Frei*' (Work will set you free) above them on the gate, then waited in line, being ordered to remove all of their clothing and hand over the little they had brought with them. They were left standing there naked, and Ibrahim was glad it had befallen him to hand them the camp clothing: one set each, and boots without socks or bootlaces. Maybe the SS were afraid they would use the laces to hang themselves. He smiled at the idiocy of that; where could they actually do it? In the overcrowded barracks? No, no space there, and certainly not from one of the three storey bunk constructions which went all around the shed.

Now he almost looked forward to being in there again, body next to body, each holding on to a blanket. He wondered whether his would be missing when he got back. It often was, but by now he had earned himself enough respect from the others to ensure it was quickly returned.

Today's distribution fell short of jackets with the yellow star, like it was his fault. Everybody had an identification marking on their clothing: different colours for different crimes, as if it mattered. He had recently moved from digging foundations to what they called a privilege. During the day he was serving food and handing out cigarettes to the SS in the large canteen. He had hoped he could remain there all winter – at least he would not freeze to death outside – and he tried to work out why he had been singled out for the evening roll call square punishment today. Could it have been the young guard? No, that man would not have given him away. Ibrahim had recognised the young man straight after he had arrived here; the blond hair and delicate features did not fool him. This one was not of pure Aryan blood.

Ibrahim had avoided him at the beginning, but it was the young man who had addressed him one day. "Do I know you?" he had asked Ibrahim, who had denied it instantly. But months later, when Ibrahim had asked him for paper, a pencil and an envelope, it had appeared soon after, which was why it was important to push all thoughts of dying here today as far away as possible. Would his letters actually leave the camp? If they did, would they ever be received? It did not matter, he kept on writing them. No point addressing them to his home, so he sent them to the hospital instead. Maybe someone there knew where she had gone.

England. Yes, Esther had promised him.

Chapter 32

Douglas, Isle of Man, England

"Yes, Aunty Anna. Did you get my letter? Yes, he is here. I will hand it over. Will you write back?"

"Friedrich is right, Anna. It is good here. Not bad at all, but I will tell you about it when we meet. How are you settling in? Anyway, Anna, I am coming your way, back to London. Trench Hall is not that far away. Have you heard from Esther?"

Anna put the phone down. They had agreed that Alexander would spend the night at the school and Anna was looking forward to seeing him. She knew no matter what, he would find a positive side to any new situation. The letter she had received from Friedrich did sound hopeful, and he certainly did not seem upset on the telephone.

Anna picked the letter up again and read it for the third time since it had arrived.

Dear Aunty Anna,
I hope you like your new school. I miss seeing you, but we are well. We arrived here from the transit camp. There it was not very good, but I cannot believe how nice it is here. We were taken by a small boat and it was only a short crossing. You could see the island in the distance. Instead of a camp, we walked through the town. People were standing at the roadside looking at us, but nobody shouted. We reached a square in the town which has very large houses. The whole place is surrounded by a wire

fence, but it does not look very secure. There are guards, but they don't march up and down all day shouting orders. It is a very big place. First they did not know what to do with us. The women and the children were taken somewhere else, I don't know where. One of the boys here is only twelve, and he was supposed to go with them. I lied and said he was with me, so they let him stay, but told me he was my responsibility.

I think everybody is from Germany, or at least everyone speaks German here. There has been a meeting in one of the houses, and it was agreed we would speak English whenever we can. They told us that nobody knows how long we might be here, and it is best we speak their language. What do you think, Aunty Anna?

There were many men here already, and we were allocated a room in one of the houses. We six share, which is what we wanted. Everybody might have to share beds, we were told, but as long as we can all keep our blankets, we do not mind.

Aunty Anna, we can see the sea from our bedroom! We played outside and we have enough food, including some strange fish for breakfast called 'kippers'.

There are men here who have agreed to teach, and we have been told by them to come and attend their classes in mathematics and science. One of the bigger boys does not want to go, so every day he goes and helps a farmer outside the camp. Yes, we are allowed to go outside to work and come back each evening. I watch out of the window in the morning and see a group of men leaving through the gates, accompanied by armed guards. I don't know what work they do, but I will tell you when

I write again. You do want me to write again? We got permission to write home, but one of the men, I think he is an artist, told us to be careful what we write. He must be a painter; he lives right on top of one of the houses and has his window open. Sometimes we can see the smudges on his shirt and smell the paint.

Here comes the best news: we are going to print our own newspaper! I asked whether I can work on it. I want to be a reporter one day. Now I have paper and a pencil, and I speak to people and write it all down. And then I will make it into stories. We have been promised two typewriters, and I will learn how to type with them.

I have got to go now. Please write back soon.
Friedrich

Chapter 33

Trench Hall, Shropshire

"This is a wonderful location, Anna. It is amazing what you have already achieved. Has everything arrived? I am really sorry I was not there to help."

"Alexander, you cannot be everywhere. They did give us three days' notice to move, after all." Anna could not resist a smile. "I was told this would not be permanent and I should get my old school back one day."

"How are the children settling in?"

"They are adjusting to the tasks they have been assigned. I believe the cleaning of the toilets, not surprisingly, is the least popular one. After Joshua tried to bribe one of the smaller English boys to take this duty off him, we changed the routine. Toilet cleaning for one day only, so it will take a long time until it is your turn again. I had to punish Joshua, of course, and left him cleaning them for three days in a row."

"I can see you have started work on converting the stables into dormitories."

"Yes, the plan is to move the children into the new rooms there as soon as possible, and leave the main house to the men released from the internment camps. I cannot believe we have been blessed with these wonderful people."

"How does the rationing work now you have moved?"

"That is still not settled. We have to reapply with a lot of form filling. And don't forget, almost every day somebody new arrives. The hold-up seems to be the allocation of meat."

"Why?"

"Their stance is that we are a Jewish school and don't

need the ham, bacon, pork allowance."

"But you are not a Jewish school. Surely they know about all the other children, the English children, here."

"Believe me, I am trying to reason with them. Plus, I have made arrangements with the local store to swap the pork items which we might not use for extra eggs, butter or flour. Don't look so shocked, Alexander, I have to think foremost about the children. Now, tell me honestly what you think about the camps on the Isle of Man."

Alexander put his cup of tea on to the dining hall table in front of him, took a deep breath and told Anna about the situation at the Hutchinson Internment Camp. He reassured her that, although it was not an ideal situation for boys who had just fled Germany to be behind barbed wire after all, he could confirm what Friedrich had said. Everybody there was treated well, and most internees with them were German Jewish men of all ages, many with outstanding qualifications and skills. However, he did worry about the long term psychological scars this internment would leave on them.

"Any news from New York?"

"I have tried many times to get a passage back for my staff without success. All the British ocean liners are being converted into troop carriers, but I did manage to get work for them at the newspaper over there. And they have found new lodgings. They now live in Greenwich Village, and I believe they have settled in well. I am glad they are not coming back."

Anna was surprised, and her look said so.

"Think about it, Anna. Both are young men with wives and children. Unfortunately, they are the age that is the first to be conscripted. No, they are far away from home, but safe nonetheless. Have you heard from Esther?"

"Not since the last letter Rebecca sent to Joshua with a note in it for me. No, not since then."

"Is it still alright that I collect Joshua on his birthday? I am planning a special treat for him."

Chapter 34

Hildesheim, Germany

"What do you think I should do with them, Hilde? Egon brought them back from the hospital today. He said they have been there for some time. His pigeonhole is next to Dr Rosenthal's. Her name is still above it."

"Dr Rosenthal. We saw her last at the railway station?"

"Yes, after the burning of the synagogues."

"I wonder what happened to her."

"Remember she told me her husband said she must take her father and go to England?"

"Do you think she made it?"

"I really hope she did. She was going to leave some information with my brother in Brussels, but who knows whether she did? That was before the war started. I don't even know where my brother is now."

"Does it say where they came from?"

Maria picked up the three envelopes and turned each of them over so that the back of them was visible as they lay on the kitchen table. She pushed her chair back and got up, taking one of the letters over to the window.

"I think it says something on this one. Hold on, Hilde, it says Dachau. Yes, look for yourself." Maria handed it over and sat down again. "I think we should open them."

"Maria, what are you thinking? We can't open them."

"Yes, we can. As a matter of fact, we have to. They are coming from Dachau, and Dr Rosenthal told me her husband was taken away by the SS, so Dachau cannot be good news, can it?"

"No, but how would it help if we open the letters addressed to her?"

"We cannot just forward them to my brother's address. Think about it. Suppose he is still there, actually receives them and there is something in them which could cause him problems. What then? I put my own brother in danger?"

"What if there is something in them which could put *us* in danger once we know about it?"

"I had not thought about that. Maybe I should just take them back home with me."

Chapter 35

Dachau, Germany, 1940

They were standing silently outside their barracks for at least ninety minutes, Ibrahim reckoned. The SS arrived later every day, but the detainees were required to line up for the roll call at first light. At least the rain in the summer was warmer, and most detainees had left their metal beakers outside in the hope of catching some of it.

The three who had died during the night were stacked behind them with others from different blocks. They needed to be counted just the same, plus the two who had been taken into the sickbay. Why they had a sickbay, he had forgotten. They must have told him when he arrived, but he had never witnessed anybody returning from there.

He turned slightly to the right, trying to see what the commotion was outside the gate. He guessed the new arrivals had walked there from the railway station, and hoped they would be added to the list after roll call.

He then heard the approaching vehicles and knew the gates would be opened. Inside him, he dared to smile. Every day the same: car doors opened by the guards for the SS Commander to step out. Others, younger men whom he believed to be of lesser ranks, spilled from their vehicles on to the forecourt soon after, following their leader like a pack of hounds as he walked up and down in his freshly pressed uniform.

Ibrahim knew the chances were he would be punished again today. Arriving late at your workstation gained you ten lashes, the same or worse if you dared to answer back.

Fifteen lashes for stealing bread.

Several of the elders had fallen forward on to the ground. They no longer had the strength to stand up. Hard labour and shortage of food had taken its toll. He watched as one of the guards went over to the first fallen man, kicking him with a boot. There was no reaction from the prisoner on the ground. He was kicked again, only this time harder.

"Move the body," the guard shouted to the two who had stood either side of him. He was picked up by his arms and legs, dragged over and added to the pile of bodies, leaving a dirty smelling smudge on the wet concrete in his wake. The commander walked over and looked at it in disgust. Two more bodies went on the pile after that. The mathematician inside Ibrahim tried to guess the number of dead for today. Twenty? Thirty? He would soon know the exact count.

The last one lying face down was not kicked a second time, but instead was lifted up and placed on a stretcher which had stood upright at the end of the buildings. Two prisoners were instructed to lift it up and carry it to the hospital wing. Maybe one of the guards had taken a shine to him. Ibrahim often wondered who had the worse fate: the dead or the living.

Nobody ever came to claim the remains of their loved ones. One by one, the bodies were carried away after the count had been confirmed and the line dismissed. Everybody rushed as fast as they could manage to their assigned work.

The flat wagons were not to be used to carry the dead bodies. Ibrahim bent down and held the first one by the collar of the jacket, dragging him along for what was that man's final journey. Before the bodies were disposed of, all of them had their clothing removed. This would be taken to be washed and recycled for the next intake; sizes no longer mattered. Ibrahim had to slow down; it was surprising how heavy a dead body could be, even one this thin. He had to drag the man by both arms to get him over the stone step. Once inside, he put the body down and went back for the next one.

When he returned, the body had already been stripped and moved further up the line. They could fit several bodies into the hot ovens at one time. Here they were allowed to take their tops off while they worked.

The only thing that would get him through today was the hope that there would be new writing paper under his blanket.

Chapter 36

Hutchinson Camp, Isle of Man, England

Friedrich tripped and swore, then looked quickly around. The normally busy square was deserted; only the guards at the gate and two guards patrolling the street on the other side of the fence were in sight, and it was beginning to get dark. Everybody has gone to the lectures, he thought, plus he had missed dinner. It was expected that everybody would be at the lectures in the evening unless they had a prior approval, but now his main concern was to retrieve the papers strewn on the ground. He should not have sent the other boy away. The boy would have been able to help him now. Instead, there he was on all fours, picking the papers up as quickly as possible. Some of the white sheets had dirty marks on them – served him right. It had taken him all morning on the typewriter to make them presentable; now he doubted whether they would be accepted after all.

'Damn!'

Had he said that out loud? He would definitely be in trouble if he was overheard.

He had been shown how to typeset: take the page and find the letters in wooden printing sets; lay them out line by line, not forgetting blanks for the spaces or the dots at the end of sentences; place them into a printing frame. It had sounded easy enough when he was first told, and the men in charge had let him do the first paragraph. After only a few minutes he had proudly asked them to come and check. He had seen them looking at each other, and one of them shook his head in disbelief. He knew he had checked the spelling several times.

"Take the roller and the ink from over there, roll it over the letters, then press the paper on top and take the clean roller for that," he was told.

"Will this be the way we are going to print the whole newspaper?" he had enquired, fetching the items he had been told to get.

"No, we are just going to do the first check. We are getting a small printing press."

He applied the ink with great care – he had been instructed before not to waste any – then took the finished sheet, shook it several times, blew on it to make it dry quicker and handed it over, only to have it given back immediately.

"A professional printer reads his work out," he was told.

Friedrich looked at it, puzzled. None of the words made any sense. The whole sentence was back to front.

"But…"

"You want to be a newspaper man, you work it out. Bring the key back to us when you lock up."

With that they had left.

He gathered the papers back together and put his first printed sheet on the top, hoping they liked what he had written.

He wanted to finish his letter to Aunty Anna tonight; a task he had neglected for some time. Friedrich wondered whether his mother had received his letter and had written back. He had asked her to address her letters to the Trench Hall School, pretending he was there. He knew Aunty Anna would keep them for him, and maybe even send them on if she could. No need to worry his mother. How could he explain to her that, soon after arriving in England, he had been taken to an internment camp? In his letters to his mother he pretended he was studying hard and Aunty Anna had decided he would be better off with her than the foster family in London.

However, he had heard that letters from Germany were opened and read before being passed on. What if Aunty Anna read what his mother said? His mother might even write to thank her for taking her boy to live with her. Yes, he must try and post Aunty's letter tomorrow, after he had worked out how to explain it without making himself a downright liar.

Friedrich wondered how much he should tell Aunty Anna about his life at the camp. Was he allowed to tell her about the doctor who had arrived at their house? He was German, but not one of them; he was a real troublemaker. He had made a complaint to the authorities that one of the guards had been mistreating them, and had picked on the best and kindest guard they had. The guard had then been investigated, and after what must have been a trial, he was dismissed. The elder of the house tried to put it right and get the guard reinstated, but he did not come back, and they were glad when the doctor was moved to another camp.

Each night at about five o'clock, before they sat down for the evening meal, a list of the names of those who would be released the following morning was read out. The internees talked about it all day. Who would be allowed to go home? At the beginning there had been so many people here that sometimes they'd had to share the beds after all, and most of the older men had decided that sleeping on the floor was a better option, but after some of them had been released, even new intakes didn't make up the original number.

Friedrich worried about the list all day, and he had missed the reading tonight. What if his name had been read out? Where would he go?

Chapter 37

Coventry, England, 14 November 1940

Alexander knew that Anna thought his choice of city was strange, but she did not object. He wanted to set off as early as possible; Coventry was nearly 80 miles away, but Joshua would enjoy the long drive, avoiding any major towns. Alexander had driven up from London in the MG Midget just after lunch the day before. The workshop had made sure the car was running well and shining when he left, but it had rained on the way so he'd had to stop and put the roof up, which spoilt the look of the car a little.

Joshua sprang into immediate action and polished the car again. Several other boys had volunteered to help him, but he declined. That did not stop them from standing around, shouting advice and pointing to a spot he had missed, laughing at him. He knew they were jealous and the older boys would make him pay when nobody was watching, but that would not be for a few days yet. Sabbath was coming up, after all.

Joshua was up at 6am, having packed his overnight bag the previous evening. He had never stayed in a hotel before, and was now pacing up and down in the large kitchen, a place he would normally avoid in case the cook roped him in for extra duties. Anna and Alexander joined him at first light, sitting around the wooden table while the breakfast was prepared. Joshua was too excited to eat, but managed some toast after Anna insisted he was not going to leave on an empty stomach. When he could not stop fidgeting, Alexander quickly finished his cup of tea, almost choking.

"I think Joshua is ready to leave, Anna."

Joshua was almost out of the door when he remembered he had not said goodbye.

"Thank you for letting me go, Aunty Anna."

"You be careful, and I expect you back tomorrow afternoon," was her reply.

Outside, Alexander stowed their luggage in the boot.

"It looks like a nice day. Shall we take the roof down?"

"He is not going without his hat and scarf." Anna had followed them and stood in the doorway.

"Aunty Anna!" Joshua protested, but ran over to his room, being aware that resisting would only waste time as he would have to take them in any case. He waved when the car set off, and looked back until they were round the corner and Anna had disappeared from his view.

"One of the English boys said there is a big old castle in Coventry. Is that where you are taking me, Uncle Alexander?"

"That and many other places. You do remember you have an agreement with your English teacher to write about your day after your return?"

No doubt Alexander had brought his notebook and pencil, Joshua thought. "Is there a Lyons Corner House in Coventry?"

"I thought you were not hungry."

"Now I am, Uncle Alexander."

"Well, it is almost lunchtime. Why don't we stop in the next village and have something to eat there? Coventry is only about thirty minutes away, after all."

"Don't we need ration coupons?"

"Let's find out." The car stopped outside a small café which looked almost empty. "You wait here, I am going to check." To Joshua's relief, Alexander added, "And see what we could have to eat."

A few minutes later, both occupied a table by the window,

cups of hot tea in front of them, ignoring the strange looks when Joshua insisted on drinking his without any milk. The beef and vegetable pie had just come out of the oven, and a big slice soon appeared before each of them.

"I have to make another stop before we go to the castle, which is not far from here. And then we will go to the hotel to check in. After that, we are going to explore the town. Does that sound good?"

"Mmmmmh." Joshua nodded; Aunty Anna always told them not to speak with their mouths full.

Joshua was amazed how large Coventry was. He did not know why, but he had expected it to be the size of Harwich. The last time he had been in a big town was when they had been to Southampton to see his family leaving for America. His missed them, especially today: his second birthday without them.

Alexander stopped and parked his car in a street with a row of shops. "Come along, there is something we have to get."

"What are we getting?"

A little bell over the door of the second shop in the row announced their arrival, and a stooped man made his way across from behind the counter, taking his apron off while he shuffled along. His body was bent forward towards the ground and he seemed to have a problem with standing tall, but he raised his head as well as he could.

His outstretched hand greeted Alexander. "Mr Borstein, I presume. And this must be young Joshua. Come in, come in, I have it through here."

The two followed him outside to a courtyard. On the opposite side was a long flat-roofed building which reminded Joshua of the stables he had kept his horse in. A memory he had tried to erase as best he could now made him stop in his tracks.

"There it is. Happy birthday, Master Joshua. You have

a very generous father. Yes, a very generous father indeed."
The owner kept rubbing his hands together as he spoke,
only stopping when Joshua did not immediately react.

"A bicycle? I got a bicycle for my birthday?" Joshua
said finally, not bothering to put the shopkeeper right that
Alexander was not his father.

"Not just any bicycle, Master Joshua. This is a Rudge-
Whitworth bicycle. Very difficult to come by, you know."
He addressed his last sentence to Alexander. "Yes, I did as
you asked. It was not easy, no. Not easy at all."

Joshua let his fingers run across the cool metal.

"Why don't you try it out, Master Joshua?" The shopkeeper's concerned voice echoed in the confined space of the
yard. Maybe he was worried he might lose the sale after all
if the boy did not like it. Children were so spoilt these days.

"Can I take it outside?"

"Of course you can, young man."

"Don't go too far," added Alexander. "I will settle
everything here. You do like it, don't you?"

Joshua had already gone, in case it was a joke and this
bicycle was not really his to keep.

Back in the car, as they were on the way to find a parking
place in the town after they had dropped off their luggage,
Joshua asked for the third time, "You are sure he said it will
be delivered to the school? He did say it was going on a lorry
and I was not to worry. That was what he said, wasn't it?"

The cinema was on Folehill Road. They found it easily
enough. *Four Feathers* announced the poster outside.

"We are going to the cinema?"

"Unless you don't want to. This film is in Technicolor."

"What is Technicolor?"

"You know, the film is in colour. Not like the black and
white ones you have seen."

"I have never been to a cinema before."

It hadn't crossed Alexander's mind that Joshua had never seen a film. He had believed that this had been one of the treats given to the children by the local council soon after their arrival at Dovercourt Camp.

The only two seats still available together were in the third row from the front. Alexander would normally have preferred to sit further back, but they had arrived a little late and the film was about to start.

"What is that sound?"

"Oh my God, air-raid sirens. Come on, Joshua, quick, quick. We have to find the shelter!" Alexander shot out of his seat and grabbed Joshua by the arm, pushing him ahead. The way out at the rear of the cinema was blocked by other cinemagoers, struggling to reach the exit as fast as they could, but the lights had not come on and people failed to see where they were going. In the darkness, Alexander sensed that somebody was being trampled on; he heard a crunch like bones breaking and a muffled moan, and held on to Joshua, pulling him back.

"We can't get out that way. There must be other doors!" he shouted. They both felt their way along the wall to their left. Just before the stage, they found a door and tried to locate a handle or a bar, anything which would open it, but to no avail.

"Out of the way, I know how it works." Several people were now behind them. The person who had spoken pushed Alexander away and reached to the top. "Sorry, mate, I have to undo the bolt. You try the one at the bottom. There must be two of them."

Alexander knelt down, searching, his shoulder being pressed against the door by people pushing. He found the bolt, but it took all his strength to slide it open as the top bolt moved simultaneously. The door flew open with the sheer weight of people, and Alexander was thrown on to the floor.

When he managed to get back to his feet, he had lost sight of Joshua, until he spotted him standing alone, gazing up.

Hundreds of flares were lighting up the sky, slowly descending downwards.

"What are those?"

Before Alexander had time to explain, the sky changed, and large black objects replaced the flares, followed by explosions of fire.

"Run, run! Follow me!" Alexander overtook Joshua, then stopped abruptly. "Quicker, Joshua, quicker. We have to find the shelter."

The firestorm kept on ahead, behind and to the sides of them. Sparks bounced off the ground, hitting Joshua's jacket, which started smouldering. Alexander put the clothing out with his bare hands, ignoring the blisters and the pain. They stumbled on, searching for people to follow. One lonely old man stood ahead, his head raised towards the sky.

"Where are the shelters?" But any reply was drowned out by aircraft noises from above combined with the sound of raging fires on the ground. No anti-aircraft guns could be heard. Where were they? It was as if the raid had taken the town by surprise.

The ground shook as the first large bomb hit. As Alexander let go of Joshua and indicated to pull up his sweater to cover his mouth and nose, protecting him as best he could from the rising smoke, they did not hear the faint 'click' from the ground when Alexander took a step forward.

Chapter 38

"You have a visitor, Dr Rosenthal."

The nurse had been looking for her, and found her in Ward 8, just finishing her rounds. Esther was tired today. It had been her turn to be on call, and she'd had to go in around midnight, which was not the first urgent call she had received since she had started to work at the Kingsbrook Hospital. A little girl had been attacked by three Alsatians in the park. What had a little girl been doing in a park after dark? Esther wondered while she got dressed and ready to go after Isabella had answered the phone.

"What are you doing here, Father? Has something happened to the children?"

Mordechai was waiting in the family room: the one used to talk to parents of a sick child, sometimes in very difficult circumstances, which was why she did not like going in there. Mordechai had not noticed her entering. He was concentrating on the fresh snow which had fallen in the early morning; the hospital grounds were covered. When he heard her voice behind him, without turning he said, "Look, Esther, it's snowing. It is early this year, don't you think?"

Esther had learned to read her father's moods well. Matters of great concern were not addressed unless he had a solution already.

"I had a visit from Thomas today." A visit from the reporter was not unusual. They had kept in touch, and often met up in Manhattan or had dinner together at Isabella's house. Later this month they would celebrate Hanukah together;

137

both Thomas and Arthur appreciated being included in the celebration by the Jewish Community, despite the Rabbi having frowned on Isabella when he'd first found out the men were of a different faith. Isabella had not been deterred.

"He spoke with Anna yesterday," Mordechai continued. Esther felt the colour draining from her face. Her legs started to shake and she had to reach for the armrest of the first chair to steady herself. Slowly she lowered herself into it, trying to regain her composure.

"Father, sit down and talk to me."

Mordechai turned away from the window, pulled a chair across and positioned himself opposite Esther, taking both of her hands into his. He let out a loud sigh.

"Joshua and Alexander are missing."

"What do you mean, missing? How could they be missing?" Esther jumped up with such a force that the armchair tipped backwards. The same nurse who had told her that she had a visitor was standing outside the door, a practice they followed whenever a doctor had to give bad news to parents.

"Is everything alright, Dr Rosenthal?"

"Calm yourself, Esther. Come, sit down again."

"Father, how can I stay calm when you have just told me my son is missing?"

"Thomas said he already knew that they could not find Alexander, but he was not aware that Joshua was with him."

"He knew Alexander had disappeared and did not think of telling us?"

"Thomas said that Anna is in a real state. Alexander picked Joshua up in his car on his birthday."

"But his birthday was almost three weeks ago. They have been missing all this time and nobody told us?"

"Now who is being unreasonable? Do you realise how difficult communication via radio waves is across the Atlantic?"

"Yes, of course. Father, please tell me everything from the beginning."

Mordechai repeated what Thomas had told him and Isabella in their kitchen: that on Joshua's birthday, he had been taken for a day out to Coventry. Anna had given her permission, and was now devastated. She had reported them missing to the police on the Saturday, not attending any prayers with the children. She'd had a bad feeling inside her, she had said. It was so unlike Alexander not to return at the agreed time, she had waited up all night, pacing up and down from one room to another.

Maybe if she had turned the wireless on she would have found out that way, but as it was, she did not. The officers at the police station told her that Coventry had been attacked by the German Luftwaffe and they did not know if the air raid had stopped.

A search party organised by the newspaper had arrived at the school three days later. Anna was determined to travel with them to help find Alexander and Joshua, but they did not get very far as the town was still smouldering in places. Only the spire of the destroyed Cathedral told them where the centre once was.

"Father, I am going back."

"Where?"

"To England to find my son. I should never have agreed to leave him there. I am going to find him and bring him home to his family. Father, that is what I am going to do."

Chapter 39

They had come here many times before, but today Times Square had lost its magic for Esther. She hurried her father along; he had wanted to stop at his favourite deli, but thought better of it. Maybe Thomas would take them there in his lunch break.

Esther had already told Rebecca and Benjamin about her plan – there was no point in lying to them – it was then when she noticed Benjamin's bruised left eye. He had been in a fight at school, Rebecca immediately told her mother.

"The other boy told me I was not Jewish and I should go to a different school. He said my hair colour was all wrong."

"You started a fight for that?"

"I would do it again."

Esther was relieved that Benjamin had started to stand up for himself, but had to make sure he learned that fighting was never an option.

"Come here!" She pulled him towards her to sit him on her knees, but stopped at the last second. "You don't have to have dark hair. Look at your grandpa, his hair is blond."

Mordechai pulled his hair up and pointed to it for Benjamin to take a better look.

"Grandpa's hair is grey, and he has hardly any left."

"I don't know about that." Mordechai had a look in the large mirror hanging on the wall in the living room.

"Will you come back, Mama?"

"Of course I will come back."

"That is what my first mama said when the soldiers took her, but she never did."

Out of the corner of her eye, Esther saw Rebecca's reaction to what Benjamin had just said. She went down on to her knees to be the same height as him and grasped both his arms.

"Benjamin, your first mama tried very hard to come back to you."

"How do you know?"

"I know because she was taken away when all she wanted was to stay with you."

"So how do you know you will come back to us?"

"Because I am not being taken away. I am going to England to find your brother. While I am gone, you will be a good boy and listen to Grandpa and Aunty Isabella, and promise me – no more fights."

Thomas's workspace was on the tenth floor; the tenth floor already, and he had started on the fifth. This was not bad going after such a short time, he had said. They had laughed together when he told them the higher up your workplace was, the more important you were, and Esther had immediately accused him of sounding like an American already. That had been such a good evening. Isabella had told Mordechai and Esther to go and enjoy themselves; the children would be perfectly fine with her. In any case, it was about time that she had them to herself; she could spoil them better that way, she insisted.

The three now sat around the table in a small meeting room, Esther facing the windows. The snow on the buildings opposite made her feel cold inside, and her father had given her a strange look when she had insisted she was not going to take her coat off. Outside on the door, Thomas had slid the sign from 'free' to 'busy', so a knock on the door almost made Esther jump.

The young man who entered went around the table, pulled up a chair and sat next to Thomas, putting a large file down. He introduced himself, stating he worked in the company's legal department.

"We have worked out that the only way to travel to the United Kingdom at present is via a convoy." He looked at Mordechai and Esther, hoping for some comments, but when none were forthcoming he looked down and shuffled the paperwork. "As I was saying, you could leave on a convoy."

"I have made enquiries already," interrupted Thomas, sensing the young attorney's discomfort. "We could join the convoy in Bermuda. One will be leaving soon, so we would have to get to Bermuda immediately."

Mordechai had given Esther a slight nudge with his elbow. Since she had received the news about Joshua being missing she had become very quiet, and he thought it was time for her to contribute to the effort which was being made on her behalf.

"I must thank you for all you are doing for me, but how am I going to get to Bermuda, and why do you keep saying 'we', Thomas?"

"First things first. Travel to Bermuda will be on one of those flying boats. They leave from the new LaGuardia Marine Airport, and we have secured two seats for tomorrow." Esther was just taking a deep breath to interrupt, but Thomas was not to be deterred, and continued, "It has to be tomorrow or not at all. The editor has used all his persuasive powers to get the passes, and most importantly let us travel on the convoy with a supply carrier."

"The newspaper has already paid 175 dollars for the airfare from LaGuardia and needs to be reimbursed." Now it became apparent why the young man had seemed uncomfortable in their presence.

"Please give him our thanks. I will return with the money in a few days. But we also need at least 200 English pounds for my daughter to take with her."

"When do you need it by?"

"Today, of course," added Thomas, shaking his head in disbelief.

While the young man gathered his paperwork and said his goodbyes, Mordechai made a mental note to make an appointment with the manager at the bank in Brooklyn. They played chess together every Wednesday and had become good friends since Mordechai first went there and opened his bank account with a deposit box. It was the manager who had advised Mordechai to change only a little into actual money and arranged for the rest to be kept in gold coins.

"After all," he had insisted, "gold will keep its value."

Mordechai now visualised the contents of his box: the money, the gold coins and, most importantly, the two remaining cuckoo clock weights, still covered with the dark colour he had painted them back in Hildesheim.

Chapter 40

Rebecca and Benjamin were allowed to come with Mordechai and Isabella to accompany Esther to LaGuardia Marine Airport. Rebecca knew that it would be hard to convince her mother to keep them out of school, so she enlisted the help of her teacher. Esther was not surprised when she was handed a note with the permission.

They spotted the airport building long before they reached it. Despite his mother leaving, Benjamin could hardly conceal his excitement. Planes which could land on water? He had never seen anything like that; he had told his friend at school, who immediately queried whether Benjamin had actually ever seen any type of plane.

"I think I saw one once, flying high in the sky."

"No, you didn't."

Benjamin quickly weighed up the consequences of disagreeing with his new ally, who was one of the tallest in his class.

"Maybe it was a bird, I cannot be very sure."

"I thought so. I have seen many planes before. My father takes me out sometimes."

Benjamin certainly did not want to be drawn into a talk which might involve questions about his own father and thought it best to change the subject.

"I will tell you about the sea plane when I come back to school, but only if you want me to."

The airport had been built recently, and evidence of the work still to be carried out was apparent. A small queue was forming outside to enter the air terminal, the hold-up caused by workmen struggling to fit the last of the doors into the frame at the entrance. The other ones were shut with a rope in front of them, indicating they were not to be used.

"When can we go inside?" Rebecca was shivering in the cold, trying to do up the front buttons of her coat. She then pulled her scarf up higher to cover her head and blew on her hands for extra warmth.

Mordechai watched her. Why had he not noticed that the children had outgrown their clothing? They had little to protect them from the icy wintery blast, which could last long into the spring. He would have to speak with Isabella on their way back home.

"Uncle Thomas! Uncle Thomas!" Benjamin had spotted him through the glass on the other side, already in the hall waiting for them. "When can we go inside?" Now it was Benjamin asking.

The men gave up on the task in hand, took the door off the large hinges and carried it away. Rebecca was through the opening and the next set of doors before the workman had a chance to change their minds and make them wait outside even longer.

Although the weather was grey and dull, it was surprisingly light inside the large round ticket hall. Esther was too preoccupied to take it all in, but the others stopped in their tracks. The first thing which struck them was the painted 360 degree mural on the upper part of the wall, the colours mixing with the light from the large glass dome that gave the hall a warm glow.

Benjamin dived for the first wooden bench. He bent over to the side and touched the inlaid propeller with his finger.

"Wait until I tell them about this at school, they will not believe me." He had joined his mother and Thomas at the round check-in desk in the middle, where it was their turn to be handed a ticket. He stared at the globe, which stood on a pedestal in the centre. "We have one at school. Come on, Rebecca, let's find England."

He did not see the porter putting the luggage on a trolley behind him, tripped over it and landed on the floor. Tears immediately formed in his eyes when he looked at the black man's face. Now his mother would have to scold him on the day she was leaving.

Chapter 41

Esther was relieved when she stood back on firm ground. She had regretted accepting the meal served soon after take-off. First she had sat by the window in the passenger's compartment right behind the galley, sure the others passengers were slightly amused when she kept on waving, knowing very well that her family could not see her. Convinced this would be a smooth flight, she had then agreed to move to the dining lounge. As soon as the starter was served, the plane started to sway a little, but Esther was quizzing Thomas again and did not notice it at first.

"I will see my wife and children first. Then I will report to the Ministry of War for duty. I was lucky to get an assignment as a war reporter. It is my duty to defend my country the best I can, Esther. I am just glad we managed to talk Arthur out of coming along as well. I am going to visit his family and explain."

The plane started vibrating and then swinging from side to side. Esther dropped her fork and her drink spilled on to the tablecloth, her terrified face looking up at Thomas.

"There is no need to worry, madam. We are just experiencing a slight turbulence. This is perfectly normal for this time of the year," the steward reassured her. "May I suggest I bring you one of our finest brandies? It will have a calming effect."

"Make that two," Thomas requested.

The table was cleared and the soiled tablecloth replaced. Esther held the large brandy glass in between her hands as if it would provide extra warmth and slowly raised it to her lips.

The smell made her recoil at first, but she took a tentative sip.

"Yes, that feels better already."

"Would madam like to lay down in the ladies' room, or perhaps in one of the berths above?"

Esther now waited in the rain on the busy dockyard. Thomas had suggested she travel ahead with the Air Force transport to the hotel and settle in while he found their luggage. The other passengers had departed as soon as the small vessel had docked. She had never questioned where the clipper plane would land, and when it did set down on slightly choppy waters she had imagined they would be driven to the Bermuda Princess Hotel. Instead, their first stop was Darrel Island, as she heard the immigration officer call it, from where it would be a short boat ride across to Hamilton. The officer scrutinised her papers, she thought, for longer than anybody else's, and the few people still waiting behind her were starting to get restless.

A second officer joined him and took the papers from his colleague. "You two travel together?" He directed his question at Thomas, who simply nodded in reply. "What is the purpose of your visit?"

Thomas cleared his throat. "Dr Rosenthal will be working at a hospital in Liverpool to care for the wounded soldiers returning from the war, and I am required to submit daily reports on our war efforts in France."

It took the second officer only a few seconds to stamp their papers, "Have a safe journey," but it was near midnight when the jeep stopped in front of the hotel. The driver unloaded their cases, saluted and drove off. The entrance lobby was buzzing with people; Esther was surprised that they all seemed to be military personnel. She was wondering which country they represented when one of them came over to greet them.

"Dr Rosenthal?" He saluted. "We have been expecting

you. We managed to find you two rooms on the first floor. Please follow me."

"Where do you all come from?"

He was taken aback by that question. "From all over the place, mam. I myself come from Portsmouth."

"Portsmouth, England?"

"Yes, mam. This is your room. Please be downstairs in the restaurant at 7.30am for your briefing. Goodnight, mam."

"It has been a long day. Goodnight, Thomas."

"Goodnight, Esther, I will see you at 7.30. Don't be late, that soldier looked like he meant what he said." Thomas smiled.

Under different circumstances, Esther would have enjoyed her stay in Bermuda, especially spending some time at the Princess Hotel.

She was awakened by a loud knocking on her door and a female voice. "Breakfast is ready downstairs, mam."

Thomas was already waiting by a small table in the dining room. He pulled up a chair for Esther, and from where she sat the view, apart from the bad weather, was magnificent.

"Good morning, Esther, I have asked for tea and toast. I hope that is to your liking."

"This is such a wonderful place, Thomas. I don't know what I imagined it would be like. I will come back here with my family one day. What do you think we will be told at the briefing?"

"It will not be necessary, I already know everything which is applicable to us. There are certain areas which are off limits. The basement, for example."

Esther took another sip of hot milky tea. "What happens there?"

"Nobody would tell me, of course, but I found out anyway." He leaned over the table so as not to be overheard, and whispered, "It is a secure area where post to Europe will be checked and decoded before some of it can be forwarded with the next available vessel. All messages to and from Europe are intercepted there."

"Our letters as well?"

"Everything, Esther."

"How do you know all that?"

He leaned back in his chair and picked up his toast, which by now was cold.

"I would be very bad at my work if I didn't." This time he laughed out loud, and several men in uniform turned round from their breakfast, looking at him in surprise.

"Another instruction I got: we are allowed to move freely everywhere except in these areas." He produced a list and handed it over for Esther to have a look at.

"Everywhere except these places on the list? We are confined to the hotel, in other words."

"Yes. Bermuda has been declared a British strategic military base. We will leave in three days. Meanwhile we are supposed to make ourselves comfortable right here."

"We are not setting off tomorrow as planned?"

"No. They are waiting for some supply vessels, which have been delayed because of the weather, to arrive from Halifax in Canada."

Chapter 42

The weather did not improve during the day, and the next morning there was a notice placed on top of the reception desk in the lobby of the hotel, warning of a storm which was imminent. Most of the staff were engaged in boarding up the large windows facing the sea, wood and tools blocking the way into the dining room.

"Come over here, young man, and clear this away, now!" The voice boomed across from the officer in charge. "All the remaining equipment in there."

Most of the crates were carried from the reception area through the front doors and loaded on to waiting lorries. Shouted orders resulted in some of the staff stopping the work in hand and rushing back and forth, confused, adding to the chaos.

"How are we supposed to the win a war with this useless lot? For goodness' sake, somebody, get that woman from the first floor." The same officer was shouting again.

Esther appeared a few minutes later. She had tried to find Thomas before she went downstairs. The door of his room had been slightly ajar, and after knocking several times, she had pushed it fully open and gone inside. The room was empty.

"Where is my travelling companion?"

"Madam, gather your belongings. We are leaving. You." The officer grabbed a passing waiter by the collar, yanking him backwards. "Help this lady with her luggage."

Out of breath, Esther caught up with him at the top of the staircase.

"What is happening and where is my friend?" she managed to ask in short bursts.

"Madam, the convoy is leaving."

"But not all of the vessels have arrived."

"I have not been told anything about that. Madam, please pack your things."

Suitcase now by her side, she again confronted the same officer.

"Will somebody tell me where I am supposed to go and where my friend is?"

"Dr Rosenthal, we don't have much time to explain this to you. Your friend has already gone. We found him a space on one of the vessels. The boat which you were both supposed to travel on has not yet arrived, but we cannot delay our departure much longer. A storm is coming, and, like it or not, the storm is to our advantage. You are crossing on a commercial vessel together with some of our intelligence staff. Be glad we found you a berth. For what it is worth, your friend was looking for you. Now, if you don't mind, we have pressing things to attend to. Have a safe crossing."

The vessel Esther was boarding reminded her of a large motor yacht, clearly converted for Navy purposes. She tried to make out the original name, but could only read the first letter E underneath the repainted grey. Her mother had told her that it was a bad omen to rename a boat, and she wondered whether this also applied to removing the name altogether.

As soon as she was on board, the boat started moving. Esther lost her balance on the narrow staircase and her left shoulder hit the side, making her lose her grip on her case. The latch opened, spilling the contents on to the floor. A woman, not dissimilar to Esther's age, must have heard the commotion because she put her head round an opening cabin door.

"Goodness! Here, let me help you." She bent down, gathering the items which had rolled across to the other end of the corridor, and immediately recoiled her hand.

"Ouch! What did you have in there?"

"At least you are not going to be seasick. Those were my seasickness drops, given to me as a leaving present by one of the nurses."

Both women looked at each other from opposite ends of the corridor.

"I am Vicky, by the way. I hope this was not the only bottle. It's going to be rough, so they say," Esther's helper said, with her finger still in her mouth.

"I am Esther."

"Come on, girls, meet Esther." Two more faces appeared behind her.

"Top or bottom bunk? You are a doctor, we have heard, so we'd better show you a bit of respect. We might need your services," Jo, the youngest of the group, volunteered, while Rosie made some space under one of the bunks and pushed Esther's case underneath.

"Let's go upstairs while the sea is still calm." When she saw the look Esther gave her, Vicky continued, "Well, relatively speaking. And we can show you the dining area, just in case you ever feel like eating anything."

Esther immediately liked Vicky, Jo and Rosie, especially Vicky, who seemed to have a wicked sense of humour.

Jo was the first through the door, bumping straight into a crew member in his starched white uniform, smudging her red lipstick across the front of it.

"Look what you made me do." She wiped the rest of her lipstick from her cheek, her green eyes blazing, and went back inside to pick the small mirror up off her bottom bunk. "And you ruined my hairstyle." Running her fingers through her curls, she tried to locate the small combs she used to hold them in place.

Jo's ginger hair matched her freckles perfectly, Esther thought, and she had a better look at her companions from her bunk opposite Jo's. Rosie and Jo looked perfectly groomed, although maybe their choice of clothes was a little unsuitable for a crossing which was supposed to be cold and choppy.

Jo had bent down with her back towards the crew member, who had not moved, and lifted her skirt a little to straighten her stockings. She heard him cough and turned her head without changing her position.

"If I've laddered my stockings because of your clumsiness you can pay me when we arrive."

"Would you ladies please come upstairs for the safety briefing and bring your lifejackets," he stammered, his face as red as the lipstick on his jacket. He shot off, not waiting for a reply.

"You wait, never a dull moment with our Jo," Vicky whispered from behind Esther as they made their way back upstairs.

The sway of the waves combining with the strong wind started to rock the boat from side to side. Esther clung on to the railing, not able to hear any of the instructions about the emergency drill and the areas which would be off limits to the people who had gathered on top. She had imagined that they were the only passengers, and was surprised to find that the group trying to hold itself upright must number about twenty, although the four of them were the only women.

Vicky nudged her side. "Look." Esther looked to her left: as far as the eye could see were vessels of all shapes and sizes. The sound of the wind almost drowned out the roaring from above, and Esther would have missed it if Vicky had not pointed upwards.

Dozens of planes were above them. "We are off," explained Vicky, and fear gripped Esther's heart.

Chapter 43

"Do you think the whole crossing will be as rough as it is now?"

"No, Rosie, trust me, it will be worse."

"I don't feel so well."

"Esther, do you still have some of that magic medicine you injected me with earlier?"

The four women had retired to their bunks, hoping by lying down they would feel less of the sway. As it was, nobody felt like going to get some of the food they were told was available from the galley.

"Maybe we should eat something. That might help?"

"Jo!"

"Jo is right, and I might have something which could help." Esther sat up and tried to get her suitcase without having to stand up first. She felt underneath the bunks and pulled a case out.

"I think that one is mine, try a little to the left."

Esther pushed it back and tried again. Pulling her case all the way out, she lifted it next to her on the blanket.

"Jo, do you think you could fill the flask with more water?"

"In my nightdress? Yes, that would be interesting." She sat up, forgetting the top bunk had very little headroom. They heard her head bumping despite the roar of the engines.

"Are you alright?"

"Don't worry, I will have one of the sailors check it out, and maybe he could kiss it better for me."

"Here, take my dressing gown."

"You brought a dressing gown, Esther? Lucky it is pitch-black in here, I hate to think what it will do to my appearance."

"Jo, just get on with it." Vicky had heard enough. She climbed down, felt her way to the cabin door and pulled it open. The corridor was dimly lit, giving a welcome glow to the inside of the cabin.

"Blimey!" Vicky recoiled in shock as Jo appeared behind her. "Where did you get this one from, Esther?"

"It's my father's."

"I am not going out in this." Jo scrutinised what she was wearing over what she thought was her very inviting nightdress.

"Jo, please." Rosie moaned. "Otherwise I will be first to use the bucket."

Vicky watched Jo staggering along the corridor, trying to hold herself upright by steadying herself with her free hand.

"Let's try and keep the door open slightly until she gets back. Esther, push Rosie's case over, will you?"

"Use your own, it is battered already. Mine is new." Vicky ignored Rosie's complaint and placed the shiny light-brown leather case in front of the door, letting the heavy cabin door go. They heard the case crunching from the weight pressing against it before Rosie's moan.

"What have you got in there?" Vicky sat herself next to Esther. Her body made the mattress sink down at the bottom end, and some of the items Esther had placed there slid towards her. "Did you bring any clothes besides the ones you were wearing?" Esther's bunk was covered in little white boxes with writing on them. Vicky had picked up one of them. "You can actually read this?"

"Here it is." Esther handed a wrapped parcel to Vicky. "You open it."

"It says 'For Anna' on the paper."

"Open it anyway."

Vicky did as Esther said. She carefully undid the red ribbon and the gold coloured paper. Straightening the paper with her hands, she folded it over in a way that left the name on the top and gave it back.

"It smells delicious. What is in it?"

"Isabella baked some ginger biscuits."

Jo appeared in the doorway with the dressing gown open, her hair slightly ruffled, looking triumphant. Holding a flask in each hand, she climbed over the raised cabin doorstep.

"Look what I got."

"What is in the other flask?" Vicky reached for it, unscrewed the top and tried to detect its contents by smelling. "Smells like tea. Did you get any milk?"

"Better than that." She reached into the dressing gown pocket and produced a glass bottle. She gave it to Esther, who removed the cork, which made a slight 'pop' when pulled out. Immediately the cabin was filled with a sweet aroma.

"Whisky? Where did you get that one from?"

"Let's just say, he will not forget this crossing in a hurry. Plus hot, sweet black tea with a shot of whisky is good for you if you don't feel very well. His mama said so."

The journey was supposed to take less than a week, but instead it took ten long days. The sea calmed down after the first night, and when the women ventured on deck their boat seemed totally isolated in the dense fog. Only the sounds coming from some of the other ships reassured them they were not alone. They tried to find out as much as they could from their fellow passengers, but these seemed to be less informed than the women themselves.

Jo became their source of up to date information. "The planes had to turn back, but will re-join later. The fog actually helps our situation. They believe a couple of the smaller boats cannot keep up, and the smoke from their old chimneys is giving their position away, placing them in extra danger. What? What, did I say?"

"You sound like a wireless operator."

"Do you want the information or not?" She looked at one of her hands and counted her fingers with the other. "Now I have forgotten what else I was told, there were five things. Ah yes, the forecast is for strong winds combined with heavy rain, which is good, apparently, otherwise there would be a lot of zigzagging on this crossing."

All four sat around a small table, biting into a slice of bread each and holding on to their cups as instructed to avoid them sliding off. Vicky heard the sirens first. The shrill sound filled the cabin, and heavy boots started running outside in the corridor.

"Girls, girls, get your lifejackets, now!" she shouted, already standing upright as best she could, the contents of their bucket spilling over. It would have been Rosie's turn to empty it first thing.

"I will never get used to the lack of headroom, I will be totally useless if we ever get there." Jo rubbed the top of her head. "What is the stuff on the floor? It's soaking." She lifted her bare feet, trying to inspect the damage.

"I told you to sleep in your clothes. Take your life jackets. Come on, quick, quick, out. We will be the last ones again."

"Attack, Attack!" they heard as soon as they managed to pull the door inwards. The boat was listing heavily to one side. More on all fours than upright, they reached the stair-case and climbed up, Vicky bringing up the rear. They had practised this drill, and it was her responsibility to ensure that everybody in her group was accounted for. In the mess quarters, the other passengers were already flat on the floor with their hands above their heads, potentially protecting them from falling debris. Why they had to lie on the floor was not entirely clear. The captain had explained that this would be their safest position, but Jo had been entrusted with different instructions, which were to ensure the passengers didn't run around like headless chickens, getting in the way.

The boat shook, and the women hit the floor in unison. They had all agreed that instead of covering their heads, they would hold hands, just in case. The dim light flickered and went out altogether. One of the men started praying out loud, and another shouted for his mother.

"Shut up!" they heard, and the calling for Mother stopped. The sound they heard next was an explosion not far away, and the boat rocked violently from side to side. Rosie was next to Vicky and could be heard crying. Vicky gave her a squeeze with her hand, and thought she received a thankful look back, but she could not be sure in the dark. They heard one of the men vomiting where he lay, and the stench drifted over.

"What is the matter with those bloody men?"

The lights came on again, and the vessel was stabilising. Jo was the first to sit upright.

"I think I wet my knickers," Rosie confessed.

"An attack in the dark is unusual," Jo reported back during the day. The women had cleaned up as best they could, and even managed to wash some small items in the bathroom at the end of the corridor, ignoring the banging on the door from angry passengers wanting to use it.

"Use the one upstairs, we are busy," shouted Jo several times.

Lying back in their bunks, trying to recover, they made plans for the future. Rosie told stories about the Christmases of her childhood, and they took it in turns to recount amusing anecdotes. Only Esther remained quiet.

"What is your tradition at Christmas, Esther?" Rosie wanted to know.

"Rosie, Esther does not celebrate Christmas."

"Why not?"

"Esther, forgive her. Rosie is not worldly wise. For somebody who is as slow as Rosie on the uptake, you would not believe her skills when it comes to numbers and symbols. She is the best there is."

Vicky laughed out loud.

They said their goodbyes at Liverpool's Lime Street Station, their vessel having been one of the first in line to be unloaded.

"It had perishables on it," explained Jo. "More I do not know, only that some boats are missing. No contact."

"I don't know what the three of you will be doing in Buckinghamshire, but from the way Jo has been reporting back to us over the last few days, it sounds precise and to the point. Please keep safe."

They had promised to write to Esther at the school, but were unable to reveal their own exact location.

"We will be in touch, I promise." Vicky hugged Esther tight before the three had to leave, turning round several times, waving.

Esther had been shocked when they arrived in Liverpool. Why had she imagined the town would have escaped the German bombs? The ticket clerk shook his head when she asked him the best way to get to Wem in Shropshire.

"Not today, love. Let me have a look in this book of mine." He produced a much-used schedule, and started flicking through the pages. "I could get you to Manchester today." When he realised Esther was wondering where to go from there, he continued, "Maybe not, as it is in the wrong direction. You want to go to Crewe, you know." He looked over his glasses through the small window, all the while pushing back his railway cap, which slipped forward every time he moved his head.

He sighed. "No, love, as I said, not today. Try again tomorrow. Next."

Esther stepped out of the line of waiting travellers, picked up her case, and was walking towards the exit when she spotted the row of wooden telephone booths. One of the booths was unoccupied, so she decided to phone the school and tell Anna she was back in England and she hoped to be there tomorrow. Tonight she planned to find a room in a large hotel she had passed which did not look to be too damaged.

A sturdy woman bustled towards her, knocking her suitcase over.

"I am so sorry, I am clumsy today." The woman picked it up. Still bending down, she took a closer look at Esther. "Do I know you?"

"I don't recall, but somehow you look familiar."

"Yes, I thought so. You are a doctor, right? I met you at Frank Kett's last year."

Esther tried to work out whom she was referring to, and then it dawned on her.

"I am sorry, it's your accent that gave you away. No, no, I don't mean anything by it, really. It is nice, and your English is excellent. I am Flo." She stretched her hand out to greet Esther.

"Don't worry, I am not offended. I am Esther, and now I do remember. It was when I dropped the children off at the pawnbroker's shop. I had forgotten his name. You came to pick up your friend who was not well."

"Yes, our Annie."

"She was pregnant, if I remember right."

"Yes, she had a baby boy, David. He is a real cutie." Flo's face lit up.

"Did she not have another little one in the pram?"

"Poor little Derek died, I am afraid, and Annie is not coping too well."

161

"I am really sorry to hear that."

"What are you doing here at the station anyway?"

"I need to get to Wem in Shropshire, but there are no trains today."

"You live nearby?"

"No, I just arrived by boat from America. I am hoping to find a room in the hotel across the road and try again tomorrow. I have to find my boy who has been missing since Coventry was destroyed. Sorry, I should not burden you with my problems."

"Nonsense. You come with me. I have plenty of space in my house. It is a couple of tram rides from here. But you have been in Garston before. I do ramble on."

"You are very kind, but I could not possibly accept your generous offer."

"Esther, believe me when I say you would be doing me a great favour. I definitely need some company tonight."

Chapter 44

Garston, Liverpool

Flo put the kettle back on to her kitchen stove. One more kettleful and the bath in front of the fire in the living room should be at the right temperature. At first Esther had protested that Flo was wasting her wood and coal, but Flo had insisted on a fire. Besides, she knew where to get some more without having to swap her ration coupons.

"Are you alright in there, Esther? Is the water still hot enough?" Esther heard Flo's muffled voice through the closed door.

"You could not possibly imagine how good this feels, Flo. How can I ever make this up to you?"

Later they sat in their nightclothes around the small kitchen table. Flo made sure they each had a blanket wrapped around their body, held together with one hand. In the other hand they held a spoon, heat rising from plates in front of them.

"This is delicious, Flo. What did you call it?"

"Irish stew, just as my mother made. Go on, eat up." When Esher hesitated, she added, "The meat is not pork. To be honest, I have no idea what the butcher handed to me, but I am quite sure it looked nothing like pork."

Esther savoured every spoonful. She took her last piece of bread and used it to wipe around the plate until it was clean, then looked up into Flo's amused face.

"A woman after my own heart, that is what you are, Esther. Would you like some more?"

"No, thank you. You are a wonderful cook, I cannot thank you enough."

"Really, Esther, I am glad to have your company. It is getting dark. We can wash the dishes later, but right now we have to do the blackout. Come on, I will show you."

There were dark pieces of fabric underneath each window. In the living room they used the blanket which a minute ago had warmed Flo.

"You keep yours. I am not cold, and in any case we are going to sit in front of the fire with a hot toddy. We Irish are a very inquisitive race – some would call us nosy. I would love to hear your story."

"Wait, I have some warm socks upstairs. Somewhere," Flo added more quietly. Esther had stepped into a wet patch on her small rug; she was not used to emptying the metal bath with a big ladle into a bucket and had spilled some of the water.

Esther was halfway through telling Flo how she had managed to come to England before the war and her journey all the way to America when the sirens started blaring.

"That is just great. Those bloody Germans again. We are supposed to run for the air-raid shelter."

Esther put her glass on to the small table which Flo had placed next to her side of the comfortable settee. It had been a very relaxing evening, and Esther was sorry to have to go out in the rain. She almost fell back on to the worn out settee, nearly dropping her drink. She lifted herself up, but Flo pulled her back.

"I don't usually bother. I did at first, but I have not been near a shelter since the night Derek died. You know, Annie's little boy."

"What happened that night?"

"I was not there, but he died of a fit in a dark shelter. George, Annie's husband, was nowhere to be seen, of course. Just Annie, their children and neighbours. I don't think Annie will ever forgive George."

"Where was he?"

"Fast asleep in their flat in the tenement upstairs. We can go to a shelter if you like, but in November an air-raid shelter in town got a direct hit. Over 160 died, so it said in the papers."

"If you believe we should stay, we will."

"We've had quite a few false alarms anyway. What I usually do is get dressed, blow the candles out and take the blanket off the window. That way I can see what is happening outside. If the bombs drop anywhere near Garston tonight, we will have to run."

"Tell me what brought a young lady all the way from Ireland to Liverpool." Both had settled down again after getting out of their nightwear and into their street clothes. Their coats were ready at the front door in case they were needed. Flo had insisted they must have another drink, then giggled, explaining they would be quite a sight: two women staggering through the streets.

Flo's story took most of the night. The all-clear had long since sounded, and still they talked. The fire had gone out and both had covered themselves again with the blankets. Esther kept asking one question after another.

"And I thought the Irish were the ones who wanted to know everything."

It was beginning to get light outside when Esther enquired, "And your Kieran, where is your husband?"

Flo turned towards the window. She did not want Esther to witness her tears.

"Kieran thought we would be better off if he went and joined the Merchant Navy. You see, the wives who are left behind get part of the wages paid out every week. And when their menfolk come home, they get given the balance and extra ration coupons."

Esther braced herself.

"My Kieran – I am afraid he is gone, Esther. The boat

got a direct hit from one of those Luftwaffe planes. A lot of the crew managed to be saved, but not my Kieran. You see, he helped others, not thinking about himself. That is what my Kieran was like, always thinking of others."

"I am so very sorry, Flo. I feel so ashamed. I should have asked you earlier. And I should not have invaded your home. Oh, Flo! When did all this happen?"

"I was informed yesterday. I had just picked up the letter when I met you."

Chapter 45

Flo waited with her until the tram to Penny Lane departed first thing in the morning. The smoke from burning buildings seemed to come from the opposite direction to where Esther was heading. She looked out of the window until Flo was a small speck in the distance, then changed trams, just as she had on her previous journey.

There was a different man inside the ticket booth at Lime Street Station who kindly explained where she had to change trains. He even took the time to write it all down, then he handed her three tickets.

"Mind how you go, Miss. Make sure you keep your tickets and your money in a safe place now. There is a lot of riffraff loitering about. And desperate times call for desperate measures, as they say. And sorry I couldn't be of more help. Hopefully the connecting trains will depart today."

Esther was relieved to hear Anna's voice over the phone. Although Esther had purchased tickets for the complete journey, Anna told her to stay at Crewe Station and not travel all the way to Wem. The small bus they had kept would be waiting for her.

Esther hardly recognised John. The strong, proud man she had last seen at Dovercourt Camp was a shadow of his former self. He approached her, dragging his left leg slightly, the scars on his cheeks distorting his smile, then stood in front of her, holding his cap with both hands and turning it round and round.

"John?"

"Dr Rosenthal, you are back."

"It's Esther. You are supposed to call me Esther."

"Yes, Dr Rosenthal. Let me help you with this." He bent down and picked her suitcase up, the pain of doing so clearly etched in his face. His limp was more pronounced with the weight he was carrying. Esther's heart missed a beat; she wanted to grab the case off him, but knew that would hurt his pride and do more harm than good. Although the vehicle was parked just outside, the walk seemed endless. Esther breathed a sigh of relief when they were inside and John started the engine.

"Don't look so worried, Dr Rosenthal, I can still press the clutch with my left leg."

"I am not familiar with driving a car, John. What does a clutch do?"

"It disengages the gears, you see, like this." The bus jumped forward and stopped. "On this old thing the gears sometimes stick, but her engine still purrs like a pussy cat. Listen." John visibly livened up in front of her.

"What do you have to do next?"

"Watch and learn." He depressed the clutch again, put the gear lever into first, eased his left food slightly while pressing the accelerator with the other and released the hand break. This time the bus rolled forward without stalling.

"You should learn how to drive while you are here, Dr Rosenthal."

"How would I get a licence?"

"You don't need one anymore. That is one good thing, I suppose. They have been suspended. The country needs drivers, but has no time to issue licences. Everybody is too busy making weapons and fighting a war."

Esther detected a bitterness in his voice; maybe Anna would be able to tell her what had happened.

"Maybe I should take some lessons."

"I could teach you."

"I would like that very much."

Anna had been waiting by the kitchen window, and ran outside despite the rain to greet them. As soon as John brought the bus to a complete stop, she opened the passenger door.

"Esther, I am so glad you came back." This was the first time Anna had addressed Esther by her first name. "I have so much to tell you."

The two women hugged each other for what seemed like a long time. The rain was dripping from Esther's headscarf on to her cheeks, mixing with her tears.

"I will take your case inside, Dr Rosenthal. Your room will be on the second floor."

Esther had the feeling of being watched. She put her arm around Anna's shoulders and had a quick look towards the upstairs windows before both women entered the house. A man was looking down at them.

"It is good to see you, Anna, I just wish the circumstances were different."

"Let's go into the sitting room. We have many things to talk about. The cook has prepared your favourite: chicken soup. You still like it, don't you? But maybe first you would like to freshen up or have a rest. You must be very tired."

"Believe me, I feel much better already just being here."

"In that case, let's have a cup of tea. That should settle your nerves. I know the way John drives round those tight bends leading up to our school."

Two elderly gentlemen rose from their armchairs when the women entered. The nearer one to Esther took a bow and offered his outstretched hand.

"Dr Rosenthal, we have heard a lot about you."

His companion joined him and nodded.

"Esther, let me introduce Edwin Schnabel and Otto Braun. Edwin and Otto are two of our residents. Since they arrived, we have regular music evenings, and some of our students have taken up learning the clarinet and oboe."

"Frau Essinger, we will retire. We realise you two have a lot of catching up to do."

"Auf Wiedersehen, Dr Rosenthal."

Both bowed again and left the room, leaving Esther standing in front of the open fire, looking slightly puzzled.

"Esther, a lot has happened since you left. I will tell you all about it later, but now there are more urgent things we need to talk about."

"Would it be possible for me to see Joshua's room first?"

Chapter 46

"This is a list of hospitals and doctors' surgeries in the vicinity of Coventry which we have not yet been able to reach. John has drawn a map and grouped them into areas which can be searched in one day."

"Are you're sure you've got them all? What about cottage hospitals?"

"We put them under doctors' surgeries. As you can see, the list covers all small towns and villages to the north of Coventry. That is the only area still outstanding, the rest have been checked."

"Anna, how did you manage to look for him in so many places?"

"We could not have done it without the help of Rabbi Jacob from Coventry. The synagogue was badly damaged, and still he spread the word. We stopped there the day after the destruction and hoped he would be able help us. He agreed immediately. John has been going back and forth to meet up with him and get updates. This is how we know which part we still have to search."

"You are sure you can spare John?"

"Esther, you and Joshua are like my family. Besides, it is my fault. I should never have agreed to let them go there. That far away in a war. What was I thinking of?"

"You are not to blame, and we are going to find him. I know we will."

"You are aware they did find Alexander's burned out car not very far from where the cinema was?"

"Yes, John told me."

"We had better get going. I want to come to the police station with you. You will need to register there. Hopefully they will be able to issue you with the papers you will need to move around. We all have those. Plus we will have to put you on the list for your ration cards."

"What exactly are the papers we need?"

Anna coughed again. This time she seemed to have difficulty breathing. Esther put her hand on to Anna's forehead. It felt hot.

"I need to examine you."

Anna shook her head, still coughing.

"I am sorry, Anna, we are not leaving unless I know what is wrong with you."

Esther helped Anna upstairs and made her take her blouse off. She then listened to her chest, asked her to cough once or twice and checked her pulse and her temperature.

"I believe you have bronchitis. You have to stay indoors and rest. The best thing to do is go to bed for a few days. I have some medicine in my case, and I am going to write on the box when to take it. You should feel better within a week."

"First I will come with you. Yes, I promise I will lie down when I get back." Esther raised her eyebrows, questioning the sense of Anna coming with her. "The inspector's son attends our school."

At the police station, they were immediately ushered into the inspector's office, offered a chair each and told to wait for a moment.

"The inspector will be with you shortly."

John opted to wait in the public waiting area and found a space on the bench opposite the booking desk. A young policeman in his pristine new uniform viewed him with suspicion.

"Can I help you?"

"You most certainly cannot." John had never trusted the police, not since his father had been arrested when he was a young boy. They had never found out why, even though he was sent by his mother every morning before school to the local station to ask when his dad would be home. One morning the policeman behind the desk had laughed when he asked again.

"He won't be coming back. You run home now and tell your mother to collect his things." They were never told what he had died of. It was claimed he had died during the night, but John's mam had seen cuts and bruises all over his body at the undertakers. No, John had no time for the police. If it were not for young Josh being missing and Dr Rosenthal desperately trying to find him, John would not be here at all. No way.

The inspector's door opened inwards, banging against Esther's chair, which made her rock forward.

"I am sorry to have kept you waiting. Frau Essinger, I hope you are keeping well. And you must be Dr Rosenthal." He greeted them with his outstretched hand, but quickly withdrew it when Anna started coughing again. "How can I be of assistance?"

He settled himself on his chair behind the desk, took a cigarette from an open packet, put it into his mouth and struck a match, then quickly blew it out again when Anna had another coughing fit.

"I'd better not." He put the unlit cigarette back where he had taken it from, pulling over a brown folder which had been placed on the side of the desk. He cleared his throat and looked at Esther.

"May I ask you whether you have any connection to Belgium?" he enquired.

"Belgium? Why do you ask?"

"Well this has arrived on my desk." He took a letter

from his folder and slid it over for Esther to see. She froze; her name was on it, above the address of Dovercourt Camp.

"Do you recognise the writing?"

"Has it been opened?"

"Dr Rosenthal, all mail from across the channel will be opened and scrutinised, especially if it is addressed to an enemy alien."

Anna stood up so quickly that her chair fell backwards against the door, almost shattering the frosted glass in the top panel. With three steps the inspector was behind her, picking up the chair and putting it back.

"Frau Essinger, please sit down. I am only doing my duty."

Esther's hands were shaking. She had not been invited to take the envelope, but took it anyway. She opened it and pulled out some handwritten notes, immediately recognising her Ibrahim's handwriting.

Chapter 47

Esther was still in shock when they got back into the bus to take Anna home before setting off for Bedworth, the first place they had decided to search. None of what the inspector had told her made any sense at all. Enemy alien, class C? What was the meaning of that? Anna seemed comfortable with it, so there was no reason for Esther to question it further.

It must have taken the best part of an hour to question Esther about the letters from Dachau. The inspector had been joined by a uniformed police officer who sat behind Esther in the corner of the room, taking notes. Esther could not see him, but he had brought paper and pencil with him when he entered and she heard him scribbling furiously, egged on by the inspector's nods.

"Please tell us again how you know this contact in Brussels. What does your husband mean when he talks about a munitions factory? Do you know what type of ammunition is manufactured there? If it is really, as you say, a labour camp in Dachau, how was he able to write to you? And if he was, as you state," another nod to the writer, "taken away by the Waffen SS on the night they burned the synagogue, how would he know this address in Brussels?"

Answering all the questions, even Esther thought some of it sounded unbelievable. But her Ibrahim had been alive when he wrote these letters. She could not know when that was or how long they had taken to reach her. The date had been blacked out, and many words were underlined in blue ink – the same colour as the ink in the pot on the inspector's desk that he kept dipping the tip of his pen into before writing on a crisp piece of paper in front of him. It went through her mind that maybe he and the uniformed officer wanted to compare notes later.

"It all seems to check out. If we have any more questions or receive further letters, we will require you to come to the station again, but as it stands at the moment, you can take them with you. The proviso is that you do not destroy them and you make them available to us again should we so require."

The inspector handed her the necessary papers and wished her a good day. Only as an afterthought, he said, "I hope you find your boy."

Esther ignored his outstretched hand when they were eventually allowed to leave.

Back at Trench Hall, they reached the conclusion it was better to defer leaving for Bedworth until early the next morning. The daylight hours were fast disappearing and it was too dangerous to travel on the roads in the dark. Any air raids they had heard about were mostly carried out during the night. Besides, it would be impossible to find lodgings if they reached their first destination after dark. The overnight cases stayed in the bus. There was no need to take them in for one night.

The boys had already eaten and were busy blacking out the windows by the time they entered the main house. Work was being carried out to convert the outbuildings and the boys had moved out of the house, so there were only eight of them living in the main building at the moment. Esther insisted Anna went straight to her room and asked the cook to bring her some chicken soup, which arrived just after Esther had checked her temperature again and listened to her chest. Anna was already in bed, leaning against her cushions, but she refused when Esther wanted to help her with the food.

"Esther, I will be fine. Please have something to eat yourself, and if you feel like meeting the other residents, they always sit and talk downstairs in the living room."

"I will check on you again when I go to bed, if you don't mind."

Downstairs, the sitting room was lit by a lamp on a small table opposite the window plus a couple of candles, and there was a warm glow coming from the fireplace.

"Dr Rosenthal, please come and join us. Here, take my seat."

One of the musicians she had met the previous day left his comfortable place and offered it to her.

"It is very kind of you, but it is not necessary. I can take a chair."

"Nonsense, nonsense. You met the inspector, no doubt. No, you sit here. Otto, go, go. Bring Dr Rosenthal a cup of tea."

"You don't have anything a bit stronger, do you, Herr Schnabel?"

"Please, call me Edwin. We took on the English custom of using first names a long time ago. Are you comfortable with that?"

"Yes, thank you, Edwin, I am. To be honest, I prefer it."

Esther accepted the hot black tea Otto carried over to where she now sat. She tasted it and immediately realised he had added some alcohol, which indeed calmed her nerves.

"That definitely feels better."

"I see Otto parted with a shot of his best whisky. He must like you. Now, tell us your story and let's find out how we can help."

"Can you tell me first what life is like for us in England at the moment? Anna was very vague about it."

"You have been called an 'enemy alien' then?"

"Yes, classified as C." She giggled; the alcohol was

starting to go to her head, and she remembered she had not eaten anything all day.

Edwin told her that, although most of them had made England their home many years ago, when war broke out with Germany the authorities were suddenly concerned about having so many Germans living among them. It had been announced in Parliament first to classify all Germans as aliens, and then transport them to internment camps for further assessment. Class C were professionals who did not present any threat and could be useful, but it had taken the musicians nearly a year to be released. They could not go back to their old teaching positions, and, in Otto's case, the orchestra he had played in declined to have him back. Since Anna had been given Trench Hall to run as her school, she had readily agreed to take them in. Edwin and Otto had met on the Isle of Man. Edwin had had the good fortune to go there directly from his home, but Otto had reached there after coming from a temporary camp in Scotland where the situation was very bad.

On her way to bed, Esther saw a dim light under Anna's door. She knocked, and found Anna still sitting up. She had a note in her hand, and was beckoning Esther to come and sit down.

"How are you feeling, Anna?"

"Much better. Look, the cook gave me a note. She forgot to tell us when we got back that there was a telephone call from Thomas. He has reached London and will call back tomorrow."

Chapter 48

John was loading the bus. They had talked about their journey again the night before, and John had suggested that it would be a good idea to take several blankets and the pillows from their beds. Why had they not thought about that before? When they found Joshua he could be injured and would need to be kept warm. Plus, there would be plenty of space in their vehicle for Esther and John to sit for a night, if they didn't find accommodation straight away.

It had started snowing again, and the light covering was making the short walk to the vehicle slippery. John almost fell while carrying a box, but was quickly steadied by one of the bigger boys who was already outside, dragging a big broom behind him, ready to sweep the steps.

The cook handed the boy a wicker basket. "Give John a hand. Place this on one of the seats and come back into the kitchen. There is one more box to go."

John had started the engine and the bus was warming up when Esther settled herself into the passenger's seat. She felt comfortable in her woollen trousers; she had meant to alter the bottoms since they had a tendency to drag on the ground, but rolling them up a couple of inches was just as good and exposed part of the brown leather boots which reached halfway up her calves, fastened securely with new laces Anna had given her. She was glad Isabella had insisted she pack sensible clothing.

"Let me check the map again. I can see you marked the places we want to visit today in red. As planned, first stop is Collycroft, the furthest north. We then travel on to Mount

179

Pleasant, Bedworth Heath and Coalpit. Last in Bedworth would be Goodyers End. As you said, we might not reach it today and may have to stop in Bedworth Heath tonight. What is in all those boxes and the basket? I thought we would take only a few items."

"You know the cook. She said what we don't need, we can always bring back. There is bread, butter, cheese and hard boiled eggs, plus pieces of cake, flasks with hot tea, not forgetting Joshua's favourite biscuits." John turned his face towards Esther and gave her a big smile. "You know we are going to find him, don't you, Dr Rosenthal?"

"Yes, we are, John, but what about Alexander?"

"The newspaper staff did carry out a thorough search, or so they said, but found nothing besides his burned out car. We are going to ask about him everywhere we go. You never know. Dr Rosenthal, I hope you don't mind me asking you. The letters the inspector gave you, were they from your husband?"

"Yes, I still cannot believe it myself. I have them with me, you know. There were three of them in that large envelope. My Ibrahim is alive."

"Where is he?"

"In Dachau in the south of Germany. There is a labour camp there – that's what they call it, but it used to be a large munitions factory, converted to house prisoners in their early thirties, I believe. Nobody knows what really happens there. It is Himmler's little showpiece."

"Maybe it is not as bad as you fear. He was allowed to write to you, after all."

"My Ibrahim is very resourceful. I am quite sure nobody is allowed any visitors or to write to their families once they are there, but my Ibrahim, he has a strong mind. I am not surprised he found a way. He told me to come to England, you know. He knew Hitler would not give up, and he wanted me to be safe."

"Did he have an address in England for you?"

"No, but at the hospital where I worked in Hildesheim I had a friend, also a doctor, whose wife's brother lives in Belgium. Watch out, John."

John's eyes had left the road for a split second, looking at Esther in astonishment at the story she told him. The bus skidded on the snowy surface of the road, but John reacted in time. The vehicle straightened up, then John switched the engine off and took a deep breath.

"I am sorry, Dr Rosenthal, I should have concentrated on where we were heading."

"Nonsense, John, I am as much at fault for talking without thought. You have been driving for hours. I think we should have a rest. According to the map, there is a village ahead. Let's stop there and find a place where we can get a hot drink, or even something to eat. We should keep our provisions until we really have nothing else. What do you think?"

"It is a good idea."

"And John, I think you should do the talking." When he looked at her with a puzzled expression, she continued, "I am aware that I still sound very German."

"You should not let your accent hold you back, Dr Rosenthal. They knew anyway."

"Do you mean it shows?"

"It is more because you refused the delicious hot slice of ham the farmer's wife offered you." John started laughing. "Next time, don't send it back."

"Do you think I offended them?"

"No, of course not. Believe me, your situation will prompt a lot of sympathy."

"Soon we have to take a left turn, John. It should be signposted to Nuneaton. It will take us a bit further up, but after a few miles there should be a right turn to Bedworth."

"It won't be long before it starts getting dark and

everybody will blacken out their windows. Nobody will open their doors to us then. We will go and visit the two surgeries in Collycroft and then find a place to stay."

They found the road they were looking for after stopping several people to ask the way. Everybody seemed in a hurry, heads down, not wanting to be engaged in conversations with total strangers.

At the first surgery, Esther showed Joshua's school photo to a kind woman at the reception. She shook her head and said she was sorry, but offered them a seat. They could wait until the doctor had seen the last patient for the day.

The doctor was very apologetic about their long wait and that he was unable to supply them with any information. He had not heard of any survivors from Coventry being taken as far as Bedworth, but that did not mean that it was not so, then he asked them where they were heading next, and Esther handed him her list. He shook his head at the next address in Collycroft: that surgery no longer existed. Advising them to stay overnight at the pub across the road that had rooms and was one of the few which stayed open at night, he gave them a note he quickly wrote to guarantee them a warm welcome. Finally, he told them he would phone some of his colleagues who did not appear on the list. Maybe they would know something.

"Please come back in the morning. My receptionist will let me know as soon as you arrive. Try to rest tonight, Dr Rosenthal. Goodnight, John."

Chapter 49

Both Esther and John were downstairs in the bar the next morning before it was light outside. The owner was not surprised to see them this early and had already prepared a large pot of tea. He poured it into their cups and put the bottle of milk on to the table.

"Sorry there is no sugar. The rations seem to get smaller every day. Would you like some toast?"

"That is very kind of you, but please don't make yourself extra work on our behalf."

"That is no problem, Miss, a friend of the good doctor is always welcome in our house."

Across the road, back in the doctor's surgery, they were ushered straight inside.

"Good morning, I hope you managed to sleep. Would you like something to drink? Freda has just put the kettle on."

The doctor then told them that he was sorry he could not be of more help. He had phoned several of his colleagues, but unfortunately they also were not aware of injured civilians being hospitalised in this area. But they promised to ask around as well. Would Esther mind giving him the telephone number of the school in case he found out more? He would like it very much if Esther would phone him when she found her boy.

The first place in Mount Pleasant was closed. They waited outside in their bus for almost an hour, but there was no sign of anybody. John had walked up and down the street several times, stopping passers-by, but most of them just shrugged their shoulders.

The snow was falling much heavier today. John came back to the bus, opened the driver's door, took his coat off and gave it a good shake. He climbed in and switched the engine on.

"We'd better be off. Maybe you could give this address to the doctor in Collycroft. He would be able to find out whether there is anybody here. We have to find a place which will sell us some petrol. Hopefully this will not be a big problem because of the writing on the sides of the bus: schools, ambulances, doctors, fire brigades and farmers get preferential treatment. It was Joshua's idea to mark the bus with our school logo. I believe they did a project about it in their art class. Mind you, that was before I got there."

The second garage they found agreed to sell them some petrol, but at an inflated price. Esther was astonished at John's negotiating skills. Although the price was far too high, they left there with a full tank. Finding the garage had taken them into a different area altogether, and it was mid-morning before they got back to Mount Pleasant. Just to make doubly sure, they went past the first doctor's office again, but it was still closed. The three places in Bedworth Heath also gave no results. One doctor told them that, doctor or not, he would not collaborate with a bloody German. John quickly put his hand on Esther's shoulder and guided her away. She seemed visibly shaken by the outburst.

"We should make our way over to Coalpit, find some lodgings and call it a day. We will have a better day tomorrow."

They found two pubs. The first one was blacked out, and there was no accommodation in the second.

"There is no room at the inn." As soon as John said it, he realised how silly he sounded. "I am very sorry, Dr Rosenthal."

"John, you must stop apologising. You are correct in your belief that I do not celebrate Christmas with my

184

family, but we are aware of others people's faith. There will be a Christmas celebration at the school, isn't that right?"

"Yes, will you be there?"

"Of course. Anna insists that everybody takes part in the religious festivals of all her pupils. She does not want Trench Hall to be a Jewish school." Esther noticed John was grinning. "Why are you smiling?"

"I am sorry, Dr Rosenthal, but the innkeeper said we could park at the back, next to the stables."

A couple of hours later there was a knock on the door. Esther had just nodded off. John talked to somebody, then came over to her.

"The landlord said we should come inside. He is closing for the night. We should bring our blankets and cushions, there are two bunks we can use."

The owner apologised for the smoke filled air and the smell of stale ale, but the fire was still glowing and it was warm inside. Two hot drinks were placed on to a small table in front of them, and he left them to make themselves as comfortable as they could. Esther heard whispered voices coming from the door to the side of the bar. She imagined the landlady was less happy to let two total strangers stay overnight in their bar alone, but before she could talk about it to John, he was already snoring.

Chapter 50

The last village on their list was Bulkington. At the pub the landlord agreed to let them use the telephone, and Esther managed to update Anna in a brief conversation. Anna understood that Esther had to continue searching. Esther said she was at a loss what to do next, and John suggested they go back to the doctor in Collycroft. Could Anna phone him with the message that they might be back there in a couple of days?

Before Esther put the receiver back, she added, "Anna, we might go to Coventry after all."

Esther was surprised to see the market town of Bulkington was so busy. They were diverted from their planned route, and stopped at the side of the road, opposite the main street. In the centre of the town, farmers had set up their stalls, selling eggs, potatoes, root vegetables and some green curly ones, similar to a vegetable eaten this time of year in Germany. John explained the name for it was kale.

"Maybe we could buy some. Do you think they will sell us any?"

"I cannot see why not. None of the products I can see from here are rationed – besides eggs, that is."

"Can you also ask for swede and parsnips? Take the money."

When John came back he had three boxes, which were carried by a young lad, similar in age to Joshua. He must be freezing in his short trousers, Esther thought. She was tempted to give him her gloves, but feared his parents might be offended by such an offer.

When he placed the last box on to the seat behind her, he said, "A nice bus, Mister, where are you going with it? Not far, I hope. Me dad says there will be a lot of snow tonight, that is why all the stalls are here today. Could not go to school because of it. Mind you, Miss, I don't care much about school. Do you have to go to school to drive a smart bus like this one?"

"You have to go to school whatever you want to be, young man."

"Train driver. That is what I want to be. It is always nice and warm in the front. I watch the trains sometimes on the way home. I sit on the wall above, on the bridge. Me and me mates, we hang our legs over. We wait for an oncoming train and they blow the whistle just as they go under. When they come out where we sit, all the steam comes up. For a moment we cannot even see each other. It is a bit scary, but warm. Here, you see, my skin on this leg is all red and cracked. Me mam would be mad if she found out that is where I go after school, and me dad would give me a right hiding. Do you have any children, Miss?"

"You run along now, lad, we have to be on our way."

"No, wait!" Esther reached for her coat, and from the pocket she produced a shiny sixpence. "This is for you."

The boy grabbed it before Esther could change her mind. "Do I have to give it to me dad?" He was already halfway down the step.

"Young man, have you forgotten your manners?" John asked him.

"Thank you, Miss." And he was gone.

The diverted route took them down Arden Road and past a large factory. "I wonder what they manufacture there." Esther looked back as they passed it.

"Bulkington is famous for their fine quality ribbons, but whether they still produce any, I don't know. Maybe it has been converted and they now make uniforms."

"I should have asked the lad how to find our next destination. It is difficult to read any of the road signs, most of them are covered by snow."

John stopped the bus next to an elderly couple, opened the door and leaned out, asking for directions. The man looked at the logo on the side, nodded and pointed straight on, left and right.

The doctor's office was open, and they did not have to wait very long before they were seen. Similar to the other surgeries, they were offered a seat and a hot drink. The doctor was very kind, but again sorry he could not help them. Of course, he would check around, and was happy to call them, if he heard anything, if they would care to leave their telephone number.

He then asked them what their next destination was to be. He was the last address on their list, they told him, and Esther said she now wanted to make her way to Coventry itself. He wished them good luck.

Outside, the snow continued to fall. They could hardly see a few yards ahead. Esther had walked on in front and slipped, steadying herself by holding on to a lamppost. John was just going to suggest they find somewhere to stay and review their plans when the young receptionist came after them.

"Doctor, Doctor, wait!"

Esther turned towards her.

"Sorry, I could not help it, but I overheard your conversation with Dr Harrison. There is a big house not far from here, up in Weston on Arden. You cannot miss it if you take the first road to the right, and then – let me think – yes, it is the second on the left after that, and then straight on all the way."

She turned and started to go back inside, brushing the snow off her cardigan. John pulled her back by her arm.

"Oi!"

"You have not told us why we should go there."

"Oh, yes, yes. The house is very big with loads of land. I think the building itself is grey. Anyway, I don't really know who lives there now, but my mam said she heard from a friend that a retired doctor is still there, and he reckons he rescued somebody after the bombing in Coventry. But my mam also said he is a bit funny in the head, so maybe he is making it up. I have got to go."

Chapter 51

"It was a stray bomb, you know."

Esther held her breath. Was John about to confide in her how he received his injuries?

They'd had to abandon the idea of driving to Weston on Arden that afternoon. It was almost impossible to open the bus doors in the storm, which was blowing directly at them from the north. John suggested they park somewhere a bit more protected and wait there overnight. He would have a look around on foot; Esther should stay inside and wait. But this time she had no intention of letting John go all by himself. It was difficult enough to walk in sturdy boots without John's additional burden of dragging one leg.

They found a building not too far away which had a drive underneath an archway. At the back was a large courtyard where several small lorries were parked, with an ideal place between two of them for their bus. The building took most of the force from the snowstorm, which meant the yard only had a light covering.

"It looks like some sort of depot. Let's go to the front and see whether anybody is there. At least we should ask if we can park here."

A set of slippery steps led to an imposing wooden door. Esther was the one who pulled down the bell handle. She could hear a faint ring inside the building.

"Sorry, mate, they are closed, and if you have any sense you will get yourselves home as well," a passer-by shouted from across the street.

Very slowly, and almost slipping twice on the road, John

drove the vehicle and parked it at the place they had found.

"Are you sure we will be alright here?"

"Let's not worry about it. At least the snowfall has raised the temperature a little, so we won't be freezing in here tonight. And we have hardly touched any of the provisions we have brought along. Plus there is another good reason we should stay here for the night."

When Esther did not ask what he meant, John continued, "I spotted an outside toilet, over in one corner."

They each occupied a seat directly across from each other, leaning on cushions against the window, legs up and wrapped in blankets. The bread was hard and the remaining tea tasted a little sour, the milk having gone off a day or two ago, but both felt content in the dark in their own thoughts.

"Yes, they said it was a stray bomb," John continued. "It was meant to be dropped on Bernhard's Uniform Factory. Not many houses got hit, but ours was the middle one. The one where not a brick is standing now. I could not help my Elsie. I tried. Believe you me, oh yes, I tried. We should not have been at home that day. Elsie was supposed to help out in the village hall. The Home Guard were having a meeting. You know: the old folks, too frail to fight. They are the ones who now protect the people here. What can those old fellows do? I ask myself. You should see some of them. Hardly able to stand up by themselves. But there they are, doing their bit, I suppose. I was called up to serve the country and it was my last day at home. So we sent a message that Elsie did not feel well and could not help out. I am sure Elsie never knew what hit her. That's what the warden said.

"You see, she was thinking about me, as always. I stayed in bed, and she had gone into the kitchen. She said I should have my breakfast in bed that day. I smelled some bacon and wondered how she managed to get any. I never heard anything, but then the bedroom was no longer on the first floor. It was where the kitchen had been a few minutes before. I did not feel any physical pain, and started digging and shouting her name over and over again. Naked, that is what they said I was. What happened to my nightclothes, I never found out. I was useless to serve our country after that. When I came out of the hospital, I was discharged from duty. I lost all track of time. I don't even recall where I stayed after that. All I wanted to do was end it all there and then. It was my fault, you see, that my Elsie lost her life."

It took a while for the door to be answered when Esther and John knocked the next morning, after having left their sheltered place before light. He opened it fully and just stood there, the old man, looking at them, his cardigan straining at the buttons over what must have once been a white shirt. The front panels did not match up, and he was missing one of the buttons in the middle. He had his glasses in his hand; then he put them on again. He looked down at his grey slippers, as if apologising for receiving guests in a state of undress, took a step back and opened the door further.

"I did my best."

He turned and walked back inside, leaving it up to them whether they followed or not, but then he must have noticed them behind him because he continued.

"I can see a resemblance. He has his mother's dark hair."

Esther's heart missed a beat.

"The lad is outside. I take him there. The fresh air will do him good. He does not protest."

"What has Joshua said?" Esther wanted to run: to take her boy and hold him close.

"Joshua? Is that what his name is? He has not told me. My German is very little, and he does not understand when I try to communicate with him. I did my best."

Esther took hold of John's hand and held it tight. The

old man looked around and saw them standing there, hand in hand.

"I will take you towards the garden door. You can see him from there. I had better go and say his name. If he does not react, he is not yours. I cannot give you a boy who is not yours."

John held Esther back. "Wait," he whispered. They could see a shape through dull glass panels, sitting in a chair with his back to them, the snow around him carefully brushed to one side. The hinges of the door made a protesting noise when the man pushed it open. There was no reaction from the child. Esther and John got as close as they dared, close enough to hear.

"Joshua." The boy looked up at him. "Your mum and dad are here." This was greeted with silence. The man looked at them and shook his head. "Not yours," he said.

"You are lying. My *mutti* and *vati* are dead. I saw it. I was hiding in the stable and I saw with my own eyes what the soldiers did to them. I never told the others."

Two steps, and Esther was in front of him, holding him tight, not wanting to let go of him. She was sobbing loudly, not caring what the man thought, tears rolling down her face, wetting Joshua's cheeks and the bandage across one eye.

"Joshua, Joshua, it is your mama. Joshua, please remember me. I am your mama. Joshua."

"Mama?" He lifted his face and bent his head to one side, trying to make out the shape in front of him with his undamaged eye. The weight of Esther holding him pushed the chair back, but John was behind him, holding it steady.

"Mama, you came for me."

He lifted his left hand and let it run over her face. The bandages felt rough on Esther's skin, yet it was the most wonderful feeling.

Chapter 52

Anna put the receiver back into its cradle. She needed a few minutes to compose her thoughts before she shared the news with the others. She felt her heartbeat increasing, and fumbled for the scribbled notes she had taken. Esther had spoken so quickly. Her hands were still shaking, and the paper slowly floated to the ground and landed underneath the wooden desk, just at her feet. That was why she was on all fours, hidden from view, when Brenda, the cook, came to find her.

"Anna, are you in here?"

Anna lifted her head and banged it on the drawer she had forgotten to close.

"Are you alright?"

"Yes, yes, I am fine. Please help me back up. Oh, Brenda, I have such wonderful news. Please gather everybody in the dining hall. Yes, everybody you can find. I will be there shortly, but first I must do as Esther asked and make a few telephone calls. Help me find my telephone book. It must be here somewhere."

Brenda found it on the bookshelf, hidden under some old newspapers. Soon I need to replace my glasses, Anna thought. It is more difficult to see every day, especially in this dim light.

She found the name she was looking for and put her index finger into the first number. The dial turned halfway, then her finger slipped. Her hands were sweaty. She rubbed them on her skirt to dry them off and tried again. This time she missed the third number. She took another deep breath, then heard the ringing sound at the other end, but nobody picked up. She would have to leave it till later. Was it possible that there had been another air raid overnight and the office was closed?

Anna heard voices outside her office. The children were obviously pleased that their lessons had been interrupted, but were unsure about the announcement to be made. The second telephone number she dialled was answered after just a couple of rings.

"Royal Salop Infirmary."

Anna left a message for the doctor to call her as soon as possible, then tried the London number again without success. She would have to call Thomas's wife; maybe she would know why Anna could not get through. In any case, she would love to hear this news, and she might have heard from Thomas by now. He should be somewhere reporting from the front.

Anna looked happy when she entered the dining hall, and the assembled group relaxed.

"Quiet, please. I want to make this as short as I can." She took a deep breath. "Dr Rosenthal and John have found Joshua." Everybody spoke at once. "Quiet, quiet!" A boy in the middle raised his hand. "Yes, Brian?"

"When is Joshua coming back?"

"I don't know yet, I don't know how well he is right now. But we do know he is alive and has been found. Let's say a prayer of thanks."

Yes, there had been another bombing raid in London overnight, confirmed Thomas's wife. She had the number of the editor in charge of the newspaper, and she would phone him at home and call Anna back as soon as she could. She was confident that he would be able to notify Mordechai in New York somehow. Yes, Thomas was reporting as regularly as he could. No, she did not know exactly where he was.

Anna looked out of the office window. Her head hurt a little. She felt a swelling and there was blood on her fingers.

She sighed. A group of the younger boys had started to build a snowman. The clock on the wall showed 11.15am and everybody should still be attending their lessons, but the teachers must have decided the news about Joshua was a good reason to celebrate and had stopped for the day. Anna smiled. She felt blessed having such excellent staff, and the older men who had arrived from the Isle of Man had so much knowledge to pass on. Yes, blessed indeed.

Brenda arrived with a cup of hot tea. Anna had always been a coffee drinker, just like her father, but had embraced the English custom of drinking tea. Tea with milk, of all things.

"Anna, your fingers. Are you bleeding?"

"It is nothing, Brenda. Thank you for the tea. Can we leave the discussion about tomorrow's lunch until later? I can see the boys are not in class. Do you still have the list of the provisions we need?"

"Yes, and it is now much longer than it was yesterday. I wanted to talk to you about it."

"Bring me the list and send Brian to gather a group of the bigger boys. Tell him they should dress warmly and get the cart out. It is time we paid a visit to our farmer."

The last call on her list was to the kind doctor in Collycroft, but before she had time to dial his number, her phone rang. The hospital in Salop put the doctor on the line. He had yet to meet Esther, but was delighted with her news. Yes, they did have the use of an X-ray machine, but he was not sure what the cost of the X-rays would be, or whether it would be possible to treat Joshua at the hospital. Did Anna have any idea of the extent of his injuries? He couldn't, however, see any problem with Joshua being admitted there if that was the right place for him. After all, his mother was a surgeon soon to join the team. Yes, he would make all the enquiries and would phone back.

Chapter 53

They made a makeshift stretcher. The old man said John could use the top of the dining room table as he had no need for it any longer, here on his own. Yes, he had been in Coventry on that day. He had sat not far behind Joshua and Alexander in the cinema; he had intended to meet an old friend, but when the friend did not turn up he had been at a loss as to what to do. That was when he had noticed the cinema. He had not even looked at what they were showing; he'd just followed everybody else.

There had been a panic when the sirens went off, people getting trampled, so he'd decided to stay in his seat. When the door opened at the front, he saw Alexander and Joshua again. Maybe they had been the last ones to leave, he did not remember.

He had thought they might lock the cinema and decided to go after them. That is when it happened. He had heard that the Germans dropped landmines. He was blinded for a minute and his hearing went – it had never come back the way it was before – and he could only see Joshua when the smoke cleared a little. There was nobody else, just a crater, fire and debris. He had shouted for help, and a warden came running, took one look at the child on the ground and said there was no way to help. It was too late. There were others out there who needed him.

"I was strong once, and God must have returned that strength to me for an instant, because I straightened up and grabbed him by the collar. I believe I lifted him off the ground. Yes, I am sure I did." The old man smiled a little.

"The warden looked scared. Can you imagine it? He looked scared of me. There was lots of wood on the ground, and we found a piece, maybe a door of a wardrobe, that was not smouldering. We took it to where your boy was lying on the ground. He had not moved. We turned him over on to his back and laid him flat on the door. I used my jacket to try to stop the bleeding on his arm.

"To my surprise, the warden was very skilful at first aid. That was the one good thing about him. He told me to take my shirt off and we ripped it apart. Placed a bandage over the child's eye. With my belt, we held it in place. Imagine me, an old man, standing there with bare chest and trousers slipping down. We slowly carried him to where I thought I had left the car, putting him down several times. I think the strength God had just given me was slowly disappearing again. Like a miracle my car was where I thought it should be, and besides being covered by bricks and rubble, it was still drivable. The warden helped me get your boy inside on to the back seat. I thanked him for what he had done, and he told me he hoped my grandson recovered. Fancy that, he thought your boy was my grandson."

The old man chuckled.

John had found a pile of wood behind the house and an axe in the yard, and had chopped some after lunch. It helped to clear his head. While Esther checked on Joshua's injuries earlier, he'd had a quick look in the old man's kitchen. It was surprisingly clean, just a couple of unwashed bowls waiting in the kitchen sink. He quietly opened the cupboards, but besides neatly stacked dishes, he did not see any provisions. How had the old man managed to feed himself and Joshua?

"Porridge. We live on porridge, bread and eggs." John had not heard him entering. "I am not a good cook. The farmer's wife brings me eggs and bread. A few times she brought some soup and fed it to the boy. She was worried that he was so thin. She tried to talk me into reporting to the police station that I had found him, but how could I with him being a German and all that? Those are the ones we are fighting, is this not so?"

"Thank you for letting us stay, Doctor. You should consider coming with us."

"I was a good doctor once, a psychiatrist. Fancy that, me now losing my mind. God must have intended that all along."

John was painfully aware that the old man still had not told them his name.

"What did your patients call you?"

"Professor."

"Well, Professor, do you still have any eggs left? I will get what we have in the bus and I am sure I can make us something we can all eat. After that I would like to go and thank the kind farmer's wife. Can you give me the directions?"

John, with his arms full of wood, knocked on Joshua's door with his elbow. Esther opened it. Somehow the professor had managed to pull a bed into what must have once been a room used for entertaining guests. The bed was placed near a large fireplace, which was not lit. Esther had pulled back the heavy curtains and opened the windows for fresh air, and the room now looked a bit brighter than when they first arrived, although there was mould on the wall and the wallpaper was peeling off. Esther thought John was right: they should convince the professor that coming with them was the right thing to do. The farmer's wife might help to persuade him.

The wood was dry inside and John lit the fire. "There you are, Josh, you will be nice and warm in a minute."

"Now I recognise you, you are John. Nobody else ever called me Josh. You look different somehow." Joshua tried to focus with his unbandaged eye.

"I am still the same old John, Josh. Glad to have you back with us."

John thought Joshua smiled and nodded.

"If you don't mind, Dr Rosenthal, I will light the fire in the sitting room for the professor, and after that I will go and see if I can find the farm."

It was dark by the time John returned. Esther and the professor were sitting in front of the fireplace, and Joshua was in the wheelchair next to Esther. He was holding on to her hand.

"It's freezing out there. The farmer's wife gave me some soup and we had a good chat."

"Why don't you and I go into the kitchen and heat the soup," Esther replied, putting Joshua's hand on to his lap. He seemed a little less anxious that she was leaving him by himself now. Esther glanced at the professor, who had fallen asleep. "What did you find out?"

In the kitchen John told her he had found the farm straight away, but at first the farmer would not let him enter his land. He greeted John with a shotgun by his side. He apologised later, but said you had to be on your guard all the time these days. They had already been broken into twice.

Over a hot tea, the farmer and his wife told him they had known the professor for many years. He used to have a really busy practice, but when he started forgetting things, patients stopped coming. His wife passed away long ago and there were no children they knew off, but some nieces and nephews came to check on him occasionally.

"We all know why they come," the farmer said. "To claim their inheritance. They hope one day when they arrive they will find him dead. We met them once or twice. Nasty lot they were, real vultures if you ask me, accusing us of becoming too close to him. Now only the wife goes."

Yes, the farmer and his wife thought it would be best if

the professor left with John, Esther and Joshua.

"The solicitor in town has all his papers and should be informed," John continued. "The farmer wrote down his name and contact details. The farmer has a key to the property – the relations do not know – and he will go and check it from time to time. Unfortunately the farmer himself does not have a telephone, but he can use one at the local store he supplies. He will speak to us from there when he delivers to check on how the professor is doing. Now we just have to find a way to convince the professor and pack his things."

John had asked the farmer how the professor managed to find enough to feed himself and Joshua besides what he and his wife had shared with them.

"You should check the cellar," the farmer had replied. "You might be surprised."

Chapter 54

"Brian, why are you loitering in the hall? Don't you have to be in study class?"

"I have heard that Joshua will be coming back today."

"Where did you hear that? Come on, you'd better tell me. Take this and you can give me a hand." The cook handed Brian a box of root vegetables and held the kitchen door open for him. "Put them over there next to the potatoes, wash your hands and start peeling."

"But I am not on kitchen duty today," he protested.

"You are now as far as I am concerned."

Brian liked Brenda and thought kitchen duty was the best duty, if there was such a thing. Still it did not do any harm to protest a little. He wanted to be a chef in a large establishment, and maybe one day own a restaurant himself. He was supposed to follow his father into the family business, but he had shared his secret with Brenda and knew she would not tell on him. As far as he was concerned, his sister could take over instead. She had shown some skills at woodwork when he had visited them last. Alright, she was a girl, but war changes things. He had heard his father saying those very words.

"Come on, out with it. What did you hear?" Brenda loved to gossip, and Brian was an excellent source of all the latest comings and goings. She had asked him once before how he was always the first to know, but he had just smiled and touched his nose with his finger.

"Do you want to know or not?" he often teased her.

He had walked over to the sink and filled a large metal bowl with clean water, then placed it on a folded newspaper on the table, careful not to spill any. He knew Brenda would not take to it kindly if he made a mess and she had to clean the table after him.

"I just overheard."

"Are you going to make me beg for it, Brian?"

"Well, you did not hear this from me. There is somebody else coming along."

"What do you mean?"

"I heard Aunty Anna asking Herr Schnabel whether there was space for another bed in their room since it is the biggest in the house. She said a professor was coming with them. You know, the one who found Joshua."

"My word! Why am I always the last to be told anything around here? Am I supposed to summon extra portions like magic? I saw that, Brian, don't touch them."

While Brenda had her back to him, he had been reaching over to the tray of biscuits she had taken out of the oven a few minutes earlier. Brenda's warning was too late; he had burned his finger, quickly withdrawn it and put it first into his mouth and then into the cold water for the potatoes.

"How often do I have to tell you before you learn, Brian? Now go and rinse the potatoes and replace the water. A fine cook you are going to make." Brenda had a soft spot for Brian. He showed remarkable skill when she let him help her prepare a meal, and she had been meaning to have a word with Anna to let him be excused of all other duties and work with her in the kitchen in his free time. Now with somebody else arriving, and she was convinced he would not be the last, she had the opportunity she had been waiting for.

"That is all I have heard, but I also saw them bringing the extra bed out of the store, and Herr Schnabel made his friend Otto beat a mattress out back."

Brian jumped up. "They are here!" He had heard the vehicle approaching and turned towards the kitchen window. "Can I?" He did not wait for a reply; he was already out of the door and back in the hall, but was beaten to the front door by Anna, Herr Schnabel and Otto. He wanted to run out of the door in front of them, but knew Aunty Anna would not approve, so he waited until the bus had stopped.

In the dark he could make out John helping an elderly man down the step. Aunty Anna stepped towards him, and Brian used the chance to pass her and climb into the bus.

"Joshua, it's Brian." There was no reply. Maybe he was asleep and hidden in the back behind all the boxes and the wood. He scrambled over them as best he could and banged his knee in the dark. "Ouch!" The top box tumbled down, opened and spilled its content. Cans rolled down towards the driver's seat. "Joshua?"

Brian got back out of the bus. John had disappeared inside the house together with the others. Some of the boys, who had been spending their free time in the common room playing scrabble, came outside and gathered around.

"Where is he? Did they not bring him back?"

"I don't know, but I am going to find out."

The hall was empty, but Brian could hear voices from the sitting room. That was the room which was used by the adults only; none of the children went in there unless it was important. Brian decided today was an occasion important enough to merit entering without knocking and waiting for a reply.

"Joshua?"

"Brian, what are you doing barging in here?"

"It's alright, John. Brian, we have a new guest, the professor. Now, please apologise for the interruption and help to unload the bus. Brenda will tell you where everything goes."

"I am sorry for the interruption, Professor, but what have you done with Joshua?"

"The boy's name is Joshua? He never told me."

John took Brian's elbow and together they left. "What has got into you, Brian?"

"Where is Joshua?"

Chapter 55

Anna agreed that Brian could accompany John to Salop the following week. John had felt sorry for him when Brian confided that he had been jealous that day; he had wished it was he going on an outing, not Joshua, and now he felt mean about it.

At first Esther had said no, Brian couldn't see Joshua. There were so many tests to be carried out, and Joshua first had to regain some of his strength. But she had changed her mind when Joshua was silent for most of the day. Maybe seeing his friends would do him good. On the way over, John briefed Brian on Joshua's condition. Brian was not supposed to react in any negative way or ask too many questions.

"But don't lie to him."

Esther waited for them in the corridor just outside the ward. Brian almost did not recognise her in her white doctor's coat with a stethoscope hanging round her neck.

"Brian, you can come in. He is awake. Don't wear him out." She opened the door, and Brian saw Joshua propped up on pillows, a white sheet pulled up to his chest, covered in most part by a blue blanket. For a second, John thought Brian had changed his mind, but then he entered confidently.

"Joshua, what are you still doing here? We have been waiting for you at school. Even shy little Philip keeps asking. Here, I have a letter signed by them all. I will read it to you."

More, Esther and John did not hear. They closed the door behind Brian and went to the canteen for a cup of tea. It was what the English did: in a crisis, they would sit down and have a cup of tea. Esther had been told that many times, and almost managed a smile.

"What did you find out from the machine?"

"The X-ray confirmed what the doctors suspected. Joshua might not be able to walk again. We have not told him yet, but I think he knows anyway. He can't feel his toes when they run some instruments to check whether there has been any change. However, they have told me about a doctor in Oxford who settled here from Germany in 1939, Ludwig Guttmann. Apparently he is the top neurosurgeon, and his specialist field is spinal injuries. I have talked to him twice, but of course he has no time to come and see us here, and it will be difficult for us to move Joshua to Oxford at the present time. He has promised to look at the X-rays we have sent over and phone me back when they have arrived."

"And his eye?"

"The professor did an excellent job and managed to save it. Joshua will never have full vision in it, but at least he is not totally blind in that eye. His hand has healed well. He lost two fingers, but has the movement back in the others. The big problem is how will he react when he finds out he is confined to a wheelchair?"

They heard the boys laughing before they entered the room. Brian was sitting on Joshua's bed. John was going to rush over and pull him off, but Esther held him back and shook her head to say no.

"You two are having fun."

"Mama, when can I go back to school? I have to catch up, otherwise I will have to repeat some of the subjects, maybe even the whole year."

"Not yet." But when Joshua looked sad, Esther added, "As soon as all your wounds have healed completely you can be discharged. That is what the other doctors said. Meanwhile, Brian can come back to visit you on the weekend. Do you mind bringing him over, John?"

Chapter 56

Esther heard about more bombing raids on Liverpool on the radio in the hospital's common room, where the doctors could rest when they were on call. Normally the radio would not be on. Some of the doctors were so rushed off their feet that they fell asleep in the big armchairs almost the minute they sat down, but the room was empty when Esther entered, and the radio had been left on.

She just caught the end of the report. "Bombs rained down on Liverpool for a third night in a row. Some targets were indiscriminately hit while others had again been selected for strategic purposes. Reports of burning factories in the dock area are still coming in. We are waiting for confirmation of last night's damage. Stay tuned to Radio Salop, your local station."

Esther went over and turned it off. She had to find out how Flo was, and hoped that she was alright. She had been so kind, and Esther knew she should have made contact with Flo as soon as she had found Joshua. She had made that promise. Maybe she could ask Anna if she still had Frank Kett's telephone number. He was not too far away from where Flo lived, and he had said when Esther had delivered the children safely that if there was ever anything he could do for her, just to let him know. Well it was time she took him up on his offer.

Esther had to collect her thoughts. She had heard from Dr Guttmann, and the X-ray had shown that the spinal cord was damaged. It was unlikely that her Joshua would be able to use his legs again, but not to despair. He would like to see the boy for himself. Dr Guttmann was a great believer that you should be able to live your life to the full even if you were in a wheelchair, and he had developed a programme of exercises which would help Joshua to strengthen and make use of his other muscles. More importantly, they would give him back his confidence. If it was alright with Esther, Dr Guttmann would travel over at the weekend. He wanted to examine Joshua himself, and thought it was prudent that he gave Joshua the news. He had found in the past that most patients directed their anger at the person who told them, often blaming that person for their misfortune. It would not be good for Joshua's recovery if he directed all his anger towards his mother.

Esther had immediately agreed, as long as she was beside her boy when he found out.

Dr Guttmann was not what Esther had expected. As a man in his position, she had thought he might be a little offhand. Instead he was modest and kind. He spoke very quietly and slowly, examining Joshua in the presence of the team who had cared for him so far, and going through all the tests again. He then nodded at Esther to sit in the chair beside the bed.

She held Joshua's hand while Dr Guttmann sat on the bed.

"Joshua, what would you like to become later in life?"

"A scientist."

"That is an excellent choice. Do you want to teach or do you want to go into industry?"

"What do you mean by industry?" The doctor now had his full attention.

"There are many fields in science, and it is most important that we learn as much as possible about – medical research, for example. Yes, most important indeed."

"I have never thought about it in detail, only that I like science. That is why I want to go back to school. I am missing too many lessons. And did you know we have a very famous scientist living with us? He now gives extra classes. He came from a place on the Isle of Man. He will help me to go to University. Oxford, that is where I will go. Did you know there is a famous boat race between Oxford and Cambridge Universities? It is held every year on the river in London. Mind you, Brian told me it is not on while we are at war. But when the war is over, he thinks they can race again. What do you think?"

"I think your Brian is right. Is he a good friend of yours?"

"My best friend."

"It is good to have a friend, don't you think, Joshua? A friend who helps you."

"You mean like pushing my wheelchair?"

"That is one type of help, but there is also another one. The one when people make you laugh when you feel sad. That one."

"Oh, yes, Brian does all that."

"Joshua." The doctor took his other hand, looked him straight in the eye and said, "Joshua, I don't think you will be able to walk again unaided." Joshua was just going to reply, but Dr Guttmann said, "Joshua, let me finish first, and then we can talk about it, alright?" Joshua nodded. "You know about the spinal cord?" Another nod. "Yours has been damaged, and the message your brain should send to your legs to walk does not get through. One day, Joshua, one day a scientist like you will find a way to repair it. This is why it is important you study hard, because we need scientists like you. Will you do that, Joshua?"

Joshua nodded for a third time.

Chapter 57

Dachau, Germany

Singing. It could be heard through the otherwise still night. From his place on top of the bunk, Ibrahim was able to see through one of the windows. Soon there would be no space left in here; below him they could already only lie side by side. He considered it a luxury to be able to roll over on to his back occasionally.

He imagined the flicker of the candles on the tree in the guards' dining hall. He knew where it stood; he had carried it in himself. Him and one other; he did not know the man's name. Speaking was forbidden again. "Especially today, Jews," they were told. They knew the guards would not want any trouble tonight. It was holy to them. Holy! What did they know about that? he wondered.

He prayed to his God, as he did every night, thanking Him that he had survived another day. He prayed to keep his Esther safe.

Ibrahim had been allowed to bury him. In a mass grave. Naked like the others. "This is where he belongs," he heard them say.

"Bloody Jew, and to think I sat with him at the same table," said one.

"I was in the tower with him. I hope I did not catch anything," laughed another, and he spat on the body before it rolled down into the ditch. Only twenty today. Ibrahim had had a quick count. All of them covered in blood from gunshot wounds. He had wondered who they were; he did not recognise any of their faces. Apart from one, dried blood

210

congealed in his blond hair. When the body turned over and over again before it landed on top of the others, Ibrahim saw the torture marks on his back. They had obviously beaten him and burned him with cigarettes. The first guard opened the front of his trousers and urinated, carefully aiming at that one body. It felt good, he had said. Shame he was shot at the end. They should have made him suffer.

"Bloody Jewish pig," said the other.

Ibrahim wondered when they had found out. He had concealed it so well. Maybe attending the Christmas party had been too much and he had refused, or found a reason to be on guard duty. They might have been suspicious of him all along, just waiting for their chance. Ibrahim was sure his family was long gone by now. Maybe they had managed to flee in time, or were perishing in another camp just like this one. There would be nobody left to grieve.

Ibrahim would. He said another prayer for his only ally.

They were allowed to stop for the day after the grave was filled in. A Christmas present from us, the guards explained. They just wanted to celebrate tonight, Ibrahim thought. He still had some paper and his pencil. He would write again. The man next to him moaned when Ibrahim stirred. Some nights they would whisper and speak about their lives back home, but most of the time they remained silent.

His Esther would not be able to read the letters now. There was nobody left here he could trust, but writing gave him hope. He often wondered whether the others had ever been posted. If they were, did they reach her? He imagined they did. In them, he had pretended all was well. There was no need to worry her.

The stench from below was sudden. "Moses? Moses, are you alright?"

Ibrahim pulled himself out of his place and got down on to the cold floor. He had taken his boots off and left them under the blanket; leaving them on all night would only make the wounds on his feet worse. They were infected already.

He shook Moses's body. No reaction.

"What are you doing?" complained the man next to Moses.

"He is dead, don't you see? Help me to move him."

The men on either side of the body got up, pulled it by the shoulders on to the floor and dragged it to the door. From there, the little air would hide some of the smell. It was a routine they followed most nights.

"I have been here longest, I get the extra space and his blanket tonight," said one of them.

'Silent night, Holy night' drifted over from the dining hall.

Chapter 58

Trench Hall, May 1941

"Esther, good to see you. Are you staying for a while? We are having a small party tonight. I hope you will join us."

Edwin Schnabel held the front door open. He could hear her arriving before he saw the car coming up the drive. That darn woman, he marvelled, she had learned to drive after all. Whatever next? God forbid there would ever be a woman in charge of a country.

She had parked the car next to the vegetable garden which they had created last year, built and cared for entirely by the students with the help of one of the younger men who had arrived from the Isle of Man. His family had owned land back in East Prussia: land which had belonged to them for generations. The family had sent him to study abroad in Russia, and he had thought that was where he would stay. He was fascinated by the richness of the culture and the diversity of the language, but he started to get a feeling of uncertainty when many of his student friends decided to leave.

Most of them had started the course in Literature together, and decided France would be the obvious place to continue their studies. Those were restless days, but since his parents had given him carte blanche to do as he pleased when their only son had shown no desire to work the land, he decided to explore Europe further. How could he have known that his parents were thinking of leaving themselves? There were not many landowners of Jewish faith in their part of Germany, as far as they knew. They sold up without telling him, maybe because they had no idea where he was at the time. Had he left France already and gone on to Italy, as he had said in his letters? The funds kept arriving, so he was not concerned.

All seemed well. He wanted to see London, and had his uncle's address in Golders Green. He wrote a quick letter home, posting it in Luxemburg before the train took him through Belgium and on to Holland. On the pretence he had to return to Cambridge University, he managed to get on a boat to Harwich. That was when Hitler invaded Poland, news he was greeted with on arrival.

He was at a loss as to what to do. Neighbours told him his uncle was working at the bank, so he decided to wait. His uncle found him asleep outside, using his rucksack as a pillow. He had never seen his nephew before and called the police, who had taken him away before he had time to protest. At the police station he joined three other young men. None of them were put into a cell, but instead waited in a large room, and the policeman's wife brought them tea and cake she had baked that day. The next morning they were hurriedly picked up by an open army truck and taken to Watford. They were interviewed and put into different categories. Nobody there seemed to know what to do with him, so they decided to class him Enemy Alien class B.

He slept the night on the floor on a mattress in the drill hall. One of the internees was shot in the leg by a soldier, who claimed it was an accident. His next stop was Lingfield Racecourse. Several hundred men were there already, housed in the stables. Groups started to form during the week he was there; one of his group was an excellent pianist and played for them each night. After that first week, they were split up yet again. His group boarded a train to Liverpool, and from there took a small ferry to the Isle of Man.

He had been in England for less than ten days, and was now at the Hutchinson Internment Camp in the centre of Douglas. Thirty men shared a house, and he soon made friends with the professors and artists, of whom there were plenty. There was a small kitchen and a living and dining room. The bedrooms contained little else besides beds. Most of them had double beds which they shared. The glass in the windows had been painted blue, and the only lightbulb had an orange covering which gave it an eerie glow at night. Soon the artists in the houses scratched the paint off the windows, creating landscapes in the paint left behind. They were magnificent, and a competition started among the houses. Now they used their blankets for black-out, but took them down when they went to bed, watching the shapes on the windows when the sky lit up outside. Who was going to check?

His language skills were impressive, and he was soon noticed by the guards when he lingered at the fence, watching new arrivals walking past. A group of Italians – he spoke their language with ease. After that, the commander made use of his skills and called upon him to translate. This gave him a certain freedom, and as a reward he was changed to classification C. This meant after four months he was allowed to apply for release, but he had nowhere to go. His young friend Friedrich suggested he put down Trench Hall in Wem as the address. Friedrich was certain Anna Essinger would not turn him away.

He was allowed to leave after having signed the papers agreeing to help the war effort. He was to report to the local police station every week until they found a position for him. It was his leaving party Edwin was referring to when he greeted Esther.

Chapter 59

She found Joshua outside. For a moment she just stood there, watching him. Anna's education plan was for the children to engage in as many outside activities as possible, including team sports. Esther knew Joshua had always liked ball games, football in particular, but the boys who were about the same age as Joshua had decided to ask for permission to change from football to basketball, a game none of them had played before. She watched as Joshua caught the ball with both hands, held it with his left hand by pushing it against his chest and manoeuvred his wheelchair with his right hand. It was difficult to move quickly over the rough ground, but he positioned himself under the basket and threw it up. It hit its target, went through the hoop, bounced back down, and one of the boys grabbed it and ran to the other end.

"Fifteen to eight."

"No it is not, that was nine."

"It wasn't."

Joshua had turned his wheelchair around and saw his mother standing there. He waved, then the game continued. Esther went back inside through the kitchen and up the ramp John had built. At first Anna had suggested that Joshua stay in the main house; they could convert her office as she had space to move it upstairs, but Joshua would have none of it. He wanted to be back in his own room with his friends.

As usual, John found a solution. He combined the first and second rooms in the end stable block into one big enough for a bunk bed, a writing desk, a wardrobe, two chairs, and Joshua could move around in the wheelchair. He then broke through the outside wall where there was space to build. John and the boys fitted a toilet and a stand for a washing bowl. The pipes were connected to the existing drainage, and the new bathroom was separated by a curtain.

Of course it was Brian who wanted to share the room with Joshua.

Anna's office was, as usual, open. Esther gave a slight knock.

"Come in, come in. Tell me how your week has been. Sit down, I will ring for some tea." She picked up the little bell on her desk, and before Esther could stop her they heard the ping. Brenda appeared with a tray holding a teapot, two cups and a bottle of milk.

"I saw you arriving. Sorry, we are out of sugar again. I used the last rations for the cakes. Would you like a piece?"

"No thank you, Brenda, and I did not use all my allocations this week. I am going to drive down to the village later. I am still registered there, I presume?"

Esther then told Anna that she could stay for two nights, but after that she would not be back for several weeks. There had been heavy bombing raids on London again and more doctors were needed at the hospitals over there, especially now the younger doctors were required to work with the men at the front. Even some of the nurses were being conscripted and placed in hospitals up and down the south coast.

"When did John find time to make those basketball stands outside?"

"You know John, he will not stop until he has done everything in his power to give Joshua the best equipment possible to aid his recovery. He has been working very hard, and quite frankly we would be lost without him."

"How can I ever repay him, Anna?"

"No need, we are all friends here helping each other. Before I forget, this arrived for you." She opened the desk

217

drawer, took out an envelope and handed it to Esther, who had a quick look at the sender and put it in her medical bag, which she had placed on the floor.

"I will read it later. I hear there is a party tonight."

"Yes, one of our guests is leaving. Our young linguist. It looks like they need him after all. He has orders to report to Bletchley House. All very secret, I believe. I only know because all the orders have to come via our police station and then are passed on to me."

"Where is Bletchley House?"

"In Buckinghamshire, I believe."

Chapter 60

"Mama, will you read me the letter again?"

"For a third time?"

Esther pulled the chair closer to Joshua's bed. Her cardigan was draped over the window, which allowed them to leave the lightbulb, swinging from the ceiling, on a little longer. Brian had stretched out on his bunk above Joshua.

"Yes please, Dr Rosenthal. I understood quite a few words. I believe my German is getting better, isn't it, Joshua?"

"It is. Mama, we have to be careful what we say in front of Brian these days." The boys laughed.

Joshua was looking at the photographs which had been included with the letter again. There was one of Rebecca at school and another of Benjamin. The third one was a group photo: Grandpa, Isabella, Rebecca and Benjamin, taken in a park. Big buildings could be seen at the edge.

"I wonder who took the photo, Mama. And where do you think it was taken?"

"There is some writing on the back."

Joshua turned it over. "It says April 1941, that is all."

"I have heard there is a big park in New York: Central Park. I have seen it in a book. Let's have a look." Brian bent down and stretched his arm out. Joshua reached up to him. "Yes, that looks like Central Park to me. I have seen it has big buildings all around it. In the book, it said, 'An oasis in an urban jungle'. Something like that, I think."

"It is hard to believe Rebecca looks so grown up now, and I cannot believe Benjamin is wearing glasses."

"I will read it one more time, and then it's lights out."

My dearest Esther and Joshua!
How we miss you both. It was so good to receive your last letter, and it only took two months to reach us. Ha, ha. Where it has been, who knows? But we have got it now; that is all that matters. We talk about you every day and you are in our prayers. I would think many things have changed for you over there since you last wrote.

"What does Grandpa mean by that?"

"I don't really know. Maybe he is referring to you getting so much better now. Don't forget the letter he refers to must be the one we wrote in January, not long after you moved back in here."

I hope I am allowed to say that now President Roosevelt has signed an agreement allowing the country to supply military equipment to Britain, we think the war will soon be over and you can come and join us here again. Isabella is looking for a good school for Joshua. She said she will select two of the best, and then you, Joshua, will be able to choose. She says you have to have your input into where you go, otherwise you might not like it here. There is lots of room here at the house, but you know that already.

"Do you think Grandpa is under Isabella's thumb, Mama? 'She says, she says', I cannot believe it is Grandpa talking. You should meet Grandpa, Brian, he would make you laugh."

Rebecca is doing well at school and has won the prize for biology for her form this year. She had the certificate framed, and it is now hanging in her room. Isabella helped her make the frame, and Isabella knew of a store who would let her have the glass for free if she agreed to babysit from time to time. Benjamin really misses his mama, but Isabella is doing her best.

"Here we go, Brian, here comes the best bit."

Well, I don't know where to begin. Maybe I should come straight to the point: I have asked Isabella to marry me. She said yes, Esther. I do hope you don't mind. I do miss your mother, Esther. Please don't think Isabella will be her replacement. But these are such uncertain times, and why should we be denied this bit of happiness? We are both widowed. I hope we have your blessing. We have not set a date yet and we are waiting until we hear from you.

"Can you believe it, Brian? Grandpa asks my mother's permission to marry. Grownups are funny, don't you think?"

Well this is all for now. I hope this letter gets to you soon. Please write back when you can.
With love from your father and grandpa

Dear Esther,
It took your father a lot of courage to ask me to marry him, and I think even more so to tell you about it. I miss you very much, and hope you and Joshua will come to join us soon. Joshua, I have heard so much about you, and cannot wait to meet you.
With love from Isabella

Dear Mama and Joshua,
Yes, please come home soon. We miss you. And Aunty Isabella is very nice.
With love, Rebecca

Dear Mama and Joshua,
Do you still remember me? I remember you. Rebecca
has a boyfriend.
Miss you, Ben

Dear Mama,
He is making it up. See, he has not changed. I don't
have a boyfriend.
Miss you, Rebecca

Esther sighed and put the letter down on her lap, then gave it to Joshua.

"Here, put it in your box."

He turned and pulled a small wooden box from underneath the bed. He then used his arms to pull himself into the sitting position, reached behind him and pulled his pillow up. Reaching down again, he retrieved the box and placed it on his blanket. Esther resisted helping him; she had already learned he valued his new-found independence.

"It's about time we switched the light off."

"Are you going over to the party?"

"Yes, mainly because I am curious about the place in Buckinghamshire. Remember I told you about the three friends I made on the crossing over from Bermuda?"

"Do you think they are at the same place?"

"I have the feeling they might be. Goodnight, Joshua. Goodnight, Brian."

"Goodnight, Mama."

"Goodnight, Dr Rosenthal."

Chapter 61

New York, 7 December 1941

"From the BBC Station, New York. President Roosevelt has announced today that the Japanese have attacked Pearl Harbor from the air. We interrupt our broadcast to give you the latest news. Stay tuned to this station."

"Ladies and Gentlemen, a special announcement. The entire sheriff and police force has been ordered to serve a twelve-hour shift. All auxiliary personnel have been directed to stand by for emergency service inspections. Citizens are urged to remain calm and avoid all unnecessary confusion because of hysteria. Citizen volunteers are asked to go quietly to the nearest police or fire stations and offer their services if they wish to help. There is no imminent cause for alarm. We return now to Hollywood."

Mordechai bent forward to turn the radio off.

"No, leave the music on for a minute. We might get further information."

They'd had a late lunch today, which was interrupted by Isabella's neighbour knocking on the door.

"Quick, put the radio on. The BBC." She was gone before she had finished her sentence. All four stormed into the sitting room; Mordechai had lit the fire before they had sat down for their meal, and the room was starting to warm up. His hand was shaking, and he could not find the correct station straight away.

"Let me do it, Grandpa." Rebecca turned the knob. They caught most of the announcement, and then remained silent, listening to the music until the programme was interrupted once more.

"This is the National Broadcasting Company. Go ahead, Honolulu."

"Several planes have been shot down and anti-aircraft gunnery is very heavy. All lines of communication seem to be down between various army posts. Everyone here on the islands was taken by surprise by the attack, and it is difficult to believe an air raid on these beautiful islands actually happened and lives have been lost. After the attack on Pearl Harbor, several squadrons of Japanese planes came in from the south and dropped bombs and incendiary devices over the city. One bomb dropped on the Governor's mansion. Traffic is almost at a standstill. At Pearl Harbor three ships were attacked. The *Oklahoma* was set on fire. There is great activity now to clear the debris. The Governor has announced a State of Emergency. The army has issued orders for all people of the civilian population to remain off the streets. After machine-gunning Ford Island, the first Japanese planes moved to Hickman field. There were 350 men killed in a direct bomb hit on the barracks."

Silence, followed by: "A Bulletin from New York. The Japanese took over the American Shanghai Power and Light Company this morning. This news comes hours after the bombing at Honolulu. This is the National Broadcasting Corporation."

The music returned. "Shall I see whether I can find another station?" Rebecca was turning the dial again, putting her ear close to the speaker. Isabella let go of Mordechai's hand.

"I will make us some coffee," she said just as the radio sprang to life again. Rebecca pushed herself back on the carpet and remained on the floor next to Benjamin. Putting her arm around him, she received a thankful smile in return.

"The White House is now giving out a statement. The President's brief statement will be read out by reporter Stephen Early, the President's press secretary."

"A Japanese attack on Pearl Harbor would mean war.

Such an attack would naturally bring a counter attack, and hostilities of this kind would mean that the President would ask Congress for a declaration of war. There is no doubt from Congress that such a declaration would be granted. Secretary Hall talked with the Secretary of War and the Navy. Now the two Japanese special envoys are at the State Department, engaged in a conference with the Secretary of State. Their appearance at the State Department on this Sunday afternoon emphasises the gravity of the Far Eastern situation, where hostilities seem to be opening up all over the South Pacific. And just now came word from the President's office that a second air attack has been reported by the Army and Navy bases in Manila. Thus we have official announcements from the White House that Japanese airplanes have attacked Pearl Harbor in Hawaii and Army and Navy bases in Manila. We return you to New York, and will give you information as it comes along from the White House."

"Grandpa, are we now at war?" Benjamin moved over to Mordechai's armchair and looked up at him from the floor. Mordechai stroked him on the head.

"I believe we are, but you are not to worry."

"Does this mean Mama will not be coming back?"

"Don't be silly. Of course she will, won't she, Grandpa?" Rebecca, still in front of the radio, had turned around, looking worried.

"Now the Americans are involved, the President is going to send our biggest tanks and planes over there with many brave soldiers who will be fighting. They will make sure that Hitler cannot hurt people anymore."

"And ships? The President will send ships, won't he, Grandpa?"

"Yes he will, my boy, and when the war is over, your mama and Joshua can come here and we will live all together. You just wait."

Chapter 62

"*Mazel tov*."

Mordechai broke the glass with his right foot. He shouted for all to hear. Rebecca later said that he sounded so loud they could hear him on the other side of the Hudson River. It had been Rebecca and Benjamin who accompanied their grandpa, leading him under the chuppah where Isabella encircled him three times. Rebecca rolled her eyes at Benjamin when she saw the way Isabella looked at her new husband. The marriage contract had already been signed, the two witnesses being friends of Isabella. The Ketubah was then read out by the chief Rabbi. He read it in Aramaic, and Benjamin sneaked another look at his sister, who just shrugged her shoulders. She did not understand what the Rabbi said either, and she teased her grandpa. Was he really married? Nobody as far as she was concerned knew what he had signed. He laughed, holding his glass of wine, and kissed his new wife on the cheek. Oh yes, they were sure they were now husband and wife. They both showed her their wedding bands again, which Benjamin had carried on a velvet cushion. Rebecca thought the plain gold rings were nice, but nothing compared to the ring with a large ruby stone which her grandpa had given to Isabella when he had asked her to marry him.

They did not have seven really close friends, so it was the Rabbi who read out the blessings. The wine her grandpa was to drink from a large cup was held by one of the witnesses, so was the cup for Isabella. The ceremony ended with the custom of leaving the pair alone, which seemed to take ages.

Rebecca wondered why; Grandpa and Isabella had spent time together by themselves many times before, and surely the food had to be eaten soon. She straightened her new dress and had another look at Benjamin. His tie had come undone again, and she could see a dirty mark on his white sleeve.

"What is that?" She tried to rub it off, and ended up with a sticky substance on her hand. She turned round to where the food was laid out as the newlywed couple re-joined the others, hoping nobody could hear the noise coming from her tummy. She was cross with Benjamin. He should have told her he was intending to sneak some food; maybe he could have got something for her as well. Now she had to wait until the dances were over.

First only the guests would be dancing in front of the married couple, who sat on a chair each, clearly enjoying the spectacle. Isabella had told Rebecca about most of the customs, and together they had danced in the sitting room some evenings. Then even Benjamin had wanted to learn, but when it came to dancing at the party where everybody could see him, he thought it was time to use the bathroom and stay there.

Rebecca waited for her chance. She held him by his arm, but not before wiping her sticky hand on his, until then, clean sleeve, and pulled him with her. He had no choice unless he wanted to create a commotion, which he knew would be wrong today. Mordechai watched his grandchildren dance, and took Isabella's hand. If only Esther and Joshua could have been here, that would have made his day complete, but Esther had insisted that they did not delay their wedding.

"You two are suited to each other," she had said in her letter. "Rebecca and Benjamin need a stable family more than anything else. Please look after each other until we can join you. Joshua and I will pray for long life and your happiness. God be with you."

She even managed to get a message to them, which said more or less the same as her letter, via the newspaper office. Arthur came over and delivered it, and they invited him to the wedding there and then. He felt honoured, he said, and as his gift, he offered to take their photographs. Maybe it had been this visit from Arthur that made the two decide to get married soon; this and the fact that Mordechai had seen a small empty store not far from the house.

"An easy walk, even in the winter," he told Isabella.

Together they had made an appointment with the owner to view it. It was ideal, with a counter and shelving out at the front, and behind a door to the back there was a small storeroom that could easily be converted into a workshop. Mordechai immediately formulated a plan for his bench and lighting. The owner was going to rent it out with a twelve-month lease agreement, but Mordechai wanted to buy it outright. The owner refused, and Isabella thought they would have to start looking again, but Mordechai said not to worry, he would be back, and then they would be in a better bargaining position. Just wait.

Meanwhile, he made an appointment with an attorney and went to the bank. Now was the right time to take the last of the cuckoo clock's weights from the safe. He had already worked out where the clock could now be placed: on the back wall for all to see, but he was not sure whether he should repair it first or leave it as it was.

Once he had purchased the store, bought all his supplies, paid for his wedding and kept some back to live on, he would still have the funds to bring Esther and Joshua back. First class cabin this time. Yes, that was what he would do. Esther had said the children needed a secure home, and he knew soon there would be college fees to be paid. It was up to him now to prepare for their future.

Chapter 63

Salop Infirmary, England

"Now with the Americans having arrived, maybe the war will be over soon and we can all go home. What has this to do with me in any case? I am Irish, for goodness' sake. I never wanted to fight this bloody war in the first place. Oh sorry, Esther, I should watch what I say."

Flo pushed a second piece of fruitcake into her already full mouth and looked around, hoping nobody had overheard.

"I am so glad you came. How did you manage to get a pass to Salop, of all places?"

"Well I did not feel like going to Liverpool this time. I told them I had a friend here, which they did view a little suspiciously – your name and all that. But when I told them you are a doctor here helping with the war effort, I have never seen them stamping a request for a leave paper as quickly as that one. Hope you don't mind me coming here?" she managed to say while taking a large gulp of tea, washing down the cake, which had become a little dry and was in danger of getting stuck.

"Definitely not, I am glad you thought of it. You can stay with me tonight."

"Are you sure? I was going to get a room not far from the hospital, I have already looked it up."

"No, I would like you to stay with me. We have a lot of catching up to do."

Flo leaned over the table and whispered, "I would have come earlier if I had known you were surrounded by dishy doctors like the one behind you. No, don't look now. He keeps staring at me. Must be my uniform."

"I can see this is going to be an interesting night. Here, take my key. I should be free in two hours. The boarding house is directly opposite. You cannot miss it. I had better write you a note to give to Mrs Fishbourne, otherwise she will freak if she sees you standing there, looking so official. Her son is fighting somewhere, she does not know where. Last she heard of him he had been to France and back."

"You mean when they evacuated all the troops from Dunkirk? But surely she has heard since then. That was almost two years ago."

"A friend of his told her he was fighting in Africa."

"That's where Annie's brother, Paddy, is. You do remember Annie?"

"Yes, you told me she had lost her little boy."

"Derek, yes he died of a fit in an air-raid shelter. Annie has never been the same since then. She now clings to her little one, David."

"I can quite understand that."

"Esther, is it alright if I go to your room now? I am really tired all of a sudden."

"How long can you stay?"

"Three days, then I have to report back."

"That should give us enough time to go to Trench Hall. I will try to change my shift. You could meet Anna and Joshua and all the others, what do you think?"

"Really, you will let me come with you? You do know I am Irish Catholic?"

Now Esther laughed. "That makes no difference in Anna's home. It never has."

Flo picked up her large duffle bag and put her arm through its handle, lifting it up so the weight was on her shoulder. She looked apologetically at Esther.

"It was my Kieran's."

*

230

Esther was loading her car. She had to check in with the hospital the next morning to make sure her shift was covered. Flo's bag had been in the room when she returned, but no sign of Flo. Esther had asked the landlady whether she knew where Flo had gone. She had left a message for Esther that she would be back as soon as she had run an errand. Esther then saw Flo through the front room window, running up the street, carrying a box and panting all the way.

"I am sorry you had to wait for me," she said, out of breath. "I had some ration coupons for milk, butter, sugar, jam and meat I wanted to make use of before we left. You see, we get extra rations because they need us to keep our strength up, I think. It is heavy work moving those big searchlights, looking for the enemy in the sky. Anyway, I noticed a Co-op on the way here. They had to give me what I asked for because I am in uniform. I got everything."

"It is all in there?"

"No, not in here. I then went to the pub across the road. See? That one, The White Horse. The landlord let me in, after I made a right commotion outside."

"Flo, have you been drinking?"

"Yes, no, wait. Anyway, I thought the pub could do with all the stuff I had just got, and the landlord's eyes lit up when he saw my goodies. He wanted to fob me off with some of his ale, but I said no, I take it elsewhere. So we started to negotiate. I had to drink some of his stale stuff. Awful it was. Must have been leftovers from the night before. He thought if he got me drunk, I'd just forget what I came for, but then I am Irish, and we can hold our liquor. Here, I got two bottles of his finest whisky. I thought the gentlemen living at the house – you know, the ones you told me about last night – could do with a nice drop."

"Get in." Esther could not help but smile.

Chapter 64

Dachau, Germany

Maybe one day you become immune, or you no longer care. He hoped it was the former and not the latter. He never wanted to stop caring. Nor did he ever want to give up hope. Hope was what kept him going. He had lost all sense of time and no longer knew what day it was. He used to count every day so he would not miss his Sabbath, then he would pray after the guards let them rest for the night. Now he prayed every day. Prayed to be reunited with Esther.

He imagined her and Mordechai in England, being safe. Did they find work over there? He was sure his Esther did, as a fine surgeon with excellent English. This was why he wanted her to take Mordechai and go. He knew nobody in England, but still he had insisted. France or Belgium were not an option. He wanted some distance between his family and the madness developing in Germany. Yes, he had to keep going. Esther would be waiting for him.

Ibrahim heard him again, the man banging his head against the wall. How long had he been in there? A week? Two maybe? Or even longer? Ibrahim wiped the floor outside the door. He whispered to the man, lying flat in the wet puddle left behind. There was a small gap underneath the door, maybe just over one centimetre – would that mean there was a little light inside? Even here, in the corridor, he could hardly see. He knew the man would be waiting for him, but it was not Ibrahim who brought him his food. Ibrahim never witnessed anything being taken in there.

But he kept trying: trying to make the man listen to him.

Trying to give him hope. He had nearly been caught once by one of the guards and had thrown himself into the wetness left by his mop, pretending to have tripped. He did not want to be removed from his duty; he knew the man was listening to him, and he imagined the man looked forward to him coming along. It was not every day he could come, but Ibrahim never let on. He just continued to tell his stories from where he had left off the previous time.

The guards were going to build more of them. Standing cells, he heard them say. Work would be starting soon. An inspection was due, he knew this much. They would get nothing to eat the day before, not even a piece of stale bread. The guards wanted to put extra pressure on the men to do as they were told at the roll call. In reality, it meant more of the prisoners would not make it through the day. They would fall down right in front of the visitors. It was then up to the prisoners to clean up with the efficiency expected. They got praised that day if they did well.

He looked at the new foundations at the end of the hall. The marked places could not be more than forty centimetres, hardly the width of a door. He would be one of those who did the work. Maybe as soon as tomorrow. He and about a dozen others, watched over by two guards. What did he know about building? He was a writer, after all.

He continued to whisper his stories underneath the opening.

Chapter 65

Trench Hall, England

Esther helped him to pack. The clothes had been donated from guests in the main house. She wanted to buy him something new and found a sweater in a store in Salop, handing a necklace over to get it.

"Clothes are rationed, and without the coupon I cannot sell you any," the woman behind the counter had insisted. When Esther undid the necklace she always wore around her neck, the woman suddenly found she could.

Esther looked at her son. How handsome he had become, and how tall he was, standing there supported by two wooden crutches. She felt at a loss; he was leaving her. He was only just eighteen and keen to be in charge of his own life.

She still could not quite believe the day she'd been told Brian had come rushing into the kitchen, running past the cook and into Anna's office.

"It's Joshua," he had shouted, and then was gone again. Anna had phoned Esther at the hospital soon after. Joshua had fallen out of his chair on the playing field and screamed in pain, not letting anybody touch him. Esther was in the ambulance when it arrived and rushed to her son's side. He was lying there, covered by a blanket, surrounded by his friends.

"He says it hurts," John had told her, kneeling beside him, holding his hand. At first Esther did not seem to take in the significance. She was already on the grass, stroking Joshua's head.

"Mama, it hurts. My foot hurts."

"The ambulance is here. Just be brave a little longer. We will take you to the hospital now."

"Dr Rosenthal, Josh said *his foot hurts*."

"I suspect it is broken, John. He must have landed awkwardly when he fell."

"Yes, but how can he feel it?"

"It really does hurt, Mama."

Esther had lost her balance then and stumbled backwards, lying on the ground in a not dissimilar position to Joshua. It was Brian who had reached under her arms and helped Anna lift her back up.

"But it can't be. It should not hurt."

"But it does, Mama, and I can wiggle my toe on the other foot. Can't I, Brian?"

Ludwig Guttmann agreed to examine Joshua again, but could not leave Oxford for at least ten days, he had told her on the telephone. There was no miracle cure, he reminded her. She must be prepared to accept that Joshua would never regain the full use of his legs.

"Please do not raise his hopes, we do not want him to have a setback later."

After the phone call, Esther decided it was best to tell Joshua exactly what she had been told, but added that he should concentrate on all his exercises. She had asked a young nurse to help him every day. Joshua thought his foot was healing far too slowly; he wanted to get back to school, and the doctors agreed to discharge him after four weeks. When John collected Joshua that day, a nurse he had not met before handed him some wooden crutches with strict instructions not to let Joshua put any weight on his foot yet.

John was just going to explain that Joshua would have no use for them, when Joshua said, "They look new, can I keep them?"

"We only need them back when you have finished with

them. Be careful how you go." The nurse seemed rushed off her feet and quickly left.

"Do you think you could help me, John?"

"I don't know, Josh, we should leave them here or ask your mother." He saw the look Joshua gave him and agreed: Dr Rosenthal would never allow Joshua to use the crutches. "The plaster was only taken off yesterday, Josh, I really don't know."

"Please."

John sighed. "This is how it will go, Josh. You slide yourself to the end of your bed. Let your legs hang over the edge and support your body with your arms. I will give you one of the crutches at a time. You do not make any silly moves until I am right in front, lifting you up while you support your weight with the crutches. Is that totally understood?"

"Yes." Joshua looked hopeful. "And only for a few seconds."

Moving his body to the sitting position was something Joshua did every day, but he hesitated when he was handed the first of the crutches. John was not sure what to do next; although he was not a religious man, he gave a short silent prayer that his own disability would not prevent his body from holding the boy's weight. He would have to lift Joshua up before the crutches were in a stable position.

He forgot about his own pain, but saw in Joshua's face how he hurt when both crutches were under his arms and he started the lift. John was dismayed at how light the child was; hardly any weight at all, and still he found the strength to stand there for a few seconds before falling back on to the bed. Beads of perspiration rolled down his face. Catching his breath, he gave John a big smile.

"That was good, we will do it again tomorrow."

Look at my Joshua now, Esther thought. He moved around his room with ease. His wooden crutches had given him a new lease of life. Although he could not walk, he could stand on one of his legs and use his crutches to swing both legs forward. He hardly ever used his wheelchair now, but Esther had insisted he would take it along. He knew better than to argue with his mother.

"How long will it take us to get there?"

"Dr Guttmann said it is about 150 miles from here to Oxford. It will take us most of the day, I reckon. John is coming along. He said we have to leave early, he does not want us to go all that way by ourselves."

"That, plus he wants to inspect my new lodgings. He told me so. I will miss John when I am gone. And you, of course, Mama," he quickly added.

"I will miss you too, my son."

"Mama, don't you think it is funny that the college in Oxford Dr Guttmann got me a scholarship for is called Jesus College?"

"Yes, who would have thought?" She smiled.

"You have never met Friedrich before, have you, Mama?"

"No, he arrived at Dovercourt Camp after we had gone. Anna could not prevent him being taken to the Isle of Man, she told me, but they have kept in contact all this time."

"I am glad he is staying here in my room for the time being. I felt a little bit awkward leaving Brian all by himself. Is it true that Uncle Alexander told Friedrich he could come to London and work at his newspaper?"

"Yes, I believe so. The prospect of working there one day was what kept Friedrich going over on the Isle of Man, he told Anna. Things were not the same during his last few months there. There was a riot one day. Another day the guards found an escape tunnel. Friedrich thought it was at the Italian camp, but he could not be sure. A lot of aggressive prisoners had arrived, and when his name was on the list of the people to leave he could not wait to get away. He still cannot believe that Alexander is dead. He had imagined he would just stay at Trench Hall for a few days and then travel down to London."

"What will he do now?"

"Anna said she is going to ask the new editor to honour Alexander's agreement. Friedrich used his time wisely and brought copies of his printing along. Maybe they can use somebody with his experience. I honestly hope so, he is such a lovely young man."

Chapter 66

"Cuckoo, cuckoo, cuckoo!"

The little yellow bird disappeared back behind the door and the flat celluloid figures began their dance to the music. Mordechai checked his pocket watch.

The clock on the wall was late again. He had still not managed to adjust it correctly, although he was sure the calculations of the weight for each function were correct when he had given them to the workshop he used occasionally. The owner was very skilful and had made them several items which needed to be replaced at the house. Using his best iron, he had said when he repaired part of the railing on the steps leading to the front door, which had collapsed after the last storm. Some storm that had been. It had snowed for days. New York seemed at a standstill, from what Mordechai could make out, and to the children's delight, all the schools were closed. They soon changed their minds about that when it became their duty to keep the steps and the walkway free of snow and ice, although at first they had thought it was great fun. Who had ever heard of building snowmen in the middle of their street? All of the children in their neighbourhood had joined in, then somebody suggested there should be a competition and several groups were formed. The judging would be on the Sabbath, but one of the real spectacles was sabotaged on the first night. Benjamin had seen it through his window, but could not identify who the culprits were. Mordechai suspected he knew, but would not say, and he was quietly delighted that Benjamin had taken that stance. The children whose efforts were now in pieces on the ground had no longer wanted to be part of the competition, but Benjamin had talked to some bigger boys and together they had knocked on the children's door. Benjamin explained to the distressed parents that he had seen a vehicle trying to pass and that had pushed the snowman over. That there were no tyre marks left in the freshly fallen snow did not seem to matter, and the building continued.

On Rebecca's instruction, groups had to include children of all ages to ensure the contest was fair. She is going to be a politician one day, Mordechai thought when he heard about it. On the day of the judging the snow started to melt. Again it was Rebecca who took over. The judging was changed from the afternoon to early morning, despite the fact that some snowmen had not been completed. That caused yet another argument and more tears, and Mordechai and Isabella were glad that they had not volunteered to be part of the judging panel. They watched the commotion with amusement from their front steps, holding a large cup of coffee each into which Mordechai had found it prudent to slip a little of his brandy, despite the early hour. That was when Isabella had slipped and tried to steady herself on the railing, which fell to the ground with a thud. Mordechai managed to hang on to her, but now all attention was focused on them rather than the slowly melting snowmen.

One of the older boys used this opportunity and made a snowball, taking a handful from the melting figure right in front of him and packing it tightly. At first the others protested, but soon they joined in the fight. No winners or losers that day.

Mordechai looked at his cuckoo clock again, waiting for the next time the little bird would pay him a visit. Isabella had accused him of treating the clock like his pet. He heard the bell which was fixed above the store door, removed his glasses, which had a magnifying lens attached to one eye, and raised himself up from his chair in front of the bench. He had told the customer whose watch he was repairing it would not be ready until the next morning, although he would do his best to hurry up. Surely the customer was not expecting it already?

"Hello, Grandpa."

"You are early today, something wrong at school?"

"You should fix that old clock of yours sometime, Grandpa. It still shows just after three when it is nearly four o'clock."

"Is it really? My, my, how time flies. How was school today?"

"Same as yesterday, Grandpa." Benjamin put his school-bag behind the counter. "I cannot wait to start junior high after the summer term. All these little children running around in the playground. A menace, they are. I almost tripped over one of them today."

"And that had nothing to do with you not watching where you were going, I suspect."

"What are you repairing there, Grandpa? Can I have a look?"

"Come along, I will show you. This is a very interesting piece. You see the little rubies in there?"

Benjamin pulled the other stool over and placed the magnifying glass his grandpa had given him last year over his right lens. He put a newspaper on the floor behind him.

"What have you got there?"

"Isabella gave it to me. I met her on the way over to the shop, and she said not to stay too long today."

"Let's have a look, there must be a good reason why she wanted me to see this." Benjamin got up again. He knew of his grandpa's bad back and that Isabella did not allow him to bend down very often, so he retrieved the newspaper, handed it over and went back to looking at the rubies.

Mordechai opened *The New York Times*. There was a map showing part of England and France. Above it, big letters said:

ALLIED ARMIES LAND IN FRANCE IN THE HAVRE-CHERBOURG AREA. GREAT INVASION IS UNDERWAY.

Mordechai refolded the paper. "We had better close up for the day and do as Isabella asked."

Chapter 67

Trench Hall, June 1944

The Daily Telegraph lay neatly folded on the small table by the window. One of the boys had put it there earlier. Edwin walked up and down the room with excitement. Maybe the end was now in sight. He wanted to share the good news with Otto, who had not been feeling well and had gone for a rest earlier.

Edwin was worried about his friend. Otto seemed to have lost a lot of weight in the last few weeks and looked awfully pale. He had already spoken with Brenda, who had noticed it as well. Edwin had told her to make sure Otto got extra meat this week and to put extra butter on his toast. He said to take it out of his rations; he could do without it. He had given his late wife's gold earrings, matching bracelet and necklace to Anna the day before. She had protested, saying they could manage, but Edwin insisted. He had nobody to leave things to, and the children here were in desperate need, he argued.

John had told Edwin that one of the farmers in a village about ten miles north had begun trading food for people's possessions, and he and one of his local friends were planning to pay the farmer a visit. It was best if two of them went together. The farmer was crafty and had cheated an old chap, saying he had never handed his watch over so he had to leave empty handed, having walked all that way. All the old chap had wanted was to put a decent meal on the table for his grandchildren. Land women, who had just walked back from the fields pushing a cart of sacks containing fresh peas, found him sitting on the roadside in distress, with no intention of returning to his family.

"I am no use to them anymore, no use," he had said over and over again.

Edwin wanted to know what happened to the old man. John had smiled and told him the farmer had not reckoned on the outrage of the small community. At first the women wanted to give the old man what they could spare, but a young lad who had accompanied them, having been classified as a simpleton not fit for the army, took his fork and spade off the cart and said he was going to sort it out. One of the women said she would go as well. Her friend worked on the farm, and had told her the women there locked themselves in their rooms every night ever since they had found him pushing a female worker into a large wardrobe with his hands all over her.

"Did they report him to the police for molesting the woman?"

"Of course not," John replied, "but he had difficulty sitting down for a while after the largest of them kicked him. You know, where it hurts. After the visit from the young man, he did not go to the police either."

The farmer had stopped dealing after that for a while, but then greed took over and now he was back in business. Edwin begged John to be extra vigilant, and was relieved to hear that John's friend had been a boxer. Now they had chickens out back; John had come home from the farm with six. To the boys' delight, instead of using them for dinner straight away, Brenda said to wait until they had stopped laying. At first Edwin had been a bit disappointed that John did not bring back a sheep as he had hoped he would, but when John said he had left the sheep with the butcher, Edwin almost hugged him. It only cost them one shoulder and a leg. The butcher had handed over the rest.

Edwin heard a noise behind him: Otto was standing in

the doorframe. Brenda had said as soon as Otto was up she would make him some tea, and she had saved him a piece of cake, the one he liked best: her finest recipe Victoria sponge without the cream.

"Otto, I have been waiting for you. Here, have a look at that." Otto reached for the paper which was in Edwin's outstretched hand and stared at the headlines:

ALLIED INVASION

TROUPS SEVERAL MILES INTO FRANCE, FIGHTING IN CAEN, 10,000 TONS OF BOMBS BLASTED WAY

PILOTS WATCHING BATTLES SAY, "BEACHES ARE OURS"

Wordlessly he handed it back. Taken by surprise at the silence of his friend, Edwin asked, "Are you not as happy as I am about this news? It means there is hope the war will end soon and we can all go back to our homes and live in peace."

"I like it here, Edwin. This is the first place that feels like home to me. And besides, where will I go? There is no place left for me."

Chapter 68

Hildesheim, October 1944

They were at a loss what to say or do. Field Marshal Rommel was dead. Their only hope was gone. As long as Rommel was alive, they had felt reassured. Now all was lost. Only madmen were left in charge.

Maria had persuaded Hilde to accompany her to the cinema. There had hardly been any coverage in the newspapers about Rommel's death, but the funeral had taken place in Ulm the week before, so there had to be some coverage in the weekly newsreel shown before the main film. They did not care what the programme was for the day; they had sworn never to visit the cinema again after the day years ago when, instead of the film they had expected to see, the programme had changed to hours of propaganda. They had wanted to leave, but their seats were in the front row, and the people behind them had kept clapping and shouting, approving of everything that Goebbels indoctrinated them with. Maria and Hilde had no choice but to stare at Hitler's and Goebbels's faces from where they sat for what seemed like forever; leaving would have meant somebody would have reported them, they were sure of that.

The coverage of Rommel's funeral was short, only a few minutes. They left after that, no longer caring what other people thought of them. Hilde's eldest boy, seven-year-old Klaus, had asked her whether the man his papa worked for was really dead. Hilde had to tell him the truth. The children had seen too much already, far more than any child ever should.

"But my papa, my papa is coming home," he proclaimed

and went back to join the other children.

Maria had received another long letter from Egon. He kept telling her to listen to the BBC German coverage every day if she could. From the way his letters were phrased, Maria knew the Prisoners of War in England were allowed to listen to it as well. None of his writing had been blacked out this time. His work as the camp doctor had become more difficult, he had said. Many more German prisoners arrived every day. Everybody was treated well, and in his block it was still only him with the others rescued when the *Bismarck* was sunk. He had been taken outside the camp one day in a military vehicle. The town had been badly damaged, which was not surprising because his camp was not far from a big and busy port, he said. They took him into the country, to a large house hidden away in woodlands. That was where the German and Italian officers were housed.

> *Maria,* he had written, *it was just like we imagine a gentlemen's club to be. They even wore their uniforms. I treated one of them who had fallen and damaged his foot. An infection had set in. He already had a high fever and kept calling for his wife.*
>
> *Afterwards I was invited to stay and eat with them, but I declined. I was handed a bottle of brandy by one of them that I took and shared it with everybody in our hut. Brandy in the middle of the war, whoever heard of that?*

Trench Hall

Anna put the letter back into the envelope, opened her desk drawer and put it with the others. The newspaper clipping which had been included was still in her hand. Maybe her eyes were deceiving her. She pushed her chair back and stood up; the light would be better by the window. She moved the curtain with her free hand. Looking back at her desk, she saw the small lamp was still on. Instead of switching the light off, she went over to the shelves behind where she kept her magnifying glass. Back at the window, she placed it over the photo which was below the article. The picture must have been taken some time ago; he was looking well. However, it was not Rommel's death which concerned her. It was the house he stood in front of.

Yes, that was her school in Herrlingen. Rommel had lived at her old school. How could that be?

Chapter 69

Dachau, April 1945

The smell drifted into the hut. Something was burning. Something was different. It was not the usual smell; this one was more pungent. His stomach turned, and he jumped down, trying to locate the bucket in time. He could see flames through the window. The fire must be large; red angry flames were rising up high into the sky. We will be burned to death if we stay in here, he thought. He shook the men awake. Some of them got up, but others refused. Several more were no longer moving at all.

Ibrahim took charge. "We have to get out of here," he shouted.

Most stayed where they were – "And be shot while trying to escape?" – but a few got down.

"Get something we can use to break down the door."

Everybody was pulled off the bunks, and now there was hardly any room to stand. Three of them started pulling on the wood at the end which held the frames together. It was no use.

"We need more space." Reluctantly several men climbed back on to the bunks, all cowering with their knees pulled up to their chins. Three younger prisoners started pushing the wood with their feet, their backs against the wall for extra force. Two others pulled. They heard the wood splinter and the bunk collapsed at one end, the loose piece exposing sharp nails. There was no time to try and do anything about it, so they quickly took their jackets off and wrapped them around the nails.

The space by the door cleared of men. The younger ones, holding the makeshift battering ram, stepped back as far as they could.

"Now," Ibrahim shouted. They ran and hit the door. It shook, but stayed shut. The smoke was now more intense and they started choking.

"We need more help."

Two more tries and the door flew open.

Ibrahim picked himself up from the ground outside. The sun was trying to shine through the smoky air with little success. Men pushed past.

"Wait."

Ibrahim retrieved his jacket, put it back on and looked around. He could see several fires to his right. Guards were running, carrying something between them and throwing it on the fire, only to return for a second time.

"Look." Ibrahim pointed to the watchtowers.

"I can't see anything."

"There is nobody up there, they have deserted their posts."

He heard loud noises from the other hut. People were trying to get out, banging on the doors, shouting and rattling at the metal bars on the windows. Somebody came running towards them.

"What is happening?" Ibrahim shouted. Too late he saw it was one of the guards: a new one he had only seen once or twice. Ibrahim noticed that he was not wearing his uniform, but instead was wearing dark trousers and a light shirt, sleeves rolled up like a farm worker. Only his boots gave him away. He hesitated and threw some keys towards him, turned around and sped away, jumping on to the back of a military vehicle which had started to move towards the gate.

More and more doors opened and the surroundings filled with people. Some walked towards the wire fences, others walked towards the gate. The dark smoke drifted over from behind Ibrahim and he moved forward. Through the smoke, he could see the few remaining guards running.

Then he heard a succession of shots. They seemed to come from the direction of the fires, which were now only smouldering. The number of people near the fence stopped him from seeing beyond.

Army vehicles started approaching the gate, arriving from the outside, trying to get in. Ibrahim was now so close to the gate that turning round and running was no longer an option. If he was to die here, he wanted to face his enemy one last time. Prisoners parted to let the vehicles enter, and Ibrahim held his ground and stood.

The driver's side door of the first military vehicle opened and a young soldier jumped out. He walked towards Ibrahim and stopped. Ibrahim fell to his knees, his head bent to the ground, blood from his damaged hands running down on to his trousers.

"What is your name?"

Ibrahim remained where he was and pushed one of his sleeves up, exposing his number.

"No, not your number, your name."

The soldier sat down on the ground, facing him.

"Your name? What is your name? We are Americans, we are here to help you."

"Ibrahim. Ibrahim Rosenthal," he whispered, and wept.

Chapter 70

Salop, April 1945

"Matron, there is a telephone call for Dr Rosenthal."

The matron looked at the new nurse. This was the second time she had been interrupted by this nurse. One more time and she would get her first official warning.

"Take a message and tell them Dr Rosenthal will call back some other time." The nurse was just going to protest, but then thought better of it. The others had warned her about the matron, so she paused. She liked Dr Rosenthal, who always had a kind word for everybody, and besides, the caller at the other end of the line had spoken with some urgency.

"And come straight back." The matron's voice boomed after her.

The matron had no intention of interrupting a doctor who was busy checking patients on her rounds. As it was she'd had to wait far too long for Dr Rosenthal to come to the ward today. The girl in the corner bed was clearly in pain. She had arrived by ambulance during the night. Stomach cramps, she had said. Nobody had come in with her, and the matron had not seen anybody checking on her during the morning.

The matron decided it was better to watch her. The girl looked like she would bolt at any minute, if the pain did not hinder her. Normally the matron would not get involved; it was not her duty, but she felt a little bit sorry for the girl. She reckoned the girl was fifteen years of age at the most. Where was her family? The girl was running a fever, and it was possible she had a burst appendix, being as she was bent over the way she was. Matron pushed the screen back, the one Dr Rosenthal had pulled around the bed to give the girl some privacy. Most doctors did not bother and examined the patients in view of all the others, but Dr Rosenthal was different.

The doctor removed her stethoscope from the girl's slightly swollen stomach.

"There was a telephone call for you, Dr Rosenthal. The caller said it was important he speaks with you. I have his number."

The young nurse had returned and decided to speak up.

"Thank you, but it will have to wait. This girl is just about to have her baby. Take her to the delivery suite as soon as you can. I will go ahead and prepare." She pushed past them and left in a hurry. The matron put both hands over her mouth. How could she have missed the symptoms?

"Quick, quick, get a trolley, now," she shouted at the nurse.

"But I am on duty at the…"

The nurse did not finish her sentence, instead doing as she was told.

It was a boy. The girl gave birth to a little boy. The delivery took hardly any time at all. Esther could not imagine what the girl must have gone through. She must have known she was pregnant. Had she considered giving birth all by herself? Esther had no time to find out how far advanced the pregnancy was. The baby was very small and did not weigh more than four pounds, but he was alive, and the first checks told her he was healthy. Most likely mother and baby would have to remain here for some time.

She made her way to the office and found the message with the telephone number in her pigeonhole. She was supposed to call the editor of the newspaper in London as soon as she could. She asked at the reception whether she could use the telephone there.

The editor picked up after a few rings, and immediately realised who it was. "Dr Rosenthal, how have you been?"

They exchanged pleasantries for a while, until Esther asked, "Was there a reason you wanted to speak with me?"

He cleared his throat. "You will tell me if I am too intrusive, Dr Rosenthal." He coughed. "News has come via the American High Commission that a concentration camp in Dachau has been liberated by the American Army." Silence. "Dr Rosenthal, did you hear me? I am sorry, I know it is none of my business, but Thomas had told me..."

"Yes, thank you. Thank you for telling me. Does this mean the war has come to an end?"

"I have no information about that, but I do know many others camps have been found by both the American and British Armies. I have a list here if you..."

"No, no, you have to understand, I always hoped to receive this news. I have to go there straight away. I have to go to Dachau."

"Dr Rosenthal, if you need any assistance, please call me. We will do all we can."

"I must thank you. Thank you for phoning me with such good news."

Esther put the phone back down. She felt dizzy and had to sit behind the desk. Two women approached her from the entrance. All they said was "Where is the delivery room?" Esther pointed with her arm down the corridor. The receptionist had come back, holding a hot drink she had clearly got for herself. She saw how white Esther had turned and put it down in front of her.

"Dr Rosenthal, are you not feeling well? Please drink this. It might help. I hope you did not get bad news."

"I have to get in touch with a colleague of mine to cover

my shifts. Do you think you could help me find his address?"

"Yes, it will be here in the box. Whom are you looking for?"

Esther gave her the details, and before she left, she added, "No, the news was not bad. Thank you, Amanda."

In the corridor, the two women who had asked her directions earlier came out of the delivery suite, holding the baby Esther had delivered only a few moments earlier.

"Where are you taking the baby?" Esther stopped them before they could get past. She recognised one of them as a woman from the orphanage with whom she had argued when a child was discharged from hospital far too early on this woman's insistence.

"We are taking him. The mother has signed the papers. It is all in order."

"This baby needs special care."

"And that is exactly what he will be getting. Now let us pass." The women carried on, ignoring the baby's desperate cry for his mother. Esther knew she was powerless. She entered the delivery room where the girl was standing up, putting her clothes back on.

"Where do you think you are going?"

"Me mam said to walk back home, like, you know, nothing has happened."

"I am not discharging you. You will have to stay."

Esther helped her back into the bed and sat with her, holding her hand and stroking her head. She waited until the girl had cried herself to sleep, and only then did she get ready to leave.

This girl would never see her son again.

Chapter 71

Dachau

"We can no longer protect you if you insist on leaving."

Ibrahim failed to understand how some people could consider staying. The American officer in charge told him it was because they had nowhere else to go to. He had a place to go, he said. He was going to find Esther.

"Once you leave here, you cannot come back. Do you understand?"

Yes, he did. This was the second time he had reported to the officer with his request for some papers which could serve as identification. They could not keep him here, he knew that much, but he also depended on them for papers in English and in German. He translated them for the Americans, who were happy to put their official stamp on them. One less person for them to have to care for.

Ibrahim did not want any of the clothing which was piled up in one of the buildings at the Dachau camp. He was adamant about that. The Americans found him some trousers, a shirt, boots, a coat and a felt hat. The trousers were too big and swamped his thin body, so they gave him some braces. All from the village, they said. Whether this was true or not, he did not know, but they smelled different when he slowly held them towards his face.

"You can take that as well." The same young soldier who had asked Ibrahim for his name on the day the Americans had arrived pointed towards a sand coloured rucksack on the floor, US stencilled on it in large black letters. Ibrahim picked it up and slung it over his shoulder. It was heavy.

The soldier led him outside and helped him climb on to the back of the first American Army vehicle. There he joined six others already waiting to leave.

"Wait, please wait," he shouted after the American. "Can we open the tarpaulin on the side?" When the soldier did not react, he added, "I need to see."

The convoy started moving towards the gate. Ibrahim's heartbeat increased. This was the first time he had been on the other side of the fences in nearly seven years. He looked back at the figures standing by the fences, none of them wearing the prison uniforms now, as slowly the place became smaller and smaller. Once they turned the first corner it was no longer visible at all, like it had never existed.

He turned round and faced forward. He could see a small village ahead, and a group of children appeared from the ditches beside the road and started running alongside, trying to keep up.

"Chocolate, Mister!" some of them shouted, stretching their hands upwards. He saw several small items flying out through the open passenger window and landing on the ground. The children immediately stopped and scrambled for whatever had landed in front of them.

When the convoy reached the village itself, he saw women standing on the sides of the roads outside their houses. Some of them had small bunches of flowers which they tried to hand to the driver and passenger. Their rewards seemed to be more chocolate. Passing through the village and out the other end, they came across more women who were working in the fields. The vehicles had increased their speed, but the women stopped what they were doing and waved. None of the people sitting next to Ibrahim waved back.

Through the hazy sunshine appeared ghost-like tall shadows ahead. He rubbed his eyes, trying to make out what they were. The other men sitting with him were pointing towards them. Then he saw: they were approaching Munich. He knew this town well; his grandfather had been born not far from Munich, and as a child he had spent many happy summers here. It had been his grandfather who introduced him to books. While the others played outside, he and his grandfather would stay in the library in the large house. On cool evenings his grandfather would light the fire, even though it was only August. In the twilight they would listen to the gramophone standing on a cabinet against one of the walls. His grandfather would wind it up using a handle on the side.

Ibrahim heard songs with words written by Heinrich Heine and music composed by Robert Schumann or Franz Schubert. This was when he discovered his love of poetry, and he told his grandfather that he wanted to become a writer. His mother used to send letters to her father after all the children had returned, complaining that Ibrahim was even paler than he had been at the beginning of the school holidays, but every year he was allowed to go again.

Later, all books by Heinrich Heine were burned in open fires in the streets, together with many other poets and writers whose work had become forbidden.

Ibrahim did not recognise any of the streets they drove through. Yes, they had heard aeroplanes above them on many occasions in the camp – sometimes the whole of the sky was filled, making the day turn into night for a brief moment – and he had even witnessed an orange glow in the sky, but he had never imagined that Munich would no longer resemble the town he once knew. As far as his eyes could see, not one of the buildings was undamaged. Some had been completely destroyed, and others were now large ruins, the remains stretching upwards like claws. His eyes followed them up to where they met the sky, as if begging to be saved.

The last air raid must have been recent. In the centre of

Munich, some bombed-out buildings were still smouldering. Here the women did not wave, but turned their backs, ignoring the vehicles passing them by, too busy using pickaxes and trowels to loosen bricks of walls which were still standing. Others cleaned them off and handed each to the next women in line, who stacked them in neat piles at the roadside. Small children sat silently on the ground.

Ibrahim was surprised to see steam from a train pulling into the station, which was now straight ahead. How could trains still be running here?

The vehicle stopped, but the ones behind overtook and turned left, disappearing from his sight. The bolts at the back were slid open and the flap was pulled down to allow the men to jump on to the ground. Ibrahim was helped again.

The soldier handed him his rucksack and pointed straight ahead. "*Shalom Aleichem.*" He had stretched out his hand for Ibrahim to take and wished him good luck. When Ibrahim withdrew his hand, he felt them. Dollar bills: the young soldier had given him some dollar bills. Before Ibrahim could thank him, he had gone.

Chapter 72

Ibrahim followed the direction in which he had been pointed and stood in line at a wooden booth, looking nervously over his shoulder, all the while believing he would be stopped. He did not notice at first when the woman behind the counter addressed him.

"A ticket to Hildesheim, please," he said softly.

"Where?"

"Hildesheim."

"I have never heard of it. Could you be more precise?"

"It is not far from Hanover."

"But that is all the way up north. If a passenger train comes, it might go as far as Frankfurt, but that depends whether they can get through."

"Thank you."

"Do you want a ticket to Frankfurt?"

"Yes, I know some people in Frankfurt. I would like a ticket to Frankfurt, please."

The woman looked at him with suspicion and reckoned something was not right. Most men his age were fighting the war. His coat was closed and his hat pulled down, obscuring his face. She repeated her question, pretending she had not heard him, so he had to raise his head and speak to her again.

She wrote out his ticket and pushed it towards him. He took one of the dollars and handed it over, but she just shook her head and pulled the ticket back. Ibrahim put a further dollar on to the counter. Still she did not let him have his ticket, but nor did she retrieve it. When five dollars were ready to be taken, she put her hand on them, keeping the other hand on the ticket.

She looked down to his rucksack. "What have you got in there?"

He got on to his knees and tried to open the belt with his shaking hands. The first thing he reached was a flat bar. Hershey Bar, it said on the wrapper.

"Do you have any sugar?"

The line which had started to form behind him pushed him further on to the counter. He had no choice but to lift the rucksack up and empty it in front of the woman. He took out several gold coloured tins, and finally four small packets of sugar. He slid the sugar towards her.

She took two, the Hershey Bar and the money, then handed him his ticket.

"I hope you find your friends." He looked at her, puzzled. "The people you know in Frankfurt." He stuffed everything back in a hurry and turned round, starting to leave.

"Wait!" He froze and turned back. "You have to go over there. We only have one track which still works. I cannot tell you when a train will be coming."

He hurried towards the platform, which was partly intact. Any rubble which would have fallen on the tracks below had been cleared away. Some children were sitting on their belongings, their mothers and grandmothers facing the direction the train would be arriving from. He felt out of place; there were no other men beside himself.

He climbed over some debris next to the remnants of the main building. From here he could see, but would not be observed. He must have dozed off, resting his head on his rucksack, and was startled by slamming doors. The female guard, the same woman who had sold him the ticket, was just going to blow the whistle for the train to continue its journey when she spotted him. When he still did not move, she beckoned him to hurry up.

Ibrahim rushed over and stood on the first step, then turned round and said, "Thank you," closing the carriage door behind him. At first he did not move, but the women and children in the carriage started to notice him so he walked tentatively along the corridor, looking right and left for a place to sit.

The train was gathering speed and he had to steady himself to stop himself falling. Halfway through the carriage, he spotted four uniformed soldiers sitting at the end. Sweat started to form on his forehead and he felt weak.

A young woman pulled her daughter from a seat opposite to her and sat the child on her lap. The little girl was chewing on the bottom of one of her tightly fastened plaits. The ribbon holding her blonde hair together had become soggy and hung limply down.

"Roswita, I told you not to do that. What will your *oma* say when she sees you like that?" Little Roswita started to cry and wiped away the tears with her dirty hands. "Look what you have done now."

The mother stood her on the floor and searched her coat pockets. Little Roswita had her back to Ibrahim, but turned her head, watching with curiosity. He smiled at her and she smiled back, then her attention returned to her mother, who was spitting on her handkerchief in a futile attempt to make her daughter as presentable as possible for her grandmother. The two women next to the mother pretended to be asleep, but when they thought he was not looking, they shot a glimpse in his direction.

He took no notice of the people sitting next to him. From where Ibrahim sat, he had no view to the outside. He closed his eyes and imagined the day when he would hold Esther in his arms.

It was getting dark when the train started to slow down and then came to a stop. He wanted to ask the young mother opposite where they were, but she had already gathered her belongings and her daughter and stood at the end of the corridor. The two passengers next to him also rose, and he quickly moved into their vacated seat and put his head against the window. It felt cool against his cheek. From where he now sat, he could see this place was also destroyed. Where would the young mother find the girl's grandmother among this rubble? he wondered.

He heard a commotion at the carriage door. The passengers had left, and two heavily armed soldiers entered. Ibrahim felt a cold shiver running over his entire body. The soldiers did not move for a while, just scrutinised the passengers still on the train.

The four in uniform at the end of the carriage pretended they had not seen them. "Get up," said the soldier in charge. The four started to rise up slowly, one of them trying to retrieve his rucksack. A gun was pointed directly at him. "Hands up," was the next command. The young men looked frightened, and then Ibrahim noticed that they were just children. They could not have been older than twelve years, he reckoned. The first one tentatively raised his arms above his head and started to move towards the exit, followed by the other three. One of the soldiers picked up their equipment and threw it after them to the end of the corridor, where somebody else retrieved it.

Then the soldier spotted Ibrahim and made his way towards him. Ibrahim remained where he was. The soldier pointed with his gun to the rucksack which Ibrahim held firmly on his knees.

"Where did you get that from?" The side facing outwards was showing the US stencil. Only now did Ibrahim realise that these were Americans.

"I have got papers," he replied in English. He fumbled in his trouser pocket, and in his panic dropped his documents on the floor. Quickly he retrieved them and handed them over. It seemed like a long time before they were given back to him.

"You have a safe journey, Ibrahim," the soldier said with a smile.

No more passengers boarded the train, which gave Ibrahim space to stretch out when it started to move again. He tried to make out the station sign, hanging down from a wall which must have once been the station's entrance.

Nuremberg, he read.

Chapter 73

Ibrahim was in England, living in a big house in the country. Looking through the window, he could see the fresh green covering on the trees and a stream beyond, a sea of bluebells in the small woodland ahead. He heard a voice and felt a hand shaking him awake. It must be Esther calling him.

"Get up," a woman said. He looked into a face he did not recognise.

"Where are we?" he asked.

"Not far from Frankfurt. The train stops here. You have got to go. My mother said just to leave you, but I came back. You have to go," she repeated.

Ibrahim heard doors opening, followed by footsteps in the distance. Dawn was breaking; the sun would be rising soon. He took his rucksack just before he heard male voices coming closer and jumped down on to the track.

The train seemed to be in the middle of nowhere. He squeezed himself between two carriages and scrambled up a bank on the other side. Woodland and bluebells: maybe it had not been a dream. He tried to find a path and kept looking towards the sky, hoping to spot the sun through the light mist which hovered just above the ground. He did not want to waste any energy walking in the wrong direction. He listened, and heard it before he could focus properly. Water. He followed the sound to a clearing ahead. A deer grazing on the bank of the stream sped away as soon as it heard the rustle of the leaves under his feet.

Ibrahim moved with care, first checking left and right, then looking straight ahead and listening again before he felt safe to move forward. He put his rucksack on to the ground and lay flat on his stomach. The grass underneath felt slightly damp, but soft. He put both hands into the cold fast-flowing stream and splashed his face, then put his hands together, gathered up some water and drank it greedily.

He opened his rucksack and removed the tins first. All of them were marked with 'US Field Ration'. One said meat and vegetable hash, another meat and beans and a third meat and vegetable soup. He would have to find a way of opening them. He placed boxes from the rucksack next to them and selected the one which said 'Breakfast'. Inside was a large dry biscuit which crumbled in his hand. He quickly retrieved the broken parts, put the box into the water and had another drink. The box seemed to hold, so he filled it again and moved back towards the woodland. There he could rest with his back against a tree; he would not be seen, but he could detect any movement.

It did not take long for the sun to appear above the horizon, and now he knew which way he should go. He raised himself off the ground, gathered his things and carried on, hoping he did not have to stray too far away from the water. The sun was high up in the sky when he paused again. He could no longer hear the stream, but the path had turned into a larger track. He kneeled down to feel the marks left by wheels: they were hard and dry. Nobody had used this way for some time, and he relaxed again.

The woodland became less dense, and by mid-afternoon he found a clearing ahead. Ibrahim scanned the horizon, and when his eyes had adjusted from the dim light in the woods, he saw houses in the distance and a road not too far away. He contemplated staying where he was and waiting until dark to continue, but he might get confused and walk in circles. No, he had to go on now.

He kept to the side of the road, ready to hide if necessary. He needed some water, but decided to search for some after he had passed the next village. A trough stood in a field which must have been used to graze cows. He shuddered, but detected no smell; the water was still good.

Ibrahim found a place to hide for the night, stretched out under some fallen trees, totally protected from sight. He planned to find the railway tracks again and hoped to continue by train. It rained during the night, and he retrieved his box from the rucksack and gathered some of the water from the puddles, but the box disintegrated after the second try. He needed the cans.

There was no sun to guide him today. He cursed, then quickly asked God for forgiveness. There was no chance he would spot any steam from engines in the light drizzle; he had to rely on his memory. His instinct told him to take the path on the left, which was steep at the beginning and Ibrahim slipped a few times, once falling flat on to his stomach and sliding back a few metres.

From the top of the hill, he had a very good view and was glad he had persisted. Sunrays were now visible through the parting clouds, and he spotted a village to his right and open fields to his left. He decided to go through the fields.

He saw a group of women; maybe he could ask for directions. On attempting to speak to them, however, he was greeted with silence. Nobody looked at him, just continued in their task of planting. He marched all day, only resting occasionally, until early evening, when he spotted a small isolated farm which he approached with caution. Washing was hanging on a rope outside, held up in the middle by a large pole. Ibrahim listened for any sound, ducked down, pulled the washing down and took the man's clothing. He put the pole back where it had been and hid behind the barn.

His breathing was heavy and it took him a while to calm down. Maybe he should stay in the barn for the night. He checked for an open door, and a couple of planks gave way, leaving a large enough gap for him to get through. He had spotted the water pump, but would wait until nightfall. He found a comfortable area behind the haystack, then changed into the clean clothes, which were not completely dry, and said a prayer of thanks. The old ones he pushed under the hay, where they would not be found for a while. He thought about Esther again and imagined their new life together.

He did not hear the barn door being pushed open until a small voice said, "I know you are in here, I saw you taking them." Ibrahim raised his head above the haystack, and in the dark could make out the small figure of a boy. "Are you going to hurt me?"

"Why would I hurt you?"

"The man did."

"Which man?"

"The man with my mother."

"Come over here, I will not hurt you."

The boy walked towards him and sat down next to Ibrahim. He pointed to the rucksack.

"What is in there?"

"Cans of food."

"Can I see?" Ibrahim lifted the first can out. "What does the writing say?"

"It says meat and it will taste really good."

"Can I have some?"

"You could, but we can't open it unless I find a tool."

"We have a can opener in the kitchen." Ibrahim held his breath, waiting for what the boy would say next. "Shall I get it?"

"Will your mother not see you?"

"She is sleeping now. She asked me to be quiet as she is very tired after working in the fields all day. That is why she forgot to take the washing inside. You know, the things the man left. She said if she washes them she might be able to sell them." Ibrahim felt guilty, depriving this family of an income. "But you can keep them, I won't tell."

The boy got up and ran towards the door. Ibrahim decided to be ready to leave quickly if he returned with his mother. In no time the boy was back, holding the can opener and two spoons.

"Which one would you like?"

The boy looked at him for a moment, then pointed with his fingers to one of them.

"This one?"

"No, wait. Eeny, meeny, miny, mo," he continued, moving his finger from one can to the other and settling on 'mo'.

"The man has gone now," he said with his mouth full. "He left his uniform behind. My mother told me to burn it, but I didn't. I hid it in my secret place. Shall I show you?" He did not wait for a reply, but crawled towards the side of the barn. "Come, it's here." He lifted two of the wooden boards away, and Ibrahim saw a space behind. "This is where I hid with my little sister when the man kept shouting for us. Look, there is plenty of space."

The boy pulled out a uniform and Ibrahim froze. It was a Nazi uniform, and one of high rank from what he could see.

"Where is the man now?"

"He took my dad's old clothes and a large fork. I heard him telling my mother he was going to work in the field. But this was many days ago – he has not come back. My mother was crying, asking my aunty who will look after the new baby growing in her belly."

"I think you should listen to your mother and burn the uniform."

First thing in the morning, the boy returned with his little sister by the hand.

"You can come out now, I am back. This is my sister," he whispered. There was no reply. He checked behind the hay, but Ibrahim was not there. "You are in the hiding place," he said and took the planks away. No Ibrahim, and the uniform had gone as well. In its place lay the last of the Hershey bars.

Chapter 74

The boy had been right. Ibrahim found the small town where he said it would be. He had also been right when he told Ibrahim his mother had called the strangers who had come English. The soldiers near the station were certainly not American.

He had buried the Nazi uniform under some leaves about one kilometre from the farm. It had pained him to touch it and carry it that far, but those children needed their mother.

People he passed in the town seemed to move freely through the streets, not bothered by him, just pushing a pram or holding on to their children, walking briskly. There was not a lot of damage here. He passed small stores, but none seemed to be open, and he did not see any goods for sale inside. He was trying to work out what day it was when he heard church bells ringing.

Two women ahead were pulling a small cart. Inside were sacks of carrots. He asked them whether they could spare any, but they declined until he remembered his sugar. He only offered them one packet, and was handed five carrots in return, although he bargained for seven. Before they left, he asked them for water.

He was directed to the town square where he found the fountain, then he savoured the sweet taste of a carrot as he walked on. The station office was closed, but a few passengers stood on the platform. An old man volunteered that he did not know when the next train would be coming. Maybe today, he added. Across from the platform there was movement around goods wagons, and at the front of them the engine was alive with steam. Ibrahim crossed to the other side and went to the last wagon in line. The door was slightly open. Ibrahim shuddered and almost turned around. He could not travel in one of them again, but then the door slid open and Ibrahim faced a group of frightened children.

A tall girl stood in front, and behind her a smaller girl of about ten. They were guarding two small brothers. Ibrahim felt the carriage jerking; the goods train was about to depart. He threw his rucksack inside and tried to lift himself up, but did not have enough strength in his arms, and he could feel the ground below him moving. Ibrahim would have fallen back if the tall girl had not held on to his coat and pulled him inside. Exhausted, he sat on the floor.

The girl was now pushing against the door, trying to shut it. "Leave it open."

They all looked at him, frightened, and moved further into the corner.

"We need to see where we are going, and nobody is going to spot us on a moving train," he explained. He slid his body to the side of the wagon now facing the opening. The train had gathered speed, and the rat-tat-tat the wheels made on the metal track had a soothing effect. Ibrahim opened his rucksack, took out the remaining carrots and handed one to each child. Then he retrieved the last of the cans and took the opener from his coat pocket, hoping the woman at the farm would not miss it.

One of the little boys came crawling over, his sister trying to hold him back by his trousers, which were soiled. Ibrahim opened the can, careful not to spill its content. It was the one containing soup. The smell of food got the attention of the larger girl, who was still eating her raw carrot. Ibrahim put the can to his lips and drank some of the soup, then he leaned forward and offered it to the children.

"You are brothers and sisters?" The children nodded. "Where are you travelling to?"

"Hamburg. We are going to live there," the little boy next to Ibrahim volunteered. "And you?"

"Not that far."

Through the open door, Ibrahim spotted hills in the distance. If his calculations were correct, these could be the Harz Mountains. He had to stay awake now, otherwise he could pass Hildesheim without realising and be too far up north. His guidance was the mountain range. When the landscape changed to fields again, that would be the right time to get off.

He must have fallen asleep. When he looked up next, the Harz had disappeared.

"Do you know where we are?" The children just shook their heads and did not reply.

He quickly fumbled with his hand in the rucksack and removed the last packet of sugar, which he threw at the larger of the girls, then he moved towards the opening and hung his legs down in readiness to jump as soon as the train slowed down. It was approaching a bend, and seemed to struggle keeping the speed up.

Now, he thought. "Good luck."

With that, he jumped forward on to a grassy bank. Before he got back up, he tried to work out where the pain was coming from. His trousers were torn and his right knee was bleeding, and so were the palms of his hands, but nothing was broken.

He tentatively stood and made his way to the other side of the track. Was that Hildesheim he could see? The large church spire he had hoped to spot was not there. Maybe he had missed the town altogether.

He approached Hildesheim from the northeast, rec-ognising the name on one of the street signs still there. Bavenstedter Strasse. There was a slight breeze, and he smelled food; somebody was cooking. It came from the direction of the small airport. Maybe he should go there. Then he heard voices, clearly English, and spotted tents. He turned away.

From there on, there was hardly anything as he remembered. He was unsure whether he had reached the right town after all. If this once was Hildesheim, it no longer existed. At first he wanted to stop and ask the women who were sorting through the rubble, but he stumbled on. Some of the craters in the road were too large to pass, and he had to walk across the small cemetery to go in the direction of where the station should be.

Everywhere he looked, not one of the buildings was intact. He went towards the Zingel, once a main shopping street. From there he could see towards the market. He had spent many happy hours there with Esther, meeting up with their friends after Esther had finished her shift at the hospital. Even from the distance, he saw it was completely destroyed. He continued until he reached the Schuhstrasse. There he turned right, but not before glancing in the direction his home should be. He did not go there, but instead made his way to the hospital, not knowing what to expect.

He ignored the curious looks some women gave him, women who had started a clean-up. One, pushing a wheelbarrow, put it down and ran towards him.

"Are you a returnee? Are there others?" Ibrahim did not know what she meant, and shook his head. Disappointed, she went back.

He spotted the hospital through the ruins of the buildings which used to stand in front of it. The hospital was damaged, but not destroyed.

Chapter 75

London, End of May 1945

"I am sorry, I don't quite understand. What do you mean, Dr Rosenthal can either travel to Dachau or Hildesheim, but cannot visit one place after the other?"

Thomas had agreed to meet Esther at the American High Commission in Grosvenor Square. The war was over. Germany had surrendered on 8 May 1945, not long after Hitler's death at the end of April, but Esther feared that too much time had been lost already. The liberation of Dachau had been a month ago. Who knew where Ibrahim was now?

After pressure from the newspaper editor, the High Commission granted her a meeting. She was glad that Thomas was safely back; they had not met since their journey from Bermuda. He had not spoken to her of his time during the war, and she was not going to ask. She just hoped that the love of his family would heal the scars left behind.

The young officer looked nervously at both of them sitting in front of his desk, then stared at the door before saying, "Madam, I have only been here for five days. I have to be honest, I think you should speak with somebody more qualified than me. Would you excuse me for a minute?" He rose, squeezed through the tight space on one side of his desk and shut the door behind him.

"How is Anna?" Thomas broke the silence.

"She sends her regards. She is coping well. But things are changing at Trench Hall."

"In what way?"

"Some of the English boys who had been sent to Anna to keep them safe are returning to their families. The residents who moved there from the Isle of Man are now free to leave. Anna said she will miss all of them. They have become her family."

"Will she stay there?"

"No, she is planning to go back to her school in Kent." Before Esther could explain more, the office door opened again. The young man was back.

"Please follow me."

Esther and Thomas walked behind him, up the stairs and along a busy corridor. Esther was amazed how young all the staff looked. Most greeted them with a smile or a nod.

At the last door, their knock was answered by "Enter."

This office was much larger than the previous one, and the first thing Esther noticed was the big portrait of President Truman on the wall facing her. On the wall to her right was a smaller one of General Eisenhower in full uniform next to President Roosevelt, which had a black ribbon attached at the bottom.

The man behind the desk stood up, reached his hand over his desk and introduced himself. He then beckoned them to take a seat.

"May I offer you a drink?"

"No, thank you," replied Esther.

"Do you have any Coca Cola?" asked Thomas.

The young man disappeared, and soon returned with two bottles, which he was just about to open in front of them when Thomas added, "Can I take mine with me?"

"How many children do you have at home?" The man behind the desk directed the question at Thomas.

"Two."

The man retrieved a piece of paper from the drawer, wrote on it, dated it and stamped it. He then handed it over to the young man, who was still standing there, holding the drinks.

"Marc, get those items and bring them back to me."

"Yes, sir."

"Dr Rosenthal, I must apologise for the long wait today. Things are still a little bit chaotic here, as you can imagine. Your situation, as I understand it, is your husband was imprisoned at the camp in Dachau. Is that correct?"

"Yes."

"I am sorry to have to ask you this, but you firmly believe he is one of the survivors?"

Esther had anticipated the question. She opened the medical bag she took everywhere and retrieved Ibrahim's letters.

"My husband wrote to me, and I know him well enough. He would find a way to stay alive."

"I see. And you have been made aware of the present situation in Germany?"

"Yes, but…" Thomas started to say, but Esther quickly put her hand on his arm, stopping him.

"Let me go over it again. The Allies have an agreement to divide Germany into zones. Each of the zones will be administered by a different authority. Dachau falls into the administration of the American Army, whereas the north of Germany, which is where Hildesheim is, I believe, is controlled by the British. At this stage it is not possible for any civilians to travel from one zone to another." He paused, but Esther did not ask any questions, so he continued. "Dr Rosenthal, as an American citizen you can travel from the United Kingdom via Belgium to Frankfurt in the American zone. You know Germany better than I do. From there you can travel by train to Munich. I believe Dachau is not far from there."

"But…" Esther shot Thomas a look, and he understood she wanted to hear the full story.

"Because you live in England at the moment, and you told my assistant that your son is studying in Oxford, you can get papers from the home office and travel to the north of

276

Germany via Holland. So far there has not been any agreement for free movement between the zones. I am sure it will be announced at some stage, but at the moment we are faced with the restrictions, as I explained."

"Will you be able to issue the required documents for me to travel to Dachau?"

"That will be my pleasure. If you would like to wait downstairs, I will have them sent to you."

A knock at the door interrupted the conversation. Marc had returned with a parcel, which he gave to his superior, who took it and passed it to Thomas.

"This is for your children."

"Will there be anything else, sir?"

"Yes, Marc. Please accompany Dr Rosenthal and Thomas to the waiting area. Make sure there are coffee and cookies available. And then come back and collect Dr Rosenthal's documents." He stood up and shook their hands again. "I do hope you find your husband. Good luck, Dr Rosenthal."

Downstairs, after eating his third cookie, Thomas asked, "You are sure about this. It is Dachau you want to go to, and not Hildesheim?"

"Yes, very sure. Why do you ask?"

"I could come with you to Hildesheim, but I would not get permission as a reporter to travel into the American Zone."

Esther looked at him, not sure what to reply at first, then she took one of his hands into her own and looked at him.

"Thomas, you have been a wonderful friend to me over the years. I would never have got this far if it had not been for you, but please understand, I must do this by myself."

Epilogue

Anna Essinger moved back into the Bunce School in Otterden, Kent, in 1946. She continued to teach there until June 1948. It is said that she ran out of funds and the school was closed, but remained her home. Most of her former pupils kept in touch throughout her life, still calling her '*Tante* (Aunty) Anna'. Many went on to become famous artists, doctors and scientists. Anna died in the Bunce School in 1960, not knowing that one day she would be commemorated in Germany.

John stayed with Anna until her retirement, before returning to Harwich.

Edwin purchased a small cottage in Otterden not far from the Bunce School. Otto moved in with him. Both wanted to stay close to Anna.

Thomas never settled back to normal life and became an overseas correspondent. His last official assignment for the London newspaper was reporting from Berlin, covering the building of the Berlin wall. He remained there until Kennedy's visit in 1963, and kept in touch with Esther. The last letters she received from him were posted in Singapore.

The newspaper editor honoured Alexander's agreement with Friedrich, and the young man started working there in June 1945. He steadily worked his way up the ladder.

Esther, on her arrival in Dachau, learned that Ibrahim had survived, but had left to go to their hometown to look for her. She travelled to Frankfurt, from where she made contact with the hospital in Hildesheim. Her former professor informed her that Ibrahim had arrived safely, and after a meeting with Maria had decided to continue to

Belgium to seek out Maria's brother. He had left a note for Esther, which he read out. Esther and Ibrahim were reunited in Brussels two weeks later. It took Esther another three months until she received permission to return with Ibrahim to England. The borders for Jewish survivors of the concentration camps had been closed.

Mordechai kept the promise he made to himself, and used the remaining money from the sale of the gold cuckoo clock weights to secure a first class cabin on a crossing from Liverpool to Bermuda. That was where Esther wanted to introduce Ibrahim to his new family.

Joshua joined them in New York years later, after having worked with Dr Guttmann at the Stoke Mandeville Hospital.

Ludwig Guttmann established the Paralympic Games in England. The first Stoke Mandeville Games were held in 1952.

Esther remained close to Anna, Flo and her friends from Bletchley Park.

And the cuckoo clock? It now has a place on the wall in the home of Elisabeth and David, who moved back to England after a brief spell managing their hotel near Tampa, Florida. It is still running slow, despite them having purchased and tried many different weights. They have come to the conclusion it will never work properly unless they find the originals.

Coming soon…

Welcome to Singapore

Prologue

Far East, 1974

He boarded the flight at Hong Kong's Kai Tak Airport. Hesitating, looking around again. Searching for the familiar face in the crowd. Too late; the flight had been called. It was time to move on. Would the departure be as dramatic as the arrival? He doubted it. He was glad that he had listened to Arthur and kept the camera. That advice had served him well, something he would never admit to. There had been many things he should have said. Arthur deserved to know the truth. Now it was too late for that.

He had stayed longer here than in any of the other places. Just one night, that had been the plan. How many times had he promised that to himself? He had lost count.

He could still feel the adrenalin rush the day he arrived. The jumbo jet flew directly towards the mountain before making a sharp turn to the right then almost touching the houses below. But a perfect landing on the runway. 'Checkerboard Hill' is what they called it. The red and white check painting. Guidance for the pilots. He had interviewed one of them. After that, he trekked there once and got as close as you could. Hidden in the bushes with Louise, no, not Louise, with Kim.

This was not her actual name, he found out later. She stayed long enough for him to be told the whole story. Yes, her real name suited her. Kimama, 'butterfly girl'.

The two seats next to him were empty. That little favour only cost him his best smile at the counter. That, and waving his press card with the promise to take her out on his return. He occupied the seat at the window, wanting one last look.

He got up to stretch his legs. He should have said no to the last large glass of brandy in the VIP lounge but then the pretty check-in girl had given him an entry ticket. There was no point in wasting it. Now he felt a little off-balance and needed to steady himself by holding on to the seats while he walked through the cabin. He failed to see the other passenger who was trying to retrieve a bag from underneath the seat in from of him. His left leg was partly blocking the aisle and Thomas stumbled.

"I am so sorry," they both said in unison. They looked at each other for just a brief moment. Had they met before? Thomas dismissed that thought and made his way towards the galley. Was the man still looking at him? No, just another trick of his imagination. The man had sat back down and was talking to the woman sitting next to him.

He must have dozed off. The stewardess shook him awake.

"Sir, the captain has put the seatbelt sign on."

"What time is it?"

"Almost 3.30 pm, sir. We are landing in twenty minutes."

Thomas did not like the restriction of a seatbelt, not since that night. He held it but left it at that.

"Sir, your seatbelt. Sir."

She bent over and took the clasps from his shaking hands. Click. "There you are."

"Cabin crew, take your seats for landing," he heard.

He was glad to be alone again. She did not witness the pearls of sweat running down his face. The plane started swaying on its descent through the formation of clouds. Thomas closed his eyes. Everything replayed in his mind in an instant. He opened them again quickly, shaking his head, trying to lift the fog and focussing on the painting on the wall three rows ahead.

With a thud, the plane landed and, like a bolt, it hit him. He remembered where he had met the man before. At Anna's funeral. Before he could linger on that day the captain's voice came through the speakers again.

"Ladies and gentlemen, we have landed safely at our destination thirty minutes ahead of the scheduled time. Please remain in your seats with your seatbelts securely fastened until the plane has come to a complete stop, and the engines have been switched off."

"Welcome to Singapore."

The Night I Danced with Rommel

Prologue

14 October 1944 – Hildesheim, Germany

"Why do people die, Mama?" I went over to where he was standing and put my arms around him. Klaus pushed me away. "The man Pappa works for, has he really died?"

How could I explain the horror of it all to a seven-year-old boy, but I could not lie to him.

"Yes, I think the man your Pappa works for, Field Marshal Rommel, he is dead."

But why, Mama? Why do people die?"

"I think sometimes God wants them to come and live with him." I hoped this would help him to understand.

"But doesn't God want everybody to come and live with him?"

"Yes he does, but special people, he might want those to live with him earlier and that is when God has to make a quick decision, you see?"

"You mean, like when he wanted Inge to come and live with him, even though we wanted Inge to stay here with us?"

"Yes, Klaus, just like it was with Inge." I had to look away, I did not want him to realise how hard it was not to cry.

"But my Pappa, my Pappa he will come home," he decided and went back into the kitchen to join the other children.

Liverpool Connection

Chapter 1

Garston, Liverpool – December 1946

He crouched behind the brick wall, which was high enough for him to hide behind, but not too high to stop him from watching the comings and goings on the pavement on the opposite side of the road. From here, he had a clear view if he stood up. Behind him was a house, but he was hidden from it by a large bush. All the leaves had fallen on to the muddy floor underneath some time ago. The front garden itself was totally overgrown. Rubble from the bombed-out building next door was covered with undergrowth. You had to have your wits about you not to slip on some of the bricks, which were slippery in the damp. Yes, he had found the ideal hiding place. He knew this place well because he had come here many times before. In fact, every day this week, straight after school, not bothering to go home first.

He was shivering. His thin coat was soaked from the heavy snow, which had started to fall at lunchtime. The coat was too small for him, the sleeves riding up on his arms and no longer protecting the cracked skin on his freezing hands. A big boy had stopped him in the playground just when the teacher had turned his back to them, ready to ring the bell to let them know it was time to go back inside. He had often wondered why it was that all the children had to be outside in the cold, when the teachers were allowed to stay in the warm Principal's office drinking tea.

He had seen the big boy before and always avoided crossing his path, but he was out of luck today. The big boy put one hand on his shoulder and lifted his warm hat off his head. "Listen, squirt! If I see you near my sister again, there'll be trouble. I told her she's not allowed to play with the riff-raff from the tenements." The big boy then laughed, took the hat away with him and walked towards his mates, who had stood guard a short distance away.

"Oi! Gimme my hat back!" he shouted after them.

"You can get it back after school, outside the gate if you dare." He couldn't recall knowing the big boy's sister. *She must be a girl in my class*, he thought. There were about twenty girls in his class of forty-five in Year 1 at Banks Road Primary School.

By now, his feet were soaking. The cardboard in his shoes, which was in there to cover the hole in the sole, had become squishy. If he stayed here much longer, he would have to take it out. *I'd be better off without it,* he thought.

He raised himself up a little to take a peek over the wall, to see whether there were any left. There had been ten at the beginning of the week, but when he got here this afternoon, only three of them were still there. If he didn't do it today, his family would be the only ones in the tenement without one again.

From what he could remember, not many of them had one during the times when the bombs fell. He had vivid memories about those days. His 'old fella' and his mam would still talk about it when they thought the kids were asleep. He knew they blamed the bombs for the death of his brother, Derek, who was two years old at the time. When he had asked his Aunty Peg about it, she told him that Derek died of a fit when everybody was inside the air-raid shelter, right in the centre of Speke Road Garden. His sister, Grace, ran through burning streets to fetch the doctor, but it was too late. He was determined to provide one for the family this year. He had promised his new little brother, Alfie, and a promise is a promise.

It was time to check again, and he slowly rose from his hiding place. Two girls brushed the snow off the wall he was hiding behind with their gloved hands. All three faced each other for a second before the first girl screamed, followed by the girl next to her, shouting, "Mam! There's somebody hiding in our front garden."

The door opened behind him, his head flew round looking towards the house. In the lit-up doorway, stood the big boy from school. In his shock, he dropped the knife, which he had taken this morning from the kitchen drawer without being seen. He had hidden it from the teachers during the day. All he could think was, *Me mam will kill me if she found out I took the bread knife to school and lost it.* He bent down quickly, feeling through the snow. He felt it cutting his finger, picked it up and scooted over the wall and legged it towards the wasteland before the big boy recognised him. Hearing shouts behind him, he guessed the loudest voice was the big boy's. He was now further away from the shops, and he knew if he didn't get back quickly, they would close for the evening, then he will have missed his chance.

He crossed the road, keeping close to the wall, all the while sucking on his bleeding finger. He re-entered Vineyard Street from the other end, trying to be invisible to the men and women hurrying past him. With his back against the houses, he slowly made his way forward. Just like his hero, Roy Rogers, in the cinema. His Aunty Flo had given him a ticket to see a film on his last birthday. He had planned to mingle with the shoppers, take it and leave. With all his running around, it was getting late, and there were only one or two people around. He could see the owner inside at the till. This was it. He took the knife and reached up as high as he could to cut the top off. He had to have several goes, but his efforts were rewarded. The top of the tree fell to the ground, at least two feet, he imagined. Just then, there were shouts from inside the shop. The owner had seen him.

"Stop! Stop that boy!"

But David had learned to be fast. Despite the weight and the prickly branches, he made off. He was cunning, in spite of his young age. He ran in a different direction to his home, back to the wasteland. He pulled his trophy behind him up the hill. All he needed to do was slide down on all fours to the other side. From there he would crawl through the hole in the wire fence. He felt his coat being caught on a piece of wire, which he should have remembered. They had put it there themselves to stop others from finding the treasure, which they kept hidden under the largest tree. They had dug themselves a really big hole, using only branches and their bare hands when the ground was still soft. He smiled at the memory of that day. He gave a pull and heard his coat rip. He tried to see the damage. *This was supposed to be for Alfie when he gets bigger*, he thought. He looked at his snow-covered tree. Like the picture in a book, he had seen in a library. The same book, which was hidden under his bed. If only it would stay that way, there would be no need to decorate it.

Printed in Great Britain
by Amazon

29808790R00169